14.

Ivory Tower

Leo McNeir

enigma publishing

Copyright

First published 2023
© Leo McNeir 2023

ISBN 9798394246036

for Steve Flint

Index

Ivory Tower

Autumn 1990s

Chapter 1

I t was first light on a crisp Sunday morning in early autumn, and mist was rolling across the gently flowing surface of the Thames as the body was recovered from the river. In the shadow of Tower Bridge a cluster of boats formed a loose circle around the still form in the murky water. Paramedics in an Avon boat of the London Fire Brigade were painstakingly attaching a recovery sling round the corpse, their yellow hi-viz jackets bright against the red rubber of the inflatable. Nearby a second safety boat loitered, backed up by two blue-and-yellow-chequered police launches. While a handful of early passers-by looked on, one of the police boats moved in to shield the activity from view. Even so, mobile phones were being raised on the bank, their owners keen to record the gruesome spectacle.

On the nearest police launch two detectives in plain clothes leaned out to speak to the officers retrieving the body.

'What have we got?' the senior detective asked.

A uniformed constable turned to reply, his expression grim. 'It's a man, sir, just like you said.'

'Can you check his pockets.'

They rolled the body into the rubber boat. The dead man was wearing a dark suit, a white shirt and navy tie. At first glance he seemed to be middle-aged with a full head of dark hair, greying at the temples. He was missing one shoe; the remaining one, a black semi-brogue, appeared to be of good quality. His socks were dark grey.

The constable reached into the inside pocket of the jacket. 'No wallet, sir.' He checked the top pocket and pulled out a business card. He read it quickly and looked up. 'It's him, sir, the one you expected.'

He passed the card to his superior and returned to his duties. An officer of the fire service manoeuvred the Avon boat clear of its neighbours and accelerated gently away. The detectives watched it go. The inspector looked down at the sodden card in his hand, read it and passed it to his colleague, a young DC.

'Get it bagged up, then contact Thames Valley. The address is Oxford, but I'm given to understand he lived in Northamptonshire, the next county. They can have the pleasure of delivering the death message.'

'Right, sir. Will do.'

As the detective inspector gave instructions to the sergeant of the river police, the DC took a transparent evidence bag from his pocket and slotted the card inside. In the gathering morning light he could see clearly the name printed on the card: Dr Ralph Lombard of All Saints' College, University of Oxford.

Chapter 2

MONDAY

The police patrol car drove slowly through the village of Knightly St John, no lights, no sirens, no twos-and-blues. Neither of the two uniformed constables sitting in the front seats was looking forward to the duty they had been sent to carry out. No one likes delivering a death message. PC Wendy Grainger and PC Ruth Wallace guessed they had been selected for the task because they were women, but in fact they were the only two officers of Northamptonshire Constabulary available in the south of the county that afternoon.

The car had turned off the dual carriageway and followed a narrow, twisty country road for a mile and a half before reaching the village. The constables hadn't visited it before. On any other day they would have been charmed by the main street which was flanked by cottages of cream limestone under roofs of thatch or slate. They were mostly set well back from the road with front gardens stocked with the flowers of early autumn: chrysanthemums, dahlias, asters, Japanese anemones and the occasional cheerful faces of sunflowers. Here and there walls were adorned with Virginia creeper, turning from green to red to burgundy.

But on that day the police officers were focused only on the grim duty that lay before them.

The village shop-cum-post-office rolled by on their left, and the pub – *The Two Roses* – came into view on their right, almost directly opposite the primary school. Beyond the school stood Saint John's church with its massive tower, standing on raised ground, dominating the skyscape of the village.

'Where now?' said Grainger, who was driving.

Wallace checked the road atlas on her knees. 'The road bends round here to the right, then look out for a field entrance on the left. We're just passing the old vicarage on our right, so it should be coming up soon.'

'I see it. There's a sign by the gate: Glebe Farm.'

'That's it,' Wallace confirmed. 'Follow the track down the hill, and the farm is at the edge of a spinney.'

'They're farmers?' Grainger sounded puzzled.

'No. It's been renovated. Marnie Walker is an interior designer. DI Bartlett says she's developed the whole place: house, barns and some cottages that she rents out. He said we can park by the farmhouse. Her office is in a barn close by. He reckons it should be easy to spot.'

They soon came upon the complex of buildings, where Grainger rolled the car to a halt on a gravel drive beside a double-fronted stone farmhouse. On the left a small stone barn, set at right-angles to the house, looked out across a cobbled yard towards a terrace of three cottages.

'That must be the barn where she works,' Grainger pointed. 'Looks like a shop front with all that glass ... tinted, too. Smart.'

Wallace unbuckled her seat belt and took a deep breath. 'Come on. Let's get it over with.'

A half-glazed door was located to the right of the frontage. They pushed it open and found themselves in a bright, spacious office with modern blond-wood furniture, neutral carpet and apricot white walls. The place looked efficient and purposeful, a good working environment. There was a desk near the entrance, unoccupied, and a second desk towards the rear of the space. A young woman stood up from that position as they entered. She was above medium height, thin and pale. Her natural blonde hair was cut very short, urchin-style. She smiled.

'Good afternoon. What can I do for you?'

The officers had been told that Marnie Walker was in her thirties. This girl looked barely out of her teens.

Grainger said, 'We're here to see Mrs Walker, Marnie Walker.'

'Sure. Take a seat. I'll get her for you.'

'You are ...?'

'Anne Price. I'm her assistant.'

'You work here?'

Anne nodded. 'Part-time. I'm a student ... art and design.'

Wallace indicated over her shoulder. 'Is she in the house? We could go across.'

'No, she's on the boat.' Anne was already pressing buttons on the phone. 'I can get her here in just a few minutes.'

'Boat?'

Anne said, 'Yeah, *Sally Ann*. The canal's just beyond the spinney. It's only about fifty metres away.' She turned her attention to the phone. 'Marnie, it's me. There are two police

4

officers here wanting to see you … No, not them, uniforms …
Okay, I'll tell them.' She replaced the receiver in its cradle. 'She's
on her way. Can I get you some coffee, or tea perhaps?'

Grainger replied. 'No, thanks. We'll not be staying long.'

They were still standing, looking uncomfortable, when
Marnie breezed in and greeted them with handshakes. Far from
putting them at their ease, this seemed to make them even more
awkward.

'I'm sure Anne has already offered you refreshment, so how
can I help?'

'Er, Mrs Walker, would you like to sit down?'

'Sit down?' Marnie looked bewildered.

Grainger continued. 'I'm afraid we have some bad news for
you.'

Marnie tensed. 'My parents? My sister?'

'No, no, nothing about them.'

'What then?'

At the rear of the office Anne too was looking apprehensive.

Grainger said, 'I'm afraid it's about your husband.'

'I don't understand.' Marnie was still bewildered.

'I'm sorry to tell you that a body was recovered from the river
Thames in London early yesterday morning. We have reason to
believe it was your husband, Ralph, Dr Ralph Lombard.'

For several seconds Marnie stared at them without
speaking. She glanced beyond the officers in the direction of
Anne, who was looking equally puzzled, before turning back.

'Ralph?' Marnie said.

'I'm very sorry,' said Grainger.

'How do you know that?'

Wallace said, 'We believe the Metropolitan Police had an
anonymous tip-off … a phone call.'

By now both officers were thinking this was the strangest
reaction to a death message that either of them had ever
witnessed. They might have expected tears, sobbing, breaking
down, collapsing in hysterics or even fainting, but this broke new
ground.

Marnie said, 'Would you like to take a seat? Second
thoughts … could you come with me for a moment?'

They followed her out of the office – it was their turn to be
bewildered – and took a narrow footpath through the spinney.
Emerging at the end, they found themselves on a grassed area,
recently mown, beside the Grand Union Canal. The smell of
freshly-cut grass mingled with the pleasant tang of burning
leaves some way off. To their left was a docking area cut into the

canal at right-angles in which lay a narrowboat bearing the name, *Sally Ann*. Over to their right on the canal's main line another boat was moored. The name *Thyrsis* was painted in gold lettering on the superstructure which was a deep sage green. Marnie advanced on this second boat with the two PCs following in her wake. She walked to the front of the vessel and tapped lightly on a window. After a few moments it slid open and a man's face appeared. He was clean-shaven and distinguished-looking, with dark hair, greying slightly at the temples.

'Back again, darling?' He spotted the police officers behind Marnie. 'Oh, we have visitors. Sorry, I didn't realise.'

Marnie said, 'Well, it appears that your dead body was pulled out of the Thames yesterday morning and these officers have come to inform me of that.' She turned to face the officers. 'Permit me to introduce my husband, Professor Ralph Lombard of All Saints' College in the University of Oxford.'

'Oh,' said Grainger. Wallace agreed.

'Do you think there might perhaps be some mistake?' Ralph said pleasantly.

ooo0ooo

Watching the two police officers head towards the path through the spinney, Marnie held back and spoke to Ralph.

'Well, that was quite surreal.'

'Not every day I'm informed that I'm actually dead,' Ralph muttered.

'Just as well, Ralph. That was seriously bizarre.'

Ralph agreed. 'If I wasn't dead I'd probably be losing the will to live.'

Marnie smiled. 'At least you won't be turning in your grave.'

'There is that consolation, I suppose.'

Marnie turned to see the police officers entering the spinney.

'I'd better see our visitors off,' she said.

'Actually, Marnie, I thought you might have been Anne bringing the post.'

'It should arrive any time. I'm sure Anne will be along directly.'

Marnie kissed Ralph quickly and set off. He called after her.

'The good news is, there won't be a copy of my obituary for me to proof-read.'

'That's a relief.' Marnie laughed and hurried on her way. It was a surreal morning.

oooOooo

Back in the office, Marnie found Anne at her desk sorting the afternoon delivery of post. Having taken leave of the police officers, Marnie returned to her seat. Anne looked up.

'So they've not carted you off to the Bridewell, then?'

'Not just yet.'

'What was all that about?' Anne asked.

'You heard what they said. Some poor devil found drowned in the Thames.'

'Yes, but why did they think it was Ralph?'

Marnie shrugged. 'You heard them say there'd been a tip-off. That's all they'd say. You know what they're like. They never give much away. Anything of interest in the post?'

'The main excitement is a reminder from the vet about Dolly's annual check-up and booster jab. Lucky cat. I'll phone them to make an appointment.' Anne gathered together a small bundle of letters and stood up. 'This lot's for Ralph. I'll take them round to him …' With a twinkle in her eye she added, '… assuming he's still alive, of course. He might want to check them out before we break for tea.' As an afterthought she added, 'I take it you don't want me to produce notes for an obituary at the moment?'

'Probably not,' Marnie said, deadpan.

As Anne was closing the office door behind her, she noticed the two constables were still sitting in their car. They appeared to be deep in conversation and seemed not to notice her. Questions floated through her mind. Why did the police accept the tip-off about finding Ralph's body in the Thames? Who had they really found? What was the connection? She knew the answers would be unlikely ever to come her way. With a mental shrug she turned on her heels and rounded the corner to take the footpath to the canal. She strode out, pleased to be in the open air after spending most of the day at college, plus driving back and forth to Oxford. She revelled in the scents of autumn, a distant bonfire, a hint of woodsmoke from cottage chimneys in the village, the dampness of fallen leaves, the cool breath of the spinney.

oooOooo

Back in the office a short while later, Anne switched on the kettle in the kitchen area a few minutes before five o'clock and laid the tray with mugs. After pouring hot water into the teapot, she

7

swirled it round before setting it down on the workbench and raising a hand to her mouth. She yawned and blinked three times.

'You're sure you're up to making the tea?' Marnie said from across the office. 'Will you stay awake long enough?'

Anne ignored the sarcasm and tipped the hot water into the sink.

'I should just about manage it,' she said. 'Actually, I want to talk to you about that.'

'Oh?'

Anne scooped leaf tea into the pot and poured on boiling water. She stirred the brew with a dessert spoon and popped the lid in place.

'It's the travelling,' she said, pouring milk into a jug. 'I seem to spend half my time driving to Oxford and back.'

Marnie looked thoughtful. 'And you're missing out on college life. I'm sorry about that. We've not organised things very well.'

'Not your fault,' Anne said. 'If the tenant in Ralph's cottage hadn't asked to stay on for another year –'

'At the last minute,' Marnie added.

'Yes, at the last minute, I'd probably have got a place in college or in a hall of residence. Then I could've spent more time with the other students and less time on the road.'

'Let's have a word with Ralph,' Marnie suggested. 'He might be able to think of something.'

Anne looked up at the clock. 'Talking of Ralph … where is he? He's usually here by now.'

'Good point. Perhaps he's stuck on the phone. If he hasn't arrived by the time you're pouring, I'll take him his tea in a picnic mug.'

Anne picked up the phone from her desk and pressed a button. She listened for a few seconds, shook her head and replaced it on its cradle.

'Straight to Ralph's voicemail,' she said and reached for a lidded mug.

ooo0ooo

Daylight was fading rapidly under an overcast sky as Marnie walked briskly through the spinney carrying the mug of tea for Ralph. It felt as if rain was threatening, and Marnie wished she'd pulled on her cagoule before setting off. She half expected to meet Ralph coming towards her on the footpath, but it was not to be.

She also expected to see lights on in Ralph's study, the front section of *Thyrsis*, but the boat was in darkness. Had he gone to the house, Marnie wondered. Perhaps he had called in there for something and that had delayed him. She was tempted to turn back but, having come this far, she decided at least to look through the study window. It was then that she had her second surprise.

Peering through the glass, Marnie saw Ralph sitting at his desk, staring down at what looked like a letter. He was utterly still, oblivious to the world and the fading light. Marnie was raising her hand to tap on the window when she changed her mind, not wanting to intrude abruptly into his thoughts. Instead she walked back and knocked three times on the centre doors. A minute passed before the hatch was lifted back and the doors swung outwards. Ralph's expression was vacant.

'I've brought your tea,' Marnie said. 'We thought perhaps you might be engrossed in something and couldn't break off.'

'Tea?' Ralph turned his gaze on the mug in Marnie's hand. 'Oh yes, thanks.'

'Are you all right, Ralph? You seem rather … distracted.'

The first raindrops began falling, spotting the roof of the boat.

'Sorry.' He stood aside and offered a hand to help her in. 'I've had a bit of a shock, actually.'

Marnie gave him the mug and began climbing down the steps into the boat, while Ralph steadied her with his free hand, then closed the hatch and doors to shut out the rain.

'What is it?' she asked. 'You're not upset at being found dead in the Thames, are you?'

Marnie could tell by Ralph's expression that her flippant tone was wide of the mark.

'I'll show you,' he said. 'I've, er … received some bad news.'

Marnie followed Ralph along the short corridor to the study which had been formed from two cabin sections combined. It was roughly sixteen feet long and almost seven feet wide. Fitted shelves were filled ceiling to floor with books, together with a built-in unit containing a printer, a cassette player, a fax machine and a small television. Ralph mainly used the latter for keeping abreast of the news throughout the day. He sat at his desk and switched on the lights. They were reflected in the rain which was now streaking the window-panes. Marnie took her place on a small sofa on the opposite side of the cabin, as Ralph handed her a letter.

'This has just arrived. It was in the bundle that Anne brought me.'

'Ralph, you've got me worried. Are you all right? You were sitting here in the gloom.'

'Read the letter. You'll understand.'

Dear Ralph,

I'm afraid I have some rather bad news that I thought you should know. I have just learnt that Rhiannon has died. I believe you knew her some years ago and I understand that for a time you and she were quite close.

You may recall that she was committed to a psychiatric nursing home for much of her life, which is where she sadly died last month. I don't have any other details at the moment. If I hear anything further I will of course let you know. Sorry to be the bearer of such sad news.

Yours ever,

Jay Harper

Marnie quickly scanned it and looked up. 'It's bad news, obviously, but I can't say I really do understand. Who is this Jay Harper? Not a name I've heard you mention before.'

'We were at university together ... well, not exactly together.'

'How do you mean?'

'Just that our rooms at All Saints were off the same staircase, that's all, oh yes, and we were in the same tennis team. We didn't attend the same tutorials as post-graduate students. His research field was history, I think. We've not really kept in touch. In fact, I haven't seen him for quite a few years, and now he's written out of the blue, as you see.'

'And ... Rhiannon?'

Ralph drew a deep breath and stared down at his hands.

'Ralph? It's a beautiful name. Did she live up to it?'

Ralph looked wistful. 'I suppose she did, yes. She was quite striking, really. She looked like a sort of ... Celtic princess, I suppose.'

'Harper writes that she's died. Why would he write to tell you that? Was she important to you?'

Ralph shook his head slowly. 'No, not really. That's rather the point ...the problem.'

'It's clearly affected you badly. Do you want to talk about it? Or perhaps you don't. Whatever's the matter, you know you can talk to me ... or not, if you don't want to.'

Silence hung in the air between them. Eventually Ralph spoke quietly.

'Rhiannon – Rhiannon Ellis, that is – was someone I knew as a postgrad.'

'A girlfriend?' Marnie said.

'Not exactly. We met at a conference in Cambridge on the economics of developing countries. Back then I was studying for my DPhil, my doctorate, at All Saints and she was doing a master's degree, an MBA, at the Highgate Business School. She'd graduated from the London School of Economics the year before. We had a brief affair ... well, really only a one-night stand. For me it was just one of those things. We'd both probably had a bit too much to drink and ... well, you can guess the rest.'

'You didn't keep in touch?'

'No.'

Marnie was puzzled. 'That must've been about twenty years ago. So why has this news affected you so much?'

'It was soon after that conference that I met Laura. I suppose you'd say it was love at first sight. Meeting Laura pushed everything else out of my mind.'

'Including Rhiannon?'

'Yes.' Ralph looked embarrassed. 'She'd decided that I was the love of her life ... kept writing to me, care of the college. On the basis of that brief tipsy encounter, she wanted us to be together for the rest of our lives.'

'Which is roughly what you felt by then about Laura, no doubt,' Marnie said quietly.

'Quite. But Rhiannon wouldn't accept that. When I wrote and explained about Laura – as gently as I could – she said she couldn't let go.'

'You eventually married Laura, so what happened to Rhiannon? Did she accept the inevitable?'

Ralph looked pained. 'I've always thought I handled the whole situation very badly. It's been on my conscience for years.'

'But you've never spoken of this before, Ralph.'

'Too ashamed, I suppose.'

'Why? Plenty of people break off relationships. In your case it wasn't even really a relationship, as such, just a passing fling. Though obviously, Rhiannon didn't think of it like that.'

'I was insensitive, Marnie. First, I stopped replying to her letters. Then one day she wrote that she was coming to Oxford to *clear the air once and for all*. I wrote back stressing my feelings for Laura, saying that there was no purpose to be served by her visit.'

'She took it badly?' said Marnie.

Ralph shrugged. 'She never wrote again.'

'And that was the last you heard of her until now?'

Ralph closed his eyes and breathed deeply several times.

'Ralph?' Marnie said.

He sighed and stared ahead. 'After Laura died I learnt from a mutual friend that Rhiannon had had a nervous breakdown all those years before. That's when she was committed to a psychiatric nursing home.'

'And then?'

'That's where she stayed until her death a month ago, as Jay says in his letter.'

'Where does this Jay fit in? I don't see the connection.'

'I seem to recall he's an old friend of a cousin of Rhiannon. They were squash partners, or something of the sort. I can't remember now; it was so long ago.'

'You lost touch with him as well?'

'I did. I'm not sure if he completed his doctoral thesis, but I think he left to go into the army … some kind of short service commission, as far as I recall.'

'Jay knew of your … liaison with Rhiannon?'

'Presumably. I don't know how. I've never told anyone until now. Not the kind of thing I'd be proud of, obviously.'

'Well, Ralph, everyone has secrets, I suppose.'

'But not all as shameful as mine.'

'Look, it could've happened to anyone. You could never have known how Rhiannon would react.'

'No, but I've always blamed myself for treating her badly. I've always thought I could've behaved better. In fact, I may well have ruined her life, and now she's dead.'

Chapter 3

TUESDAY

Marnie enjoyed working with Anne; they were more like sisters than colleagues. They had developed Walker and Co, design consultants, into a successful operation for the past few years, ever since Marnie left her well-paid job in London to set up her own company in rural Northamptonshire. Anne was nominally Marnie's assistant, though in fact she was much more than that. She regarded herself as a kind of apprentice, like her predecessors in centuries past. True, she was learning the business of interior design and was encouraged by Marnie to contribute to their projects. On the other hand, she also dealt with the post and correspondence, kept the filing up to date, handled the bookkeeping, issued invoices and cheques, the latter always signed by Marnie. Anne even kept the office clean and tidy, giving it what she described as a 'good seeing-to' on a regular basis. In short, Anne had become indispensable.

But on the following morning Marnie was glad that Anne had left straight after breakfast for art college in Oxford. It gave Marnie time to explore her thoughts in isolation, to work out what she could do to comfort and support Ralph who had slumped into the depths of despair. She was consoling herself with the thought that at least things couldn't get much worse. But then, they actually did.

In Anne's absence, Marnie picked up the phone when it rang soon after eight o'clock. It was Beth, Marnie's sister. She sounded excited.

'Have you heard the news? I've just read it in *The Guardian.*'

'Oh well, in that case, it *must* be true.'

'You really think so?'

'Enlighten me, Beth. I can't wait.'

'You don't seem too fazed.'

'I'm not. This is how I sound when I'm dying of boredom. Why don't you just spill the beans?'

'Okay. There's an article on page seven referring to a – quote – *reliable source*, suggesting that Ralph – *your* Ralph – was guilty of plagiarism when he wrote his first full-length book.'

'You mean the one entitled, *We're going Wrong*?'

'That's the one. It made him famous, didn't it?'

'I think he would probably say it made him *infamous*, Beth. It was a scathing criticism of the economic policies of the Thatcher government. And at the time, Ralph had only just completed his doctorate. Some parts of the press – not the Tory papers, obviously – described him as a raising star in the world of economics.'

'Seems like his reputation might be getting a bit of a dent if this so-called *reliable source* can produce any evidence.'

'Who wrote the article?' Marnie asked. 'Ralph will probably know them.'

'Er, let me see. Ah ... it just says Our Staff Reporter.'

'Presumably, the so-called *reliable source* is also anonymous?'

'No, the writer quotes a name. Hold on a sec, I've got it in front of me. Yes, here it is.' Marnie heard the rustle of paper. 'The source is named as a Dr Roland Haddow.' Beth pronounced the name slowly and carefully.

Marnie was stunned. 'I know that name ... vaguely. Can't think how, but I'm fairly certain I've heard it... from Ralph, I expect.'

'Well,' said Beth, 'he won't be on your Christmas card list, that's for sure.'

Marnie pricked up her ears at the sound of a car crunching over the gravel drive beside the farmhouse.

'Beth, someone has arrived. I'd better go. Thanks for letting me know about the article.'

'Okay. Has Ralph seen it yet?'

Marnie ran her eyes over the pile of newspapers on her desk. They had just been delivered by the paperboy, and in the past it had been one of Anne's first jobs to take them through the spinney to Ralph in his study on *Thyrsis*.

'Not so far. Oh!'

'What is it, Marnie?'

'My visitors. It's the two police officers from yesterday back again.'

Marnie was hanging up as PCs Grainger and Wallace knocked and entered. She stood up.

'Hello again. What can I do for you?'

'Morning, Mrs Walker. It's your husband we've come to see.'

'Sure. Have a seat. I'll get him for you.'

The constables glanced at each other before taking the visitors' chairs. Marnie pressed a button on the phone and asked Ralph to come to the office.

'He'll be here directly. Can I get you something ... coffee, tea, water?'

No, thanks,' said Grainger. 'It's just a quick visit.'

'Fine. Can I just mention something?'

'Go ahead.'

'My husband has had some bad news. Don't take it amiss, but you may find him rather subdued.'

'Understandable,' Wallace said. 'Not every day someone comes to tell you you're dead.'

'No. I didn't mean that,' said Marnie, 'though it did rather come as a surprise, of course. No, he's just had the news that er ... an old friend has died.'

'Sorry to hear that,' said Grainger. 'A serious illness?'

Before Marnie could reply, Ralph came through the door. He looked less ebullient than usual.

'Good morning. Hope I haven't kept you waiting long. What can I do for you?'

The two WPCs got to their feet.

Grainger said, 'We've come to ask if you'd mind performing a service for us, Mister er ... Doctor ... Sorry. I'm not sure what to call you.'

'Technically it's professor, but let's not worry about that. What is it you want me to do, exactly?'

'Would you be willing to try to identify the body found in the Thames two days ago?'

Ralph gulped. 'You think I might know this person?'

Wallace replied. 'The Met had a tip-off that, as you know, the body was ... well, you. They were told that you carried business cards in your top pocket. That's what they found. At the moment, professor, you're the only lead we have.'

'I see.'

'Of course it's entirely up to you, sir. We can only ask you to do it. No obligation.'

'Obviously I'll do what I can to help.' Ralph's tone was subdued. 'So how do we organise this?'

'Thank you, sir. An officer from the Met will be in touch from London. If you need a hotel reservation for an overnight stay, that can be arranged.'

Ralph shook his head. 'That probably won't be necessary. We have a flat in London if I need to stay. Do you know where I'd have to go to do this?'

Wallace said, 'We understand the morgue is in the district called Bermondsey.'

'That's all right. Our flat is near there, close to Tower Bridge.'

The constables traded glances.

'Tower Bridge?' Wallace repeated.

'Yes. It's on the right side of the river for Bermondsey.'

The two constables were looking perplexed as they took their leave.

Chapter 4

W hat time do you have to be there?' Marnie asked over breakfast.

They were sitting at the kitchen table in the Docklands flat that Marnie had inherited from her late husband, Simon. He was in fact her late *ex*-husband and had died young, himself a victim of murder. The window looked out over the river and for a moment, when Ralph turned his head, Marnie thought he was uncharacteristically ignoring her question, taking in the view downstream towards Canary Wharf. After a few seconds he cleared his throat and spoke quietly.

'I'm due to meet a Dr Haskins at nine-thirty in the entrance to the morgue.'

'And it's near here?' said Marnie. 'You're sure of that?'

'I've checked on the A to Z. It's on the site of the hospital, not far down the road from Tower Bridge.'

'Can we park there?'

'I thought I'd leave the car here and walk. It's not much more than half a mile, I think.'

And that was the plan for the morning. They cleared away the breakfast things and sat in the lounge to watch the news channel on television. The flat was spacious with high-quality furnishings, sumptuous cream leather sofas and Oriental carpets. The walls were adorned with large-scale oil paintings of Docklands and river scenes. No expense had been spared. Everything had been chosen by Simon with exquisite taste; Marnie wholeheartedly approved. She had been surprised to learn that Simon had left it to her in his will and, after an initial reluctance, she had decided to keep it as her London *pied-à-terre*.

Shortly before nine Ralph got ready to leave. As usual he was formally dressed in a dark suit. He had put on a light blue shirt with a Burgundy silk tie and shiny black wingtip shoes.

Marnie had chosen a navy velvet trouser-suit for the visit. As the weather was mild, neither Ralph nor Marnie wore a coat.

'You don't have to come, Marnie,' he said.

'I want to. Let's go. Let's just do it … get it over with.'

They held hands as they strode along without speaking and reached the designated rendez-vous at the appointed time. Dr Haskins was waiting for them inside the entrance. A compact, youngish man of medium height, thinning hair combed forwards and a serious demeanour, he signed them in and asked if they would both be viewing the body.

'Would you like me to come in with you, Ralph?' Marnie asked. She noticed that he was very pale, and knew what an ordeal he was facing. He was a brilliant economist and, in Marnie's eyes, a wonderful man, but she had no doubt that he was well out of his comfort zone in that environment.

'No. It's okay.' He coughed. 'I'll just go in. I won't be long.'

Marnie gave his hand a squeeze and smiled encouragement. He put on a brave face as he turned to Dr Haskins.

'I'm ready.'

Haskins looked at Marnie. 'If you'd like to take a seat Mrs Lombard, your husband will be back in a few minutes.'

Marnie didn't explain that she continued to use the name Walker, by which she had been known professionally for some years. She simply nodded and sat in the small waiting area.

Haskins gestured towards double doors. 'It's this way, Dr Lombard.'

Marnie was momentarily puzzled as the two men exited through the doors. A bell was ringing faintly at the back of her mind. She wasn't quite sure what it signified and wondered if it had something to do with being called *Mrs Lombard*. She tried to fathom it out but gave up and thought no more of it.

Dr Haskins led the way down the corridor. The building was old, probably Victorian, though it was well maintained and seemed to have been recently repainted. The walls were a restful pale green under a white ceiling, but Ralph found the lighting rather harsh. It made him want to close his eyes. In fact at that moment he wanted nothing more than for the whole situation to go away and leave him in peace. Yet he walked on, one foot before the other, until Haskins stopped outside a door that bore neither name nor number. He turned to face Ralph.

'I understand you've done this before, Dr Lombard.'

'Once before, yes.'

Haskins continued. 'Facilities vary from morgue to morgue. Here I'll escort you into the room where the body is lying. I'll draw back the sheet so that you can see just the face. I'll replace it as soon as you indicate, and you can tell me if you recognise the person. Just take your time. There's no rush.'

'I understand.'

'Ready?'

'Yes.' Ralph hoped he sounded definite.

Haskins opened the door and they entered the room. Ahead of them on a dissecting table lay the quiet shape of the dead man under a white sheet. His feet protruded from the end; a label had been attached to a toe. Ralph instantly felt sick and would have taken a deep breath but for the chemical smell in the room. It added to his feeling of nausea. Haskins walked to the other side of the cadaver and glanced across at Ralph, raising an inquisitive eyebrow. Ralph nodded, and Haskins slowly uncovered the dead man's face. As Ralph looked down and briefly studied the man's features, his eyes widened in surprise and shock.

ooo0ooo

Marnie was checking her watch for the third time when the doors into the reception area swung open and Ralph and Haskins emerged. She was at once taken aback by Ralph's grave expression. She had expected him to look at least partly relieved that the ordeal was over. Instead, he looked stunned and distressed. Haskins himself looked bemused.

'Thank you, Dr Lombard,' Haskins said.

The two men shook hands.

'Is that everything?' Ralph asked. 'Is there no paperwork, a statement, something to sign, perhaps?'

'That's all for today, thank you. I expect the police will be in touch to take a statement. It's just a formality. We're grateful for your help.'

Marnie rose and guided Ralph towards the exit. 'How was it?' she asked quietly.

'Let's just go,' Ralph said under his breath.

Behind them Haskins said, 'Goodbye, Mrs Lombard. Thank you for coming.'

Marnie wondered very briefly about correcting him and giving her regular name, but then she realised what had earlier sounded in the back of her mind. She stopped and turned.

Haskins was walking away but, seeing her movement, he paused.

'Dr Haskins, can I ask you something?' Marnie said.

'Certainly. What is it?'

'You address my husband as Dr Lombard.'

The pathologist looked perplexed. 'That is correct, isn't it?'

'Not entirely. His actual title is professor.'

'Oh, I'm very sorry, I didn't –'

'It's all right, I'm not complaining. It's just that people in our area know him as *Professor* Lombard and I was curious to know if there's a reason why you address him as you do.'

Haskins frowned and considered the question. 'I see what you mean, Mrs Lombard.' Again, Marnie let it go and waited for Haskins to reply.

Beside Marnie Ralph said quietly, 'I don't mind what I'm called, to be honest.'

'I know, Ralph, but I was just wondering. I do have a reason.'

Haskins looked up. 'I know what it is. Yes. The police believed that the deceased was you and understood that you kept a business card in your top pocket. The name on the card was Dr Ralph Lombard. I'm sure of it. If you like, I can show it to you – the deceased's personal effects are still here in the evidence locker – but I'm quite certain about that.'

'Interesting,' Marnie reflected. 'But thank you, I don't really need to see it. You've answered my question.'

They took their leave again and stepped outside. Marnie linked arms with Ralph as they set off down the road.

'Are you feeling all right, Ralph?' she asked. 'That was quite an ordeal.'

Instead of replying Ralph said, 'Why did you ask Haskins about my title? Did it strike you as important for some reason?'

'It may be. I think it's certainly interesting.'

'In what way?'

'Don't you see? If the card describes you as *Dr Lombard*, it must date back a few years to the time before you got your chair as visiting professor.'

'I suppose so. You think that's significant?'

'It could be. It could throw light on how this man came to have the card in his possession. Apparently he wasn't carrying anything else that might identify him, which is certainly unusual these days. That makes you the only link to him.'

'Not quite, Marnie.'

'Why not? Am I missing something?'

'Yes, and it is rather pertinent.'

'How do you mean?'

Ralph spoke softly. 'I was able to identify him.'

Marnie stopped abruptly, her eyes wide. 'You were?'

Ralph nodded. 'It was Roland Haddow.'

'Roland ...' Marnie began. 'Oh, you mean the man who's supposed to have accused you of plagiarism?'

'The very same. It means I think my statement to the police will be more than just a formality.'

'But surely it must be some time since you last saw him.'

Ralph looked Marnie in the eye and said softly, 'It was quite recent. You remember the day I came to London for a meeting and stayed overnight in the flat? That evening I had dinner with Roland. The next morning the police found his body in the river.'

Chapter 5

THURSDAY

When the police arrived at Glebe Farm the following day it was not in the form of two women constables in uniform. Detective Sergeant Jack Marriner and Detective Constable Cathy Lamb parked beside the farmhouse and crossed to the office barn soon after nine o'clock. It was a path they had trodden several times before. When they knocked and entered the office, Marnie stood up. Their visit was not unexpected.

'Good morning,' she said, her tone neutral.

'Morning, Mrs Walker.' Marriner glanced across to the empty desk on the other side of the office. 'No Anne today?'

'She's gone into college in Oxford. She's only here a few hours a week during term-time. By now she would've offered you tea or coffee.'

Cathy Lamb chimed in. 'And by now we would've declined.'

'So it's that kind of visit?'

'I'm afraid so,' said Marriner. 'Is your husband about?'

'Not at the moment. He's also on his way to Oxford. Can I help you at all?'

'I'm afraid not. It's really him we need to see. When do you expect him back?'

'Probably not until some time this evening. He's chairing a seminar. They can occasionally drag on till quite late. Would you like him to call you when he gets back?'

Marriner hesitated. 'Er … no, it's okay. Will he be here tomorrow morning?'

'Yes. He'll be wanting to catch up on his research work after being away for a day.'

'Good,' said Marriner. 'We'll see him then.'

'Don't mind me saying this, but it seems rather … portentous, two detectives to take a statement.'

'There's more than that. We need to have a word with him, really.'

'He'll be here.'

'We'll be back.'

After the detectives left, Marnie sat deep in thought. She and Ralph were still troubled: how did Roland Haddow come to have Ralph's card in his pocket? The fact that it was out of date by a few years could explain why Ralph had no memory of giving it to him. Marnie thought it was extraordinary that Haddow had apparently alleged that Ralph had plagiarised ideas for his book, *We're going Wrong*. Many years had passed since its publication, so why would anyone make such an accusation now? The whole thing made no sense.

Marnie checked her watch. Ralph would probably have arrived in college by now, and the seminar might not have started. She grabbed the phone and dialled his mobile. He answered on the third ring.

'Marnie, you've just caught me. Problem?'

'The police have been here.'

'Not just wanting to take my statement, presumably?'

'No. More than that. It was DS Marriner and Cathy Lamb. They want to talk to you.'

'CID ... just as I expected.'

'That's what I thought. I told them you'd possibly be late getting home tonight.'

'Mm ... I should be back in time for dinner. So how did you leave it?'

'They're coming back tomorrow morning.'

'Lucky me. Okay, I'd better go.'

'Have a nice seminar.'

'I'll try to stay awake.'

Marnie had hardly begun working on a new design when the phone rang. She picked up the receiver, connected and announced herself. A woman was on the line.

'Good morning. I'm phoning from the vets in Stony Stratford in reply to a message left by Anne Price on our voicemail. The annual appointment for your cat, Dolly?'

'Sure. Anne's out of the office today, but I can bring up the diary.'

They fixed a date two weeks ahead and Marnie settled back to her work. At that moment the sturdy black cat herself leapt up onto the desk and took up station under the lamp. With the warmth on her fur she blissfully closed her big amber eyes. Marnie worked on to the accompaniment of the cat's gentle purring. Concentration was not easy as the same old questions about Haddow, the business card and the accusation of plagiarism swirled around in her head. Absent-mindedly she reached over and stroked Dolly's thick-pile fur. The cat blinked twice before closing her eyes, and the purring grew louder.

Marnie said, 'What do you think, Dolly? Someone's said Ralph stole somebody else's ideas when he wrote a book. We know he'd never do that, don't we?'

The amber eyes opened slowly and stared back at Marnie. They were full of meaning without any need for words.

'Yes, you're quite right,' said Marnie. 'Of course we do. Ralph's never short of ideas, is he? He doesn't need to pinch anyone else's.'

That look again. It said it all. Dolly closed her eyes, while the purring droned on. Marnie quickly scribbled a note for Anne about the vet's appointment and took it across to her desk. She was on her way back when the phone rang again. Sighing at yet another interruption, and wishing Dolly could be trained to answer the phone, Marnie speeded up and lifted the receiver. Before she could announce herself, she heard Anne's voice, rapid-fire, staccato.

'Hi. It's me, just on my way to a class. Listen, I've had a message from Donovan. He's asking about coming up for the weekend. Would that be okay?'

'Anne, you know Donovan's welcome to come any time. You don't have to ask.'

'Well, with me being away much of the week, I thought you might want to catch up with designs and stuff over the weekend.'

'No, it's fine. But what about his own university work?'

'He says it's not a problem. His final year is mostly project-based anyway and as usual he's well ahead there.'

'How's he coming … by train?'

'He'll give one of the cars a run out, I expect. I think his usual parking space in the garage barn is cleared.'

'Probably. I'll check it out. When are you expecting him?'

'Well …'

'I think the term *short notice* is about to pop up,' Marnie said. 'Am I right?'

'If it isn't too much trouble …'

'You're thinking, what … today?'

'Marnie! That would be *totally* unreasonable.'

'So what time's he coming?'

A pause. 'This afternoon, after classes finish?'

'Sure. That'll be fine.'

'Thanks, Marnie. That's great! There is one other thing.'

'Go on.'

'Ralph.'

'What about him?' Marnie knew what was coming.

'He seemed very subdued last night. I didn't like to ask, but was it to do with identifying that body?'

'He was quite badly shaken.'

'I guessed he would be. He's not as tough as –'

'No, Anne. He was shaken because he ... he recognised the body.'

'No!' Anne's voice was a hoarse whisper.

'That's why we avoided the subject.'

'Was it a friend of his? Oh, sorry. I shouldn't ask. You probably don't want to talk about it.'

'Actually, Anne, it's worse than you could imagine.'

'Really? How could it be worse?'

'The body was Roland Haddow.'

Anne hesitated before replying. 'Wasn't that ...?' she began, tentatively.

'Yes. It was the person who's supposed to have accused Ralph of plagiarism.'

'Oh my God!' Marnie could almost hear Anne's brain whirring. 'That's awkward, isn't it?'

'I think I'd put it stronger than that. And it gets worse. The police want to talk to him. They're coming back tomorrow morning.'

'Holy moly!'

'You could say that. And it gets even worse. The body was pulled out of the river by Tower Bridge, about two hundred metres from our Docklands flat.'

'Blimey! That's an unfortunate coincidence.'

'It's not a coincidence, Anne. You're not going to believe this. Haddow was in the area because he'd been to the restaurant by Tower Bridge on Saturday evening. He'd had dinner there ... with Ralph.'

Anne said, 'The actual evening before his body was found?'

'You've got it.'

'Bloody hell! Does Ralph know the police are coming tomorrow?'

'I rang to tell him a few minutes ago.'

'How did he take it?'

'You know Ralph. He takes most things in his stride. Identifying a body would disturb him a lot, but when it comes to arguing his corner, defending himself against unfounded accusations, he'll be as solid as a rock.'

'And we know where he finds his strength, don't we, Marnie?' Anne said pointedly. 'Oh! Gonna be late for my class. Gotta dash. Bye!'

Marnie was smiling when they disconnected. But she also had her fingers crossed.

ooo0ooo

It seemed strange these days, being alone in the office at lunchtime for much of the week. With Anne at college and Ralph off to various meetings, Marnie was usually joined only by Dolly. She was well trained; she normally gave the cat her bowl of Whiskas or Felix before making herself a sandwich or a bowl of soup. Lunch was eaten to the accompaniment of Dolly's steady contented purring. It seemed to be the soundtrack to Marnie's life at that time.

Marnie's intention that day was to eat a tuna and salad pitta with a glass of what she called sparkling *designer water*. Instead, she found her thoughts wandering over a myriad distractions. Her main focus was on Ralph's dilemma. What would the police make of the coincidence that Ralph had dined with Haddow the very evening on which he had presumably been murdered? Even she had to admit to herself it seemed unfortunate that the man who had apparently accused Ralph publicly of cheating had met his end at that time and in that place.

Then another thought struck her. Had anyone stated in fact that Haddow had been murdered? The police constables had come to tell Marnie that her husband was dead; no mention of murder. Ralph had been invited to identify a body; no one had said it was a murder victim. Marnie reached across the desk for her notepad. On it she wrote:

Haddow

Murder?

She took a bite from the pitta as another thought came into her mind. If the police weren't treating the death of Dr Haddow as suspicious, why did two detectives want to 'talk' with Ralph? She swallowed and took a sip of mineral water. The situation was all such a muddle and so perplexing. Marnie was pleased that Donovan would be coming for a few days. His presence would be a welcome distraction from their confusion. More than that, he had a way of paring things down to basic essentials. He

26

always brought a calm objectivity to bear on any problems; an old head on young shoulders.

Marnie's thoughts strayed to Donovan. He had come into their lives a few years earlier and now seemed to be a fixture. They all liked him, especially Anne. He was her boyfriend, her lover, a force for good in her life, in everyone's life. Marnie smiled again as she conjured up an image of him. Not quite as tall as Ralph, he was slim-built with a pleasant face and blonde hair. In view of his build and colouring, some people had taken him for Anne's brother. That amused them both, given the true nature of their relationship.

When Marnie, wearing her designer's hat, thought of Donovan, one word came into her mind: monochrome. He always wore black or dark grey clothes, and even his narrowboat was painted in the same colours. Anne continued to refer to his narrowboat, *XO2* – pronounced *Exodos* – as the *stealth boat* or even the *U-boat*, in view of his background.

Donovan's late mother was German, a professional translator, his father Anglo-Irish, a university lecturer. They had been killed in a coach crash while on holiday in South Africa when he was ten years old. He had survived the accident and been brought up in Germany by a sister of his mother and her family. His full name was Nikolaus Donovan Smith, giving a nod to all his roots, and he was bilingual in English and German. He had inherited not only the family home in west London but also the family car – a 1971 Volkswagen Beetle – plus a 1955 Porsche Speedster and a 1954 BMW motorcycle. All of them had been his father's restoration projects, his hobby, his relaxation, and all were painted black.

ooo0ooo

On Thursdays Anne was usually back at Glebe Farm in the early afternoon. On that day she parked the Mini in her usual place in the garage barn, cast an eye over the space reserved for Donovan's car and headed for the office with a spring in her step. Marnie stood and hugged her as she came through the door.

'Has chaos reigned in my absence?' Anne asked, exuding saintly forbearance.

Marnie sighed theatrically. 'It's been an utter shambles, Anne. Thank *God* you're here. I don't know what I would've –'

'Okay, okay. I get the message.'

Marnie laughed. 'Well, if you will bounce in like Mary Poppins what d'you expect? I'm guessing you're looking forward to seeing Donovan?'

Anne tried – and failed – to look nonchalant. 'I might be. Is that a pile of messages I see on my desk?'

'Usual bumph, plus one or two that need attention. I'm sure you'll take it all in your stride, Miss Poppins.'

Poppins took off her blouson jacket and hung it by the door. Reaching her desk, she sifted through the messages while her computer powered up. 'Oh yes, Dolly's trip to the vet. I see you've fixed an appointment in the diary for the week after next. It's just routine, isn't it?'

Marnie shrugged. 'Annual service and check-up, that's all.'

'Oil change, spark plugs, that sort of thing?'

'That sort of thing,' Marnie repeated. 'You *are* chirpy today.'

'Just getting my priorities sorted.'

As she spoke, the phone rang. Reaching for the receiver, Anne said, 'By the way, Marnie, I don't *bounce*, I glide sylph-like through the ether.'

At that moment the vet's receptionist announced herself. Anne hoped the receptionist didn't hear the loud raspberry emanating from Marnie's side of the office barn. It was a short conversation. The vet had had a cancellation for Saturday morning. Would Anne like to take it? They agreed on a routine check-up appointment for Dolly at ten o'clock.

Anne was replacing the receiver and typing a note on the computer-diary when she caught sight of movement through the window. The door opened and Angela Hemingway, the vicar, entered in a splash of clerical grey.

'Sorry to bounce in unannounced,' she said, 'but I've just heard about this awful business with Ralph.'

'Which awful business do you have in mind?' Marnie asked. 'We have a plentiful supply. Is it the unfounded allegation of plagiarism or the finding of Ralph's dead body in the river Thames?'

Angela raised a hand to her mouth, eyes widening, plus a loud intake of breath. 'Oh my dear Lord! Ralph …Is he really …?'

'No. In fact he was able to explain that to the police in person. More to the point, they took his word for it.'

Angela gasped. 'Marnie, you're *dreadful*! But was there really a body found in the Thames?'

'There was, yes. Ralph was just asked to identify it.'

'How awful! Whose body … do you know?'

'It turned out to be the man who'd apparently accused Ralph of plagiarism.'

Angela's eyes grew even wider. 'No! Are you sure about that?'

Marnie nodded. 'Yep. Ralph identified him yesterday.'

'How absolutely *awful* for Ralph,' Angela said.

'Not a barrel of laughs for the victim, either,' Marnie observed dryly.

In the background Marnie heard Anne snort.

'I suppose not,' said Angela. 'Well, obviously not. So Ralph knew this man?'

'He did. What's more, Ralph had a meeting in London on Saturday, the day before the body was found, and the two of them had dinner together that evening.' Angela was speechless; her jaw dropped. Marnie continued. 'That possibly explains why the police are coming to talk to Ralph tomorrow.'

Angela emitted a strange sound, somewhere between a squawk and a cough. Marnie took it to be her response.

'Are you okay, Angela?'

'Slightly overwhelmed to be honest, Marnie. I had no idea about ... all that.'

'I expect things will sort themselves out eventually.' Marnie hoped she sounded optimistic. 'So what's your news, then?'

'Nothing so dramatic.'

'That's a relief.' Marnie hoped she sounded encouraging. 'How are things with Randall?'

Angela looked pained. 'Well ...'

'Oh dear, Is there a problem?'

'Not ... as such.'

'I feel a *but* coming on,' said Marnie.

'I was only going to say it's not easy, living as we do ... twenty miles apart. There's Randall in his rectory in Brackley, serving as parish priest as well as rural dean, plus running his hostel for homeless people and itinerants.'

'The drop-in centre for drop-outs,' Anne offered from across the room.

'Quite.' Angela sighed. 'I sometimes find life rather ...'

'Frustrating?' Anne suggested.

'I was going to say ... lonely, actually. Randall is so busy, really bound up in his work. He's clearly a high-flyer in the church. Did you know he's started writing a book on Saint Augustine? I don't know where he gets the energy.'

Marnie said, 'And it leaves you feeling isolated, left behind ... left out?'

'Don't get me wrong, Marnie. I love my work, the church, the people, this lovely village.'

'But Randall's down there, you're up here and you're both rooted in your communities.'

Angela made a gesture of resignation. 'Here I am, going on about my trivial problems when you've got all that accusation to deal with, not to mention poor Ralph having to identify the dead body of his friend.'

'His friend?' Marnie said.

'Well, I'm assuming they were friends. You did say they'd had dinner together on Saturday. You don't spend the evening with people you dislike, do you?'

'Good point,' Marnie murmured.

Angela looked up at the clock. 'My goodness! Is that the time? I must fly. I'm supposed to be visiting sick parishioners this afternoon.'

After Angela left, Marnie and Anne both sat looking thoughtful. Marnie broke the silence.

'Interesting what Angela said about Haddow being Ralph's *friend*.'

Anne said, 'Funny sort of friend who goes around accusing him of pinching other people's ideas for his book. That's pretty serious in Ralph's world.'

'*Allegedly* accusing him, Anne. Remember it was someone writing in the newspaper who said their *source* was Roland Haddow.'

'Even so,' said Anne, 'whoever wrote that must've had a reason, which is presumably why the police are treating it as murder.'

'We don't know that they are,' Marnie protested.

'So why are two detectives coming to see Ralph? I can't imagine DS Marriner is popping round to offer his condolences to Ralph on the loss of his … friend.'

'Oh God,' Marnie muttered. 'I wish we knew what was going on.'

'Sorry, Marnie. I didn't mean to be depressing.'

'No, but you're right, Anne. There must be a good reason for the CID coming to see Ralph.'

As Marnie slumped forward on the desk with her head in her hands, Anne made a valiant attempt to lighten the atmosphere.

'Anyway,' she said, 'that wasn't the only interesting thing we learnt from our favourite local vicar.'

Marnie looked up. 'Oh? What else was there?'

'She said she *bounced* in unannounced.'

'So?'

'It's vicars who *bounce*, Marnie. Whereas I glide sylph-like through –'

Anne didn't get to complete the sentence. She had to duck below the desk to avoid being hit by the rubber lobbed across the room by Marnie. The two of them were laughing when Anne surfaced. Sensing that playful atmosphere, Dolly the cat leapt onto Anne's desk and pushed her furry face into Anne's. It was a subtle hint that tea-time was upon them.

ooo0ooo

At about the time when Anne was switching on the electric kettle, Donovan was trundling up the M1 motorway from London in his aged but sprightly VW Beetle. It was running steadily and smoothly at a constant seventy miles per hour. Over the past few years he had completed the restoration of the car that his late father had begun and had improved its performance and specification, with upgrades to the engine, brakes and suspension. Donovan relaxed in his Recaro sports seat, gripping the polished wood-rim steering wheel, while a cassette-tape of Vivaldi's *Four Seasons* issued quietly from the Pioneer sound system.

On the back seat lay a box containing an assortment of German goodies: wine, bread, cakes, coffee, biscuits, sausage and cheeses, bought from a delicatessen near Donovan's west London home. The shop was owned by an ageing Austrian Jewish couple who had escaped to Britain to start life anew after fleeing Vienna from Nazi persecution. They always enjoyed serving the polite young man whose excellent German brought back memories of their homeland.

Despite the tranquil atmosphere in the car – thanks to an upgraded silencer and exhaust – Donovan's mind was in overdrive. His thoughts – when traffic conditions permitted – were centred on Ralph's predicament. Anne had outlined the situation during their regular late evening phone conversations. She seemed to think, like Ralph, that he could brush aside any accusation of wrong-doing on the grounds that he was manifestly innocent. Ralph was renowned for his original, often controversial, opinions and judgments.

Donovan thought otherwise. He knew the police had suspicious minds; that was their default setting. They would almost certainly try to lure Ralph into a position where honest denial was not convincing enough, where reputation alone counted for little or nothing.

As the miles rolled by, Donovan was all too well aware of loose ends floating around that simply didn't tie up. The evidence against Ralph, however circumstantial it might seem, could easily lead to the not unreasonable assumption that he was implicated in the death of the man who had accused him of an offence that could ruin his career.

ooo0ooo

Meanwhile, at the police station in Towcester, the team of CID detectives assigned to work on the case had reached much the same conclusion, though with certain reservations.

The senior investigating officer – the SIO – was DCI Ted Bartlett, head of a small syndicate. His right-hand man was DS Marriner supported by eight detective constables, including Cathy Lamb. Bartlett had assembled the group in the team's main office after telephone calls to his counterparts in the Met and Thames Valley. It had been decided that for the time being Bartlett would lead the investigation, while liaising with the other two forces.

'Why us, sir?' Marriner asked, reflecting the view of the whole team. 'The body came out of the Thames, and the deceased was a lecturer at Oxford. Our only suspect at the moment is Lombard, and he's also an Oxford man.'

'Fair comment, Jack, but Lombard lives in our patch and, as you say, he's the nearest thing to a suspect we've got for now. You're meeting up with him tomorrow, so let's wait and see what that brings. You're taking Cathy with you, right?'

'Yes, sir.'

'Well, there's no question of door-to-door up here.' Bartlett glanced at Marriner, who nodded his agreement. 'So the rest of you can check background on Haddow, research what was said about this book that Lombard's supposed to have cribbed and follow up on the newspaper article. Who wrote it, do we know yet?'

'Not attributed, sir, and I can't see the paper giving us any names.'

Bartlett shook his head glumly. 'We can't reveal our sources,' he mimicked in a Mickey Mouse voice. 'It'll be the usual bullshit, I expect. But worth prodding. You never know your luck. Okay. Any questions?'

One hand rose slowly. It was a young detective constable who had recently transferred from Uniform and was keen to make a name for himself. Bartlett nodded towards him.

'Just to be sure, guv. Are we treating this as a murder enquiry?'

'Not *guv*, Martin. You're not in the Met … yet.'

'Sorry, sir.'

'As for your question, it's a fair question … the cause of death was drowning. The post-mortem revealed an injury to the back of the head, but it could've been caused when he fell in.'

'So maybe not a murder, sir?'

'We have to consider a fundamental question, which is …?' Bartlett looked around the room. 'Anyone?'

'How did he come to end up in the river in the first place?' said DS Marriner.

Bartlett nodded. 'Exactly. Thank you, Jack. So we're keeping all options open for now. Any more questions, suggestions, brilliant deductions?' He paused. 'No? That's it, then. Go to it.'

As the meeting broke up, Marriner allocated tasks individually to the team then sat on the corner of Cathy Lamb's desk. 'We'll go in your car tomorrow, Cathy, set off at nine after morning briefing.'

'Fine, sarge. What's our line going to be with Lombard?'

'Take it from the top. Get him to tell us about the book he was accused of plagiarising, his relationship with Haddow, his movements around the time Haddow died. Usual stuff.'

'What's your gut feeling, sarge? Murder or accidental death?'

Marriner shrugged. 'I've been in this game long enough to know it's best to keep an open mind, all options open, like the SIO said. One thing's for certain, Cathy. We'll need our wits about us, dealing with the likes of *Professor* Ralph Lombard.'

ooo0ooo

At supper time in the farmhouse Marnie brought Donovan up to date on all the recent goings-on. Sitting in the comfortable living room after their meal, with table lamps glowing, logs blazing in the wood-burner and the aroma of coffee in the air – *Jakobs Filterkaffee*, brought by Donovan – the troubles of the world seemed far away.

Ralph gave every appearance of having recovered from the ordeal of identifying the body in the morgue. He shrugged off the plagiarism as obviously unfounded, though Marnie wondered if he had come to terms with the news of the death of Rhiannon so easily.

For her part, Marnie was worried about the impending visit by the detectives. Ralph's outward calm did little to reassure her. She knew he was troubled below the surface, though whether it was on account of his sense of guilt about Rhiannon or the potential damage to his reputation as an economist, she was uncertain. At the back of her mind was the question of how Roland Haddow had met his end. Marnie knew perfectly well that Anne was right; the police didn't make social calls. Was Haddow's death suspicious? If it was, there were too many factors pointing at Ralph to make Marnie feel at ease.

Anne was snuggled up on one of the sofas next to Donovan. She had drunk two glasses of wine at dinner and was feeling pleasantly lethargic, a condition heightened by the slow steady purring of Dolly who was curled up beside her.

The atmosphere in the room, with its warm lighting, comfortable sofas and Afghan rugs, may have been soporific, but Donovan was far from drowsy. Sitting back beside Anne with his legs stretched out before him, he was listening to everything that Marnie said. It was obvious to him that there were turbulent times ahead. The arrival of the detectives the next day would open up all sorts of awkward questions. Why else were they coming, he thought. Donovan was far from taken in by Ralph's composure. He knew nothing of the death of Rhiannon, but he could sense an inner turmoil in Ralph's mind. As usual, Donovan looked on quietly, sipped his coffee and kept his counsel.

Chapter 6

FRIDAY

After breakfast on Friday Ralph walked across to the office barn with Marnie. It was just on eight o'clock as Marnie unlocked the front door while Anne and Donovan slid open the barn doors to reveal the plate glass frontage. Ralph looked at his watch.

'Did the police say what time they were coming?' he asked.

Marnie thought for a moment. 'No. They just said they'd be back this morning. I can't imagine they'd be as early as this. Will you be on *Thyrsis* till they arrive?'

'I suppose so.'

'You won't want your concentration interrupted in the middle of something important, your research, something complicated.'

'No, but there is something else I have to do. I still haven't written to Jay Harper in reply to his letter about the death of Rhiannon.'

'Well, that shouldn't take long,' said Marnie.

'Really? You don't think so? I've been putting it off. I find it quite difficult to choose the right words.'

That was unusual for Ralph, Marnie thought. She perched on the edge of her desk. 'Isn't it just a matter of thanking him for letting you know? After all, he wasn't a relative, as far as I understand, so a full-blown condolence letter isn't needed. Have I got it wrong?'

'No, but even so ...'

'What is it, Ralph?'

Ralph took a deep breath. 'I've got all kinds of thoughts going round in my head. I suppose his letter has stirred up my sense of guilt ... a lot of painful memories.'

'I can see that.' Marnie was aware that Anne and Donovan had come in and were on the other side of the office by Anne's desk. 'Do you want to talk about it?' she said softly. 'I could walk with you to the boat and we could chat, if you like. But of course I don't want to intrude.'

'Perhaps I'll just go and sit quietly and make a few notes.'

'Okay. I'll call you when the police get here.' Ralph nodded. Marnie reached forward and touched his arm. 'I could sit in with you when they come if that would be helpful.'

'Thanks, but I'll be all right. See you later.'

As Ralph went out, Marnie found Anne at her side.

'Is Ralph okay?' Anne said. 'He seems down in the dumps. Not worried about the police, is he?'

'No. It's just … he has a lot on his mind at the moment. I'm sure he'll be fine.'

oooOooo

It was not long after nine o'clock when Marnie rang to tell Ralph the detectives had arrived. In between writing notes for a seminar, he was working on the letter to Jay Harper and making only slow, painful progress. He had made numerous amendments to the text of the letter on the computer and would have been glad to be left in peace a while longer to achieve an acceptable first draft. He saved the file and set off through the spinney.

Trying to look more relaxed than earlier that morning, he entered the office to greet his visitors with a smile and an extended hand.

'Good morning, Mr Marriner, Cathy. How are you?'

The confident entrance temporarily caught the detectives off-guard and they shook hands. It was as if they were attending a social function.

'Very well, thank you, Ralph … er, professor.' Marriner felt outflanked and unbalanced, and struggled to regain his composure. 'Sorry, but this is a formal visit.'

Cathy Lamb just smiled and nodded as she shook Ralph's hand.

'No,' said Ralph. 'I should be sorry. This is a sad affair and I'll be glad to help in any way I can.'

'I'm sure we appreciate that,' Marriner said.

Before he could get down to business, Ralph gestured them to sit.

'Have you been offered coffee or tea?' he asked.

They felt wrong-footed again, more so when Anne called out from the rear of the office. 'White with one sugar for you, sergeant, white without for you, Cathy?'

Cathy Lamb gave a thumbs-up while Marriner was still lowering himself onto a chair.

'Now,' Ralph began briskly, 'what can I do for you? I take it that the fact that you've come – two detectives, as it were – means you don't just want a simple statement.'

Anne brought him a visitor's chair while the kettle began rattling in the background. From behind her desk, Marnie wondered if Ralph was deliberately throwing the detectives off-balance. This is not exactly the third degree, she thought.

Despite everything, Marriner did his best to rally. 'Like I said, sir, this is a formal visit, and I need to ask you some questions about your relationship with Dr Haddow, also your encounter with him last Saturday.'

Ralph was nodding. 'Our meeting, you mean, yes, I understand.'

'How would you describe your relationship?'

'Roland's subject was economic history, so we had an overlap to a certain extent. I must say I thought he was very sound. He was not only impressive in his analysis of subject matter, but an excellent communicator, a good teacher, I'd say.'

'I was thinking more on a personal level,' Marriner said.

Ralph hesitated. 'Socially we didn't see each other very frequently, being fellows of different colleges. He was a senior fellow at Cranmer College, of course. Ironic, really.'

'What is?' Marriner asked.

'Just that Cranmer was tried, imprisoned and executed in Oxford. It's always struck me as odd that he should have a college named after him here.'

'I see.' Marriner did not sound convincing.

'He was a Cambridge man, as you probably know.'

Marriner didn't know. 'Dr Haddow?'

'No, Thomas Cranmer. Jesus and Magdalene Colleges, I believe.'

Marriner was frowning. He shook his head, as if trying to clear his thoughts. 'Can we get back to your relationship with Dr Haddow?'

'Certainly.'

'How did you get on socially?'

'Quite well, though we mainly just saw each other at college or university functions.'

'Is that all?'

'We exchanged correspondence from time to time.'

'What about? Can you give me some examples?'

'I wrote to congratulate him on books he'd written. As I said, he was very sound in my view. I wrote the occasional review of his books for academic journals. It was that kind of thing on a professional level.'

'Yet he accused you of plagiarism.'

'He didn't.'

Ralph's reply was so plainly put and so immediate that Marriner and Lamb both sat up in their seats as if startled.

Marriner said, 'But the whole issue surrounding his death was this article in which he accused you.'

Ralph sat forward with a serious expression, steepling his fingers, his head cocked slightly to one side. Marnie could imagine that was how he reacted when a student made a contentious point in a tutorial.

'Not quite, sergeant. If you remember, it was *alleged* in a newspaper article that Roland had accused me of plagiarism. That's not the same thing at all.'

Marriner opened his mouth to speak, but no words came out. Ralph continued. 'That's another odd thing. Usually the writer of the article is named, but withholds the name of his source for reasons of confidentiality.'

Marriner was now looking flummoxed. Cathy Lamb came to his rescue.

She said, 'Yet despite that alleged ... er, allegation, you still took him to dinner.'

'Yes.'

'That's rather an expensive restaurant, isn't it, the one near Tower Bridge?'

'It is, but it's very good and not far from our Docklands flat, so it's quite convenient.'

'But didn't you tell DS Marriner that you normally only met at college functions?'

'Quite right, Cathy, though I think I said *mainly* at college functions.'

'So, why invite him to dinner on that occasion after he'd *allegedly* attacked you in public?'

'That's simple. I'd phoned Roland to ask him about the article. He straight away denied ever accusing me of anything, and we agreed to meet at the restaurant to try to iron things out. We were both by chance going to be in London at the same time, so it made sense to meet for dinner that evening.'

Marriner now seemed to have regained his wits. He said, 'As a matter of interest, who suggested the restaurant by Tower Bridge?'

'I did.' No hesitation.

'A restaurant close to the river,' Marriner added.

'A feature it shares with Tower Bridge,' Ralph said with a straight face. 'And also, of course, our flat.'

Marriner continued unabashed. 'You said you thought he hadn't in fact accused you of plagiarism.'

'Not quite,' said Ralph. 'I thought I'd made it clear that I *believed implicitly* that he had made no such accusation. I absolutely accepted his word on that, naturally.'

Marriner nodded. 'Fair enough. There was just one other thing for the moment. Would you know how we can get in touch with Dr Haddow's family? They haven't yet been informed of his death, and we've rather drawn a blank in trying to locate them.'

'There's a good reason for that,' Ralph said. 'To the best of my knowledge Roland had no family, at least no one close. I know his parents are long gone; he had no siblings and never married.'

'Well, that simplifies matters, I suppose,' said Marriner.

Just then the phone began ringing. Anne answered it and withdrew to the kitchen area at the rear of the office. Marriner was gathering his thoughts when Anne emerged with a hand over the receiver.

'Sorry to interrupt,' she said. 'It's a call for Ralph … urgent.'

With his usual impeccable manners, Ralph stood and said to the detectives, 'Sorry about this. Would you excuse me for a moment?'

He made his way to the kitchen area. As Anne handed him the receiver, he whispered, 'Who is it?'

Anne murmured, 'Roger Broadbent.'

If Ralph was surprised to receive a call from their solicitor, he didn't show it, but retreated towards the shower room in the furthest corner of the building. There he was able to speak without being overheard. The call was brief, and he reappeared after two or three minutes. In his absence Anne had offered more coffee, but it had been declined.

'I'm sorry about this,' Ralph said. 'That was Roger Broadbent – you've met him, of course, our solicitor – and he says he's on his way here. He's asked me not to answer any questions until he can be present.'

'That's all right,' said Marriner, rising from the chair. 'I think we've covered enough ground for the moment. We will need a formal statement from you, though.'

'Would you like me to draft something and let you have it?' Ralph asked.

This was not normal procedure, but Marriner said, 'That would be very helpful, thank you.'

39

ooo0ooo

Roger Broadbent arrived shortly before eleven. He was more than just their solicitor. Marnie had known him for a few years, ever since he handled a valuable bequest made to her by an old boatman in London's Little Venice. When Marnie took over *Sally Ann* on her mooring in that part of the Regent's Canal, she discovered that Roger and his wife Marjorie kept their narrowboat *Rumpole* nearby. In his fifties, he had an avuncular manner, and Marnie always felt she was in safe hands when Roger was around.

She decided to leave Anne in charge of the office while she and Ralph decamped with Roger to the farmhouse. Unlike the detectives, Roger never declined to accept refreshment – his favourite Earl Grey tea – and the three of them settled in the comfortable living room. Ralph outlined the conversation he had had with Marriner and Lamb while Roger nodded approvingly.

'That seems all right,' he said. 'Nothing incriminating there.'

'Surely,' said Marnie, 'there can't be anything incriminating when Ralph hasn't done anything.'

Roger gave her an old-fashioned look. 'Marnie, things can often be interpreted in different ways. The main thing is not to leave yourself open to misinterpretation or worse, misrepresentation. You seem to have covered all your bases, Ralph, quite firmly, in fact.'

'So I can write my statement along those lines?' Ralph said.

'I'd like to run an eyeball over it before you send it off, but I don't see any problems.'

'Good.'

Roger's expression was serious. 'Well...' He sipped his tea, looking thoughtful

'Not good?'

'I'd like to know more about this plagiarism business. You say Haddow denied accusing you.'

'Emphatically,' said Ralph.

'Had anyone ever levelled such an accusation against you in the past?'

'No, never.' Ralph laughed. 'I've never needed anyone's help to be contentious.'

'And you don't know the name of the author of the article in question?'

'No. It was by-lined as – quote – *our staff reporter.*'

'Can you hazard a guess who it might've been?'

Ralph shrugged. 'Not a clue.'

'Mm ...' Roger murmured. 'I'd like to see a copy of the article. Forgive me, Ralph, but I have to ask you –'

'The answer's no again, Roger. In the book all the facts are in the public domain, and all the interpretations and opinions were mine alone. That's precisely why I was widely ostracised at the time. My views were original and broadly regarded as controversial, even heretical in some quarters.'

'By whom?'

'Academic rivals ... the political establishment ... the right-wing press – the usual suspects.' Ralph grinned.

'Which book was this?' Roger asked.

'It was called *We're going Wrong*.'

'That sounds familiar.'

Another grin from Ralph. 'Now that, I *did* borrow. It was the title of a nineteen-sixties song by the rock group, Cream. But I say again, all the views put forward in the book were entirely my own.'

'Well, there's no copyright on titles,' Roger muttered. 'It rather sounds as if you wanted the book to be provocative.'

'I suppose I did. I was a young academic with a freshly-minted doctorate and I wanted to make a bit of a splash. All my books have more or less argued against the conventional wisdom. I should've known *We're going Wrong* would upset the applecart to some extent, but that didn't bother me at the time.'

'You didn't perhaps quote someone else's argument without acknowledging it?'

Ralph shook his head. 'No, definitely not.'

'You say your views upset some people. Can you give me an example ... without too much technical jargon?'

'Sure. Let me think.' Ralph paused before continuing. 'Okay. This is grossly over-simplified, but here goes. The European Commission offered fifty per cent grants to fishing fleets to upgrade their boats. The Dutch, the Belgians and others accepted and built bigger, better boats. The Thatcher government refused to pay their fifty per cent share, so the Brits continued with smaller less efficient vessels. They were uncompetitive so they ended up selling much of their quota – in other words, their fishing rights – to their Continental rivals. It was short-sighted, and our people lost out. Some of the tabloids tried to blame Brussels; I got tarred with the brush of being unpatriotic.'

'Could the accusation of plagiarism be a way of getting back at you, Ralph?'

41

Ralph made a face. 'I suppose so, but after all these years, why?'

Roger looked pensive. 'Mud sticks, of course, but like you I can't see why the accusation should be made public at this particular time. And, Ralph, can you think of any reason why Haddow might wish to accuse you?'

'Roger, I've already made it clear that he didn't.'

'Of course. I worded that badly. What I meant was, if you could think of why anyone might feel confident enough to *say* that you'd plagiarised material.'

Ralph looked blank. 'Frankly, I'm at a complete loss.'

'Tell me what Haddow said about it.'

'Well, over dinner I asked him outright. He'd already denied the accusation when we spoke on the phone. I asked if he'd had any further ideas since then.'

'He repeated the denial?'

'Totally and unequivocally. He denied everything. In fact, when the article came out, he wasn't even in the country. He was spending a semester at Brown. That's an Ivy League university in America ... Rhode Island. He'd not long returned to Britain when we had dinner together.'

'He couldn't have said something to a journalist that could be misinterpreted while he was away?' Roger asked.

'Not much scope for that,' said Ralph, 'especially when he didn't believe it to be true.'

'Fair enough, Ralph. Had you been contacted by a journalist before the article came out?'

Ralph reflected. 'No, and that's rather odd.'

'In what sense?' said Roger.

'In my experience, if a journalist is going to mention or quote you in an article, they normally contact you beforehand to give you a right of reply, or at least to comment.'

'Do they need your permission?' Marnie asked.

It was Roger who replied. 'No. There's broad agreement in law about freedom of speech. As long as you don't libel someone you have the right to quote them – as long as you do so accurately – or refer to them by name if you say something about them.'

'Presumably,' said Marnie, 'you can sue them if they go too far.'

Roger nodded. 'Yes, though it rarely happens. Tell me, Ralph, did Haddow have any inkling at all of who might have written the article?'

'No. He said he hadn't been approached by anyone and had certainly never criticised me. He stood by that ... very firmly, as I've said.'

'Okay.' Roger raised the cup to his lips and drained the Earl Grey.

Marnie reached for the pot to top him up. She said, 'Can you stay, Roger? It's almost time for lunch.' Roger thanked her and accepted. What Marnie thought was, could Haddow have been murdered to shut him up? If so, by whom and why?

Chapter 7

SATURDAY

D o you think Sergeant Marriner will be at the station this morning?' Ralph asked Marnie. They were clearing away after breakfast.

'On a Saturday?' Marnie thought about it. 'Could be, I suppose. My guess is they work shifts rather than normal office hours. Are you planning to make a confession?'

Ralph smiled. 'Not exactly, but I'm wondering what to do with my statement, now that Roger's approved it. I could fax it to Marriner, but I suspect he probably needs the original with an actual signature.'

'Not the sort of thing you could just pop in the post, is it?' said Marnie. 'I think you should phone and ask him. If he's not there, someone in CID will be able to advise, I'm sure.'

And so it was that Ralph printed and signed his statement before making the call.

Meanwhile, across the courtyard in the office barn, a small drama was being played out. In preparation for Dolly's trip to the vet, Anne had brought in the cat carrier to check it over. Dolly had jumped up onto Anne's desk to take up her usual station under one of the lamps. Instead of closing her eyes and purring with satisfaction after her breakfast, she was eyeing the carrier with interest bordering on suspicion. It didn't escape her notice that Anne and Donovan had taken care to shut the office door quickly behind them when they came in. Dolly suspected that her escape route had been blocked.

When Marnie and Ralph came over from the farmhouse, they lingered chatting in the open doorway. Dolly stood and stretched and began padding to the edge of the desk. Seeing her, Donovan called over to the entrance to ask Marnie and Ralph if they would like to talk inside or outside the office. Grasping the situation, they stepped out and hastily pulled the door shut. Dolly sat and observed. She was not to be deceived; she recognised a manoeuvre when she saw one.

ooo0ooo

Dolly was not a good passenger. Understatement. Placid and calm in any other situation, when transported by car she made everyone within earshot fully aware of her displeasure. The whining began within seconds of being lowered into the pet carrier, and she kept up the serenade intermittently for the entire journey. Anne and Donovan were thankful that the vet was only fifteen minutes from Glebe Farm in the nearby small town of Stony Stratford.

To reduce the disturbance to Donovan who was at the wheel of the Beetle, Anne sat on the rear seat with Dolly in the pet carrier on her lap. She made soothing sounds to the cat in the hope of reassuring her that they were just out for a drive. Dolly was not taken in by this subterfuge.

Donovan found a parking space in the high street a short distance from the vet's surgery. He walked round to the pavement and took the carrier from Anne, holding the passenger door open while she clambered out from the back seat. Anne headed off to the vet's with Dolly while Donovan stayed behind to lock the car doors.

He was turning to follow Anne when the door to the vet's surgery opened and an old lady stepped out. She looked up and down the street, clearly agitated. This piqued Donovan's curiosity; he stood on the pavement beside a shop window, watching her.

Some minutes went by, and still the old lady scanned the high street, now anxious to the point of distress. Donovan wondered if she found it uncomfortable standing there and he was thinking of asking if she would like to sit in the car when Anne emerged with the pet carrier. She looked pleased.

'All done,' she said as Donovan approached. 'Clean bill of health, and she's had her booster.'

As if to confirm this, at that moment Dolly let out a loud meow. This brought about a strange reaction. While Anne smiled happily, the old lady turned sharply and her face crumpled. Tears streamed down her cheeks and she began to sob. Anne immediately thrust the pet carrier at Donovan and stepped closer to the old lady.

'Are you all right?' she said.

At first there was no response other than a series of rapidly drawn breaths. The old lady shook her head and struggled to speak.

45

'They've taken her,' she gasped. 'My Dorli. I know they are going to put her to sleep.' She spoke with difficulty and with a strong foreign accent.'

'Dolly?' said Anne. 'That's the name of our cat.'

'No, *Dorli.*' More sobbing, more distress. 'And she is only six years old.'

Donovan's eyes narrowed as he looked on in silence.

'Who's taken her?' Anne asked gently.

The old lady turned her head towards the door. 'The vet. She cannot come with me, and they said I had to bring her here.' More sobbing. Her accent seemed even more pronounced. 'Ach, my heart, it is breaking.'

'Who is Dorli?' said Anne.

'My cat. I must go to the elderly home. No pets allowed. I don't want them to put her to sleep. She is so lovely. She is my dear, dear friend. The only friend I have left.' Tears were pouring down her face.

Donovan moved nearer and said, 'Dorli?'

'Yes.'

'Like Dorothea?' He pronounced it as *Do-ro-tay-a.*

The old lady said nothing but stared at Donovan as if seeing him for the first time.

'*Sind Sie Deutsche?*' he said to her. Are you German?

She replied in German. 'No, I'm from Austria … from Salzburg. Dorli was named after my mother. She was Dorothea and always called Dorli, as we do in Austria.'

Donovan looked aside to explain to Anne, only to find that she had disappeared. He turned back to the old lady and continued in German. 'I'm very sorry for your problem.'

'Are you German?' she said.

'Partly, yes … my mother.'

She looked over his shoulder. 'Your … sister? She has gone into the vet's.'

Donovan wondered what Anne had in mind. Then he guessed. Anne grew more like Marnie every day, adopting the motto of what Marnie called the 'Royal Marines School of Management': *seize the high ground.*

He said,' She is in fact my girlfriend, and I think you will be seeing her in a moment.'

'It is good of you both to speak with me. I am very sad, I'm so sorry.'

'Why did you bring Dorli here?' Donovan asked.

'I didn't know what to do. I hoped they would find a home for her, but I think now …'

Passers-by on the pavement stepped round them, with the occasional glance on hearing a foreign language spoken in the high street.

'Where are you moving to?' said Donovan.

'To a home in Brackley. It is very nice but they will not permit animals, even a little cat who does no harm to anyone and ...'

The old lady fought to control herself and her breathing. Donovan reached forward and touched her lightly on the arm.

'I understand.'

Behind them Donovan heard a door opening and looked round to see Anne emerging. The door was being held open by the receptionist. Anne was carrying a large basket pet transporter and a carrier bag. At the sight of them, the Austrian lady drew a sobbing breath and rushed forward.

'*So*,' said Anne in German. '*Hier ist Dorli.*' After a moment's thought, she reverted to English. 'I think we now have to find a nice home for her.'

Donovan said in German, 'This is Anne, my girlfriend.' He pronounced her name the German way, like Anna.

The reply came in English. 'And I am Frau Kreisler, pleased to meet you, Anne.'

Anne smiled and glanced at Donovan. 'And my boyfriend ...' She decided that a degree of German-style formality was required. 'Nikolaus.'

'Nikolaus,' Frau Kreisler repeated, nodding towards him. She returned her gaze to Anne and Dorli and spoke again in English. 'But what will you do?'

'Ah, there you are! Sorry I took so long. The opticians couldn't find my new glasses.'

No one had noticed the sudden arrival of a rather breathless, rather flustered, rather plump middle-aged woman. She glanced in the direction of Dorli's cat basket.

'Oh, Mrs Kreisler, you haven't been in yet. I know it's hard for you but –'

'You're mistaken,' said Anne. 'Frau Kreisler has found a new home for Dorli already.'

'I see ... but that's wonderful.'

'I'm Anne and this is my friend ... Nikolaus. We're taking care of her now. It's been agreed with the vet.'

'Well, my dear, that's very good of you. I'm Mrs Reeves, by the way.'

'We'd shake hands,' said Donovan, 'but we're rather encumbered, as you see.' He glanced down at the pet carrier that he was holding in his arms. 'This is our cat, Dolly.'

'What a coincidence.' Mrs Reeves smiled. 'Same name. Well, we'd better be going. We've got to drive to Brackley.' She turned to Frau Kreisler. 'Do you want to say goodbye to the cat?'

Before Frau Kreisler could reply, Anne intervened. 'No need for goodbye, we'll be keeping in touch.' She carefully lowered the cat basket to the ground and reached in her shoulder bag for a business card. She handed it to Frau Kreisler. 'You can phone me any time and I'll let you know how Dorli is getting on. What's the name of your new home in Brackley?'

'It's called Autumn Lodge.'

'I'm sure it's very nice.'

'Yes.' Frau Kreisler shrugged in resignation. 'But sadly, no pets allowed.'

ooo0ooo

Meanwhile, back in the office at Glebe Farm, Marnie's mobile rang. The caller ID announced that Ralph was on the line. He was phoning from *Thyrsis*.

'Marriner's just rung me back. He's on duty this weekend and he'll be at the station for the rest of the day. I've printed off the statement and I've said I'd drop it in on him, so I'll drive over this afternoon.'

'Oh well,' said Marnie, 'I suppose it's a good sign that they're not sending a hit squad to drag you off to the clink.'

'Don't even joke about it, Marnie.'

'You think I'm joking?'

Ralph was chuckling when they disconnected.

ooo0ooo

'So now we have two cats,' said Donovan, driving back to Knightly St John.

Anne was sitting beside him for the return journey. The rear seat was occupied by two pet transporters, separated by a carrier bag containing cat food, a bag of cat litter and a litter tray. Anne had carefully positioned them so that Dolly and Dorli were not facing each other. A bemused silence, probably a blend of curiosity and suspicion, radiated from the back of the car.

'That poor lady, Frau Kreisler,' Anne said. 'She seemed so unhappy, I couldn't let her think they'd put her cat to sleep.'

'Would they do that?'

'No. They were going to take her to the animal shelter and hope to find her a new home.'

'But you wanted to rescue her.'

'I felt I had to do something.' Anne looked over her shoulder at the two felines. 'What colour is Dorli, would you say?'

'I don't know much about cats, but I think she's maybe a tortoiseshell.'

'She's got nice markings,' Anne observed, 'a nice mixture of colours.'

'And you no doubt have a master plan in mind?'

'Er ...'

'You do have a plan, don't you, Anne?'

Donovan's question was met with silence. They were now turning onto the narrow country road leading to Knightly St John.

'Anne?' Donovan repeated.

Anne said nothing, playing for time. She knew Donovan would need to give all his concentration to the twisting road with occasional wider sections for passing. At any minute they could round a bend and encounter horse riders, tractors or even a dreaded combine harvester occupying the whole roadway. It was only as they reached the outskirts of the village that Anne had a flash of inspiration.

'Take the first left,' she said suddenly.

Donovan reacted quickly. He signalled, braked, changed down and turned into a small estate of modern family homes.

'This is the plan?' he said. 'We're going to knock on doors till we find Dorli a home?'

'Down to the end, last house on the right,' Anne said decisively.

'Isn't that where ...? Ah, I get it.'

Donovan knew the house quite well. He drove confidently onto its drive, stopping behind a maroon Ford Escort that he also knew well. They were parked outside the house of their friend Angela Hemingway, the vicar.

'Please don't tell me you've come hoping for divine inspiration, Anne.'

'Trust me,' said Anne. 'I'm an agnostic.' She undid her seat belt, reached for the door handle and climbed out. 'I'll ring the doorbell. You bring the cat basket and the paraphernalia.'

'Don't you think ...?' Donovan began, but Anne was already approaching the front door.

ooo0ooo

'What did she say?' Marnie asked, pouring coffee into four mugs. It was a short while later.

Anne said, 'To be honest, I suppose Angela was rather taken by surprise at first, though she handled it quite well.'

'You presented her with a cat basket, complete with cat, just like that?'

'Plus food, cat litter and litter tray,' Donovan chimed in.

'I refer to my original question,' Marnie persisted.

'Before she could say much, I told her that if she had a pet she wouldn't feel so lonely, living such a long way from her boyfriend.'

Marnie passed round the mugs of coffee on a tray. 'So as a substitute for Dr Randall Hughes, Rural Dean of Brackley, former incumbent of this parish, she gets a cat. Have I got that right?'

'Sounds like a fair trade to me,' said Ralph, grinning.

'Actually,' Donovan said, 'there is a logic to this.'

'There is?' Anne, the author of the plan, looked dubious.

'You could at least try to look convinced,' Donovan insisted. 'You didn't explain why you suddenly thought of Angela.'

'Oh yes. I see what you mean. It's that Frau Kreisler –'

'*Frau?*' said Marnie.

'She's Austrian. I forgot to mention that as well. Anyway, the old people's home where she's going to live is in Brackley. That made me think of Randall and I made the connection with Angela.'

Ralph was nodding. 'I can see a measure of logic creeping in here.'

'That's encouraging,' said Anne. 'I thought Angela might be able to take Dorli on visits to Brackley so that Frau Kreisler could still see her cat from time to time. And it would give Angela a reason for maybe extra visits to Brackley so that she could see Randall more often.'

'Excellent – if slightly devious – reasoning,' said Marnie. Anne looked delighted. Marnie added, 'And you're sure Randall isn't allergic to cats?'

Anne gasped. 'Blimey! I hadn't thought of that. D'you think he might be?'

'Surely Angela would have said so, if that was the case,' Donovan said.

'She might've been too polite to say anything,' Marnie murmured. 'After all, she is a vicar.'

ooo0ooo

Ralph thought he was just going to hand in his statement at the police station in Towcester and that would be that. He was mistaken. On arrival that afternoon he presented himself in reception and was asked to take a seat. A few minutes later DC Cathy Lamb came to meet him. She was rather more formal than usual and not her habitual relaxed, friendly self.

'Would you like to come through?' she said.

'I've brought my statement, Cathy. Can't I just hand it to you?'

'DCI Bartlett would like a word,' she said. 'It won't take long.'

She led him down a corridor painted in institutional pale green, which reminded him of the mortuary in Bermondsey. He took that as a bad omen and tried not to shudder at the thought. The door that she opened bore the label: 'Interview room 2'.

'Please take a seat. The DCI will be with you directly.'

After Lamb withdrew, Ralph slid a copy of the statement out of its transparent pocket and laid it on the table in front of him. It was succinct, covering the bare facts without embellishment. He had read   halfway down the page when the door opened and in walked DCI Bartlett and DS Marriner. Ralph rose to meet them, smiled and stuck out his hand. The detectives shook hands awkwardly and took their seats. Ralph slipped the paper back into its pocket and slid it across the table.

'I've run off three copies in case you need them for circulation,' he said.

'That's very thoughtful, professor. Thank you.'

'I've signed all three in black ink in case you need to make more copies.' Ralph made to stand up but Bartlett raised a hand; Ralph settled back onto the chair. Bartlett quickly scanned the statement.

'Was there something else, chief inspector?'

'Just one or two things,' said Bartlett. 'That evening when you had dinner with Dr Haddow, what was the atmosphere like between you?'

'Cordial, as usual. We'd been colleagues and on friendly terms for years.'

'And at the end of the evening?'

'The same.' Ralph lowered his voice. 'It was the last time I ever saw him ... until that day ... in the mortuary.'

'You didn't leave the restaurant together. Why was that?'

Ralph reflected for a moment. 'Yes, you're quite right. How did you know?'

Bartlett shrugged. 'We ask questions.'

'Of course.'

'So why did you leave separately? You haven't mentioned it in your statement.'

Ralph recalled the scene that evening. 'Mm ... I suppose I didn't think it important. It must've slipped my mind.'

'It was only a short time ago,' Bartlett prompted. 'Think back.'

'Oh, I do remember. I had a discussion with the sommelier.'

'The who?'

'The wine waiter,' Ralph explained. 'We exchanged a few words when I was putting on my coat. Roland was dashing out.'

'Why was he dashing out?'

'I understood he was rushing off to catch a train back to Oxford.'

'So why were you chatting to this ... waiter?'

'The sommelier,' said Ralph. 'Roland had remarked on my choice of wine when I ordered it at the table. We had a bottle of claret ... red Bordeaux.'

Bartlett frowned. 'Go on.'

Ralph said, 'It was nothing really. Roland had misheard, that's all. He asked if I'd actually ordered a bottle of *Château Pétrus*. I assured him I'd ordered *Château Sables Peytraud*. There's a slight similarity in the names, you see.'

'Yes,' said Bartlett. 'I did spot that.'

'Well, the sommelier had remembered and joked about it as I was saying goodnight.'

'I don't get the joke,' said Marriner.

'It's just that for *Pétrus* you could pay around £25,000 for a case ... somewhat beyond my means, even for just one bottle.'

'So what's this other wine?' said Bartlett.

'A rather more modest claret that I know and like from a small vineyard in the *Entre-Deux-Mers* district. *Pétrus ... Peytraud*. You see the similarity '

Bartlett was looking puzzled. 'That's when Dr Haddow dashed off, leaving you in the restaurant.'

'Yes, chief inspector. We parted as friends, as we always had in the past.'

oooOooo

Supper was courtesy of Donovan from the items he had brought from London. It was a typical German evening meal – known as *Abendbrot*, literally, evening bread – and comprised a delicious spread from which participants could help themselves. Sliced dark rye bread in a basket took centre-stage, beside a crock of Austrian butter. They were surrounded by platters of sausage and cooked meats, three types of cheese, hard-boiled eggs, gherkins, pickles and tomatoes, accompanied by two bottles of dry white wine from the Rhineland.

'Donovan, you really don't have to do this every time you come to visit us,' said Marnie.

'I like to make a contribution, as long as it's all right.'

'More than all right, I'd say,' said Ralph, appreciatively.

Anne cut herself a slice of Austrian smoked cheese. 'It's a kind of family thing, isn't it? Reminds you of your relatives in Germany.'

'You're right, Anne. It's not quite the same when you're living alone.'

'Talking of living arrangements ...' Marnie began, looking meaningfully in Anne's direction.

Anne shook her head. 'Oh, I don't want to bore everybody with my petty concerns.'

'But you're right,' Marnie said. 'It's not much fun having to drive back and forth to Oxford every day. You're missing out on student life.'

'Well there's not much I can do about it right now, at least not for this academic year.'

'Not necessarily ...' It was Ralph's turn to look meaningfully, but in Marnie's direction.

Anne said, 'Nice of you, Ralph, but I don't really want you using your influence to sort out my trivial problems.'

Ralph nodded at Marnie. She said, 'That's not what we have in mind.'

'We?' said Anne.

Donovan grinned. 'You 'ave zee master plan?' His accent was a cross between Inspector Clouseau and Hercule Poirot.

Marnie looked over at Ralph. 'Shall I?'

'Go ahead.'

'Well, obviously we can't magic a room in college or in hall out of thin air, so unless there's a sudden vacancy, that isn't an option.'

'No,' Anne agreed. 'And I've been looking out for some place where I might move in as a flatmate, but so far, nothing doing.'

'Well, there might be another possibility and in fact it's staring us in the face.'

'So what is zee master plan?' Anne mimicked Donovan's Clouseau/Poirot accent.

'What if you took *Sally Ann* down to Oxford and used her as your base?'

Anne looked confused. 'I don't get it. I mean for a start, do you think we could find a mooring?'

'We've made some enquiries. There is a possibility.'

Anne frowned. 'But what if you wanted to use *Sally* yourselves?'

'Easy,' said Ralph. 'If we want to use a boat, we've got *Thyrsis*.'

Anne looked thoughtful. 'You really think it could work?'

'I stay on my boat in London sometimes,' Donovan said, 'and I don't even have a proper mooring. I have to move it about.'

'Is that practical?' Anne asked.

'Why not?' said Ralph. 'After all, I work from a boat.'

'But I'd have lectures and things,' Anne persisted.

'I go in on my bike,' Donovan said. 'You can use your Mini.'

Anne still looked doubtful.

'I know what's bothering you,' said Marnie. 'But you can sleep on the boat from Sunday to Wednesday and come home on Thursday afternoons. I mean, come back to Glebe Farm.'

'This is my home now, Marnie. I don't want to let you down by not pulling my weight here.'

'Sure, I understand. Why don't we give it a go this term and see how it works out?'

Marnie could tell by Anne's expression that she was coming round to the idea, or at least thinking about it..

'There is just one thing,' Anne said. '*Sally Ann* is here and Oxford is there. Where is this mooring, this *possibility*?'

Marnie produced a cruising guide to the canal, opened it and pointed.

'Here, not far from Duke's Cut, just a couple of miles out of the city. There are some moorings on the main line plus a workshop and a dry dock. It's got electricity and water supplies and its own private car park.'

'And the cost?' said Anne.

'Certainly not as dear as university accommodation or digs. We'll cover it.'

'But you pay for so much already.'

Marnie raised a hand. 'That was always the deal.'

Anne frowned and looked Marnie in the eye. 'I sink vee 'ave zee master plan,' said Clouseau and Poirot with one voice.

ooo0ooo

The phone call that evening came as no surprise. Anne was expecting it. She didn't recognise the caller ID number on the screen of her mobile, but she could guess.

'*Guten Abend, Frau Kreisler*,' she began.

A second or two of silence before, 'Ah, yes. But I speak English with you, no?'

'Thank you. That would be best, I think. You want to know about Dorli?'

'Of course.'

'I can tell you that she is well and is now living with the vicar in our village.'

'He likes cats, your vicar?'

'It's *she* and, yes, she likes cats.'

'A *woman* vicar?'

'Yes. Her name is Angela Hemingway. She's a friend of ours.'

Donovan was sitting close to Anne, listening to the conversation. As Anne glanced at him, he made the sign of the cross and pointed at the mobile. Anne remembered that Austria was a mainly Catholic country.

She added, 'I hope you don't mind that it's not a Catholic vicar.'

'No, no. That is quite in order.' She chuckled. 'I don't think Dorli is a practising Catholic cat.'

'I must tell you this, Frau Kreisler. Angela is a good friend of the vicar in Brackley. He's a man.'

'The vicar here ... in Brackley?'

'Yes, so you'll be able to see Dorli when Angela visits her friend.'

'*Wunderbar!* I am so pleased. And I hope I will see you again also.'

'Definitely. Dorli will bring us on her visits.'

'You have been so kind.'

'Glad to be able to help, Frau Kreisler.'

'I will remember you in my prayers.'

'Oh ... er, thank you.'

'And also your vicar friend ... Angela is her name, *ja*?'

'That's right, Angela Hemingway. I'm sure she'll be ... pleased.'

As they ended the call and Anne pressed the red button on her mobile, she was wondering about ecclesiastical protocol, Angela being included in Catholic prayers. Was that, as Frau Kreisler would say, 'quite in order'?

Chapter 8

MONDAY

On Monday morning Anne set off for Oxford after an early breakfast, while Donovan left for London. Marnie was alone in the office, but not for long. She was so totally focused on her design for a boutique country hotel in the Cotswolds that she failed to hear a car roll to a halt on the gravel drive beside the farm house. Her first awareness of visitors was a knock on the door of the office and the entry of PC Wendy Grainger and PC Ruth Wallace. Marnie rose from her seat to receive them. Grainger was the first to speak.

'Good morning, Mrs Walker. We're here to see your husband.'

Marnie reached for the phone. 'Sure. Take a seat. I'll tell him you're here. He'll be pleased you've not come to tell him he's dead.'

It was a quick call, after which Marnie asked, 'Would you like coffee … tea? Ralph will be here in just a minute.'

The constables looked at each other before Wallace replied, 'Coffee would be good, if that's all right.'

Marnie was laying the tray when Ralph came through the door. As usual he thrust out a hand. 'It's PCs Grainger and Wallace, am I right?'

'Yes, sir, quite right. Good memory.'

Ralph smiled as they shook hands. 'Oh, I always remember people who've come to inform me of my death. Please sit. I see Marnie is looking after you.'

'Yes, thank you.'

Ralph drew up a chair. 'So what can I do for you today?'

Grainger said, 'We've come about your statement, sir.'

'I rather guessed that,' said Ralph. 'Do we have to be so formal?'

'Sorry?'

'Can't we drop the *sir* … unless you've come to arrest me, of course?'

'Quite the opposite. We've come to let you know that witnesses have upheld your account of what happened in the restaurant on the evening when Dr Haddow was killed.'

'Witnesses *plural*?' Ralph looked surprised.

Grainger nodded. 'The head waiter overheard your conversation with the wine waiter ... something to do with two wines with similar-sounding names?'

'Château *Pétrus* and Château Sables-*Peytraud*,' Ralph added helpfully.

'If you say so,' Wallace said. 'It was the head waiter who also heard Dr Haddow say he had to rush to catch his train. He said you shook hands and it was all very amicable.'

By now Marnie was handing out coffee. 'Is that an end to it, then?' she said.

Grainger replied. 'As far as we're concerned it is. The Met CID are dealing with the murder investigation.'

'So it is being treated as a murder?' said Marnie.

'Oh yes.'

Marnie smiled across at Ralph and was surprised at his expression. She had expected him to look at least relieved. Instead, he seemed deep in thought, his mind far away. She had to give his arm a discreet nudge when she offered him the plate of biscuits.

ooo0ooo

Marnie held Ralph's arm as they stood at the office door watching the police car manoeuvre on the drive and head off up the field track. She thought net curtains would no doubt be twitching all along the high street at the sight of the car with its blue and yellow checkered markings and the blue light-bar on the roof. It would be the talk of the village in the shop and at the school gate that afternoon.

'Well,' she said, 'that seems to be that. You don't need to worry about the police any more.'

'No.' Ralph's voice was flat.

'Are you okay? I noticed you were looking a little thoughtful back there.'

'Was I?'

'Am I missing something?' Marnie asked. 'I thought you'd be pleased that the matter had been resolved.'

Ralph turned to look at Marnie. 'There never was going to be a problem for me in relation to Roland's death. Apart from the fact that I knew I had nothing to do with it, I knew that no actual evidence connecting me with his death could possibly be found.'

'Of course not.'

'But don't you see, Marnie? The accusation of plagiarism is still hanging over me. That hasn't gone away.'

'But it's not true. Haddow said as much. You know it isn't.'

'Of course I do, but the one person who could refute the accusation beyond any doubt is now dead ... apparently murdered. Roland Haddow can't explain to the world what he said to me, that he never did allege plagiarism, that it was all a lie or at best some sort of misunderstanding. As far as the world is concerned I still stand accused. That's what people will remember.'

'So what do you think you can do about it, Ralph?' Marnie tried to sound positive.

After a short pause Ralph said, 'I think my first port of call ought to be the Master at college. I'll look in on him tomorrow.'

'That sounds like the way forward. He's always been a good friend.' Marnie added, 'Are you going in to see your postgrad students?'

Ralph nodded. 'One or two, yes. And there are some books in my study that I'd like to bring back.'

'You've got space on the shelves in *Thyrsis*?' said Marnie, dubiously.

'I'll have to make space if necessary. I've got boxes of stuff still cluttering up my room at All Saints. I keep meaning to sort them out.'

Marnie grinned. 'It's always useful to have plenty of ballast on a boat.'

'There's something else I have to do.' Ralph frowned. 'I still haven't sent that letter to Jay Harper to thank him for letting me know about Rhiannon.'

Marnie gently squeezed his arm. 'I'd offer to help you, but that wouldn't really be appropriate. Were you on friendly terms back in those days?'

Ralph shrugged. 'I suppose we mixed in roughly the same circles. We both played tennis for the college.'

'What was he like?' Marnie asked.

'He was a nice sort of person, actually ... shy and somehow awkward. I can't say I've thought much about him in recent years. We lost touch. You know how it is. Life takes you in different directions.'

Marnie said, 'Apart from shy and awkward, what else was he like?'

Ralph paused to reflect. 'I mainly remember him as tall and thin … lanky and gawky … good at sport: tennis, squash, that sort of thing. And rather self-conscious.'

'In what way?'

More reflection by Ralph. 'I seem to recall he had a vivid birth mark on the side of his neck. I think he was rather uncomfortable about it.'

'He must have been academically bright, though,' said Marnie, 'I mean, to be at All Saints.'

'Oh, yes, quite a scholarly chap, rather intense … got first class honours in history. I seem to recall he got one of the three best firsts in his subject since the war.'

'Scholarly and intense could describe a lot of you academics, Ralph.'

Ralph grinned. 'I suppose so. Jay was a bit of a loner, too.'

'Well, it was good of him … thoughtful … to write to you about Rhiannon.'

'Yes, it was. That's why I've felt embarrassed about not replying as promptly as I should. It's bad that I've been putting it off for the past week.'

'But understandable,' said Marnie, 'in view of everything that's been happening.'

'Yes, but that's just an excuse. The truth is, I have been holding back.'

'Why?'

Ralph shook his head slowly. 'I'm finding it difficult to know what to say.'

'We've talked about this,' said Marnie. 'A simple note of thanks for letting you know is all that's needed, surely.'

'Then how is it that each time I start to draft something I find myself at a loss for words?'

Chapter 9

TUESDAY

On Tuesday morning Ralph felt a chill in the air for the first time that autumn as he walked to the garage barn after breakfast. It was a foretaste of things to come. Until that day the weather had harked back to the warmth of summer, but now he was glad to be wearing a driving jacket over his suit as he unlocked the Jaguar and climbed in.

Leaving the village behind, a light frost dusted the ground in the fields that he passed on the narrow country road up to the dual carriageway. This was the first leg of his long-familiar journey to Oxford. Reaching the main highway, he saw mist cloaking the trees in the woods and spinneys flanking the road, though the sky was clear, and the sun was lighting up the foliage, yellow and red and orange.

In the briefcase lying on the passenger seat beside him lay the draft of an article on monetarism for the journal *Economic Analysis*, the outline of a new book on the 'tiger' economies of the Far East and an envelope addressed to Jay Harper. The latter contained Ralph's reply, thanking Harper for informing him of the death of Rhiannon Ellis and expressing his sorrow at the news. He had kept the message brief and yet tried to make it personal; he hoped it was not too curt.

On a good day, Ralph could make the journey to his college in forty-five minutes or so, depending on traffic. That was proving to be a good day, at least so far.

ooo0ooo

It took all Anne's efforts to concentrate on her driving as she too headed for the art school in Oxford that morning; so many thoughts were swirling around in her brain. She worried that she had complained too much about the time she had to spend travelling and was feeling guilty about borrowing *Sally Ann*. She felt uneasy about depriving Marnie of her boat, knowing how much Marnie liked to use *Sally* for *tootles*, short outings, a source of relaxation in a busy life.

She worried too that she had drawn Donovan into her problems when he had enough on his plate in his final year at university. Then of course there was Ralph, hard-working, brilliant, dedicated, now faced with an undeserved accusation of plagiarism hanging over him. Anne reflected on her own good fortune. She had a place at a top university, a guaranteed career path, a wonderful room of her own at Glebe Farm, a car bought for her by Marnie and Ralph, even a cottage given to her by Marnie which provided her with rental income, a long-term asset for her future. Was she paranoid? Worse, was she becoming a spoilt brat?

Anne realised too late that she was rapidly approaching the roundabout over the M40 motorway that led on to the northern Oxford ring road. With traffic all around her, she was hemmed in and inevitably found herself stuck in the wrong lane as the lights turned red. Could this be a metaphor for my life, she wondered.

It was starting out to be a day for rhetorical questions to which she had no immediate answers.

ooo0ooo

On the M40 motorway heading south towards west London, Donovan was cruising steadily in the aged but nimble and rejuvenated VW Beetle. He knew that Anne was fretting about her accommodation problem, probably wishing she had never raised it with Marnie. But that thought was not uppermost in his mind. As far as he was concerned, the major issue facing them at that time was the damage to Ralph's reputation caused by the accusation in the press. Knowing Ralph as he did, he was convinced he was completely innocent of the charge of plagiarism. Ralph's professional integrity was solid. There was no question of that.

The problem for Ralph was that not everyone knew him personally. Not everyone who read the item in the press would be able to reach a balanced judgment and throw that charge in the bin along with yesterday's papers. It was plain to Donovan that it was not only Ralph's reputation that was at stake; it could be the entire career on which his life was based.

If Roland Haddow had really not made such an accusation against Ralph, then who had? Whoever that person was, he or she was still presumably alive. Donovan found himself wondering what that person might do next.

oooOooo

Ralph followed the signs into Oxford city centre. It was a route he could manage with his eyes closed. Oxford had been the hub of his life since he first went up to read economics at Balliol College at the age of eighteen. He had transferred after graduating three years later to study for his doctorate – his DPhil – at the equally prestigious All Saints' College and had remained there ever since.

Now, with the status of visiting professor, he still enjoyed certain privileges which included his own allocated parking space. He eased the Jaguar into it that morning and was pleased to see the Master's Saab occupying its reserved slot close to the main entrance. Ralph plucked the briefcase from the passenger seat, locked the car and made for his office. He had considered giving the letter for Jay Harper to his departmental secretary to type, but decided that a hand-written reply was more appropriate, more personal.

After exchanging a few words with the secretary and checking the messages in his pigeon-hole, he hung up his driving jacket and walked the short distance along the corridor to the Master's outer office. He knocked twice, went in and greeted the two secretaries seated at their desks. They looked up expectantly.

'Good morning Clare, good morning Rosemary. Would it be convenient to have a word with the Master some time this morning?'

Clare Goodall, the Master's secretary, shared the office with the Dean's secretary, Rosemary Martin. Ralph thought they looked uncomfortable, exchanging hurried glances before Clare replied.

'The Master is out this morning, professor. I'm … er, not sure when he'll be back.'

'Do you think he might possibly be in this afternoon?'

'He's actually at a meeting in London, and he's asked me to keep his diary clear today.'

'In London? Ah … In that case would you please let him know I'd like to speak to him when it's convenient, some time this week if possible.'

'Certainly, professor. I'll pass on your message.'

Ralph walked slowly back to his office. He wondered if it was his imagination or if there had been some sort of atmosphere in the room between the secretaries when he'd walked in. It was as if he'd intruded in a private conversation. The thought floated through his mind that they may have been talking about him and the accusation against him that by now everyone in the academic world must have heard.

Then he remembered seeing the Master's car in its usual place in the quad. Surely the Master would have driven to the station to catch the train to London? In fact, had he really gone to London or had Clare Goodall been stalling him? It was all very strange. Ralph put the thought out of his mind and set off towards his first tutorial of the day.

ooo0ooo

Anne had a brainwave. She was sitting in the wrong lane at the junction crossing the M40 motorway, waiting for the lights to change to green. Sandwiched between two enormous juggernauts, she was hemmed in on both sides by a solid wall of traffic. Desperately trying not to fume, she took a series of deep breaths and urged herself to calm down. A glance at her watch told her that she was well ahead of herself, with masses of time before she was due at college. As usual she had set off absurdly early for the daily commute. And then it dawned on her. Another glance at the watch was followed by a calculation. Yes … it was definitely feasible.

She had easily enough time to scope out the marina that Marnie had mentioned as a possible base for *Sally Ann*. It would only take a short detour from her normal flight-path to head in the direction of Duke's Cut.

And so it was that ten minutes later, after a very deft – if slightly unorthodox – change of lanes at the traffic lights, Anne's red Mini rolled through the gates of the small marina. She brought it to a halt beside the dry dock and its adjacent portacabin office. As she climbed out of the car she heard banging somewhere nearby. Her first destination was the office, which she found locked. Pinned to the door was a handwritten card.

When office unattended try dry dock

Anne followed instructions and wandered round to the dry dock. Its structure was little more than a kind of domed tent, from which the banging was emanating. There was just enough room for her to walk in, bent forward under the curve of the roof. Looking down, she saw a man in overalls and safety helmet standing below her on damp concrete. He was hammering at part of the hull of a tatty boat roughly the same length as *Sally Ann*. He spotted her from the corner of his eye and looked up. .

'Looking for me, love?' His accent was warm north country. Anne guessed he was in his fifties.

'I've come to look at a mooring. I think one's been reserved for me.'

'Give me a minute to knock off this anode and I'll be up to see to you.'

'Okay.'

The place smelled pungently of old rusted steel, oil and diesel, and Anne was glad to come out into the fresh air while she waited. She surveyed the area and counted no more than a dozen boats lining the canal. The man was true to his word. Anne heard three more bangs, then the sound of metal hitting the ground. The man joined her outside, wiping his hands on a rag. He didn't offer to shake.

'A mooring?' he said. 'That would be for *Sally Ann*, right?'

'That's right. I'm Anne, Anne Price. That's Anne with an "e".'

'Well, Anne with an "e", it's name of Walker in the book.'

'Marnie Walker,' Anne confirmed. 'She's my employer. It's her boat.'

'Residential, is it?'

'Part of the week, yes, but only in term time. I'll be away otherwise. So will the boat.'

'You a student, then?'

'Art student.' Anne realised she was falling into his sparse way of speaking.

He began walking along by the canal. 'You'll be on the main line. That all right? It's just here.' He pointed to a gap between the boats already lined up. 'You've got mains electricity on its own meter. I can run a hose to fill your water tank. Car park included.'

'That seems fine.'

'When you coming?'

'At the weekend or soon after. Is that all right?'

'It is.' He reached in his pocket. 'Key for the car park gate. Locked overnight, six till six.'

Anne took the key. 'What about payment?'

'Taken care of. I'm dealing direct with your Mrs Walker.'

'Is there anything you need from me, Mr ...?'

'No, nothing, and it's Harry.'

'Thanks, Harry. I'll see you soon, then.'

'Aye. Just ... one thing.'

'Yes?'

Harry looked sheepish. 'It's er ... well, it's just we don't allow drugs or that kind of thing. I have to mention it, you know. Sorry.'

Anne beamed him a wide smile. 'Not a problem.' She held out her hand.

Harry hesitated, looked at his right hand and wiped the palm down the side of his overalls before extending it. As they shook, he smiled back. 'We have a deal.'

'Deal,' Anne said.

They walked slowly together towards the car park. Anne was starting to feel that her accommodation problem was solved. As Harry set off back to the dry dock, Anne glanced at her watch and opened the door of the Mini. She would time the journey to college in preparation for the new arrangement. She was feeling relaxed and happy, unaware that she was being observed from a window on a boat moored just two places from her slot.

ooo0ooo

It was an evening for making plans. Anne phoned Donovan as soon as she got back to Glebe Farm. It was like plotting a military exercise. In fact they dubbed it Operation Great Move. Marnie was to set off solo on *Sally Ann* on Thursday morning with the aim of reaching the locks near Stoke Bruerne by early afternoon. Anne and Donovan would converge on the marina, Anne's new base, around lunchtime. Ralph would pick them up soon afterwards on his way home from college. With Anne's Mini and Donovan's Beetle ensconced in the marina car park, Ralph would transport them to Stoke Bruerne where they would board *Sally Ann*. There he'd collect Marnie and drive her back to Glebe Farm.

After supper Anne retired to her attic room to write up an itinerary for Thursday and beyond. She could definitely feel a list coming on and would print a timetable for each of them. Anne was in her element.

Marnie and Ralph lingered with coffee by the wood-burner in the farm house sitting room and chatted about their day. Marnie had made good progress with two designs and had been approached by two potential new clients. Business was steady, which was how she liked it. Ralph, on the other hand, seemed less relaxed than usual. Marnie picked up on this.

'How did your day go?' she asked.

65

Ralph paused before replying. 'In the car coming home I was wondering how best to deal with the plagiarism thing.'

'Did you reach a conclusion?'

'I was starting to wonder if I should just let the whole thing blow over.'

Marnie looked doubtful. 'Is that what you want to do?'

Ralph took a sip and put the coffee cup down. 'I'm not sure if it *will* just blow over.'

'Has something happened, Ralph?'

'I thought I'd have a word with the Master. His thinking is usually very sound.'

'So is yours, Ralph.'

Ralph smiled. 'I'd hope so, but the Master would be able to bring a certain objective detachment to bear on the subject.'

'So what did he think?'

'That's just it. When I went along to his office there was an odd atmosphere. His secretary told me he was out ... a meeting in London, apparently.'

'Is that so surprising? He is quite an eminent person, after all.'

'I saw his car in its reserved parking space.'

'Ah ... You thought you were being fobbed off.'

'It was more than that, really.'

'What then?' Marnie said. 'What was the odd atmosphere in his office?'

Ralph frowned. 'I've known the two secretaries who share that outer office for a few years now. We've always got on well. But today they were ... how can I describe it? ... they were somehow sheepish ... uncomfortable.'

'You think they'd been talking about you ... about the plagiarism business?'

'I did wonder about that.'

'So how did you leave it, Ralph?'

'I just asked them to pass on a message saying I'd like a word when the Master was free.'

Marnie nodded, looking thoughtful. 'Yes.'

'Do you think I'm being paranoid?'

Marnie smiled. 'If you were, you'd have every right to be, but no. I realise how important such an accusation can be in your line. I'm sure the Master will be supportive. You've got to get this whole thing sorted as soon as you can.'

Ralph finished his coffee. Easier said than done, he mused. But he kept that to himself. Then he had an afterthought. His briefcase was lying on the floor beside the sofa. He reached down, picked it up and placed it on his lap. The two catches snapped open and he raised the lid.

'Synchronicity,' he muttered.

'That's a very gnomic utterance for a Tuesday evening,' said Marnie.

'But relevant,' Ralph insisted. 'Look what I've found.'

He passed her a slightly faded colour photograph of four young men dressed in white shirts and flannels, standing together. They were obviously posing for the photographer in a college quadrangle, with attractive buildings in the background. The image was clear enough for Marnie to be able to recognise a much younger Ralph Lombard smiling for the camera.

'Who are these fine fellows?' Marnie asked. 'I can see you're one of them, but who are the others?'

Ralph pointed. 'That's Toby Wellman on my right and Josh Harrison on my left. Toby went into banking in the City, and Josh is an MP. The man on his left is Jay Harper.'

'The man who sent you the letter about Rhiannon?'

'Yes, that's him.'

They gazed at a tall, thin, beaky young man with a shock of dark wavy hair and a serious expression, his head tilted to one side.

'He's the only one not smiling,' Marnie observed. 'In fact, he looks rather anxious. What is this group?'

'All Saints' College tennis team,' Ralph said.

'You're all smartly turned out but not in tennis gear. No shorts and not a racket in sight.'

'That's because we'd won an inter-college tournament and we're dressed to receive our trophy. You see that rather impressive cup on the ground in front of us?'

'Oh, yes. It's magnificent. So why is Jay looking so awkward? Did he lose his match or something?'

'On the contrary. He was a star in the team, a very good player.'

'But the way he's holding himself ... so self-conscious.'

'He was always like that in photos. I think he tried to conceal the birthmark on his neck.'

Involuntarily, Marnie reached up and touched her own neck. 'Oh.'

Ralph turned to look at her. 'What is it?'

'Nothing really. Just a crazy thought.'

'Go on,' Ralph urged.

Marnie took a breath. 'It's silly, but it occurred to me that ...' She shook her head.

Ralph said quietly, 'I had the bizarre idea that the birthmark would make it easy to identify Jay if his body was found.' Ralph shuddered as the image of Roland Haddow lying on a slab in the mortuary drifted through his mind.

'Oh my God,' Marnie muttered. 'It's weird, Ralph, but I had exactly the same thought.'

For a few seconds their eyes locked before Ralph spoke. His tone was subdued.

'Synchronicity,' he murmured.

Chapter 10

WEDNESDAY

On Wednesday morning Marnie had barely had time to sit at her desk and switch on the computer when the phone rang. It was Beth breathing heavily, as if she'd just completed a marathon. Marnie wondered fleetingly if her sister was about to become hysterical.

'Slow down, Beth. You're going to blow a fuse.'

'But it's true.' Pause for panting. 'I've just heard it … on the radio. I wanted to make sure you knew.'

'I hope these are glad tidings, Beth. We could do with some jollification right now.'

'Well, hardly.'

'So what is it? I didn't catch it first time round, so could you just run it past me again … slowly this time … perhaps the edited highlights?'

Beth waited a few moments to catch her breath. 'Okay. Listen up. They've found another body. Well, not exactly a body, just part of one.'

Marnie grimaced. 'And you're telling me this because …?'

'They pulled it out of the Thames close to Tower Bridge.'

'You mean …?'

'Yes, where they found those other remains.'

'Roland Haddow?'

'That's the one. And it's near your flat, isn't it?'

'Too near,' Marnie said. 'Has the body been identified?'

'Marnie!' Beth sounded exasperated. 'They've only found a torso. It's got no head, no arms, no legs.'

'Bloody hell!'

'My thoughts exactly.'

'So why are you telling me this, Beth? Don't tell me you think I might know this … person.'

'Well, I thought it sounded a bit of a coincidence after that business with Haddow and Ralph.'

'Beth, the demise of Roland Haddow had nothing whatever to do with Ralph. And, in any case, we don't have a monopoly on dead bodies pulled out of the Thames.'

'It was by Tower Bridge,' Beth protested, with a logic all her own.

'Even at Tower Bridge,' said Marnie.

oooOooo

Ralph checked his watch. He had nearly thirty minutes in hand before his first postgrad tutorial. Reaching across to the front passenger seat for his briefcase, he spotted the Master's car parked close to the entrance to the college. He climbed out and headed straight towards the Master's office. Curiously, Ralph felt a faint twinge of nervousness as he approached the door into the secretariat. His sense of foreboding proved to be correct. He knocked once and entered.

'Good morning Clare, good morning Rosemary.' He tried to sound upbeat and positive, though he felt neither. 'Could I possibly have a brief word with the Master?'

Their expressions as they looked up were less than jovial. Clare Goodall, the Master's secretary cleared her throat before replying.

'I'm sorry, professor, he's in a meeting at the moment.'

Ralph's smile faltered. 'Any idea when he might be free?'

'Er ...' A quick glance in the direction of Rosemary Martin, opposite. 'He's in with the Vice-Chancellor, and then they're having lunch together.'

'I see. I'm sure they have plenty to discuss. Would you please mention that I'd like to talk with the Master about a rather delicate matter and I'll be back in college next week.'

'Certainly, professor. I'll let the Master know.'

Walking slowly down the corridor, it occurred to Ralph that both secretaries looked relieved when he said he wouldn't be back until the following week. Something was going on, and he had a pretty good idea what it was.

oooOooo

At roughly that time, Marnie was picking up the phone in the office. Anne was ringing, obviously hurrying, no doubt on her way to a class.

'Did you hear about the body pulled from the river in London?'

'I did. Beth thought it was somehow relevant to us, so she phoned this morning with the gory details. As a matter of interest, Anne, why are you phoning about it too?'

'Er … well, it's such a strange coincidence, isn't it? I mean, another body pulled out of the Thames just by Tower Bridge like that.'

'Not actually a body,' said Marnie. 'Just a torso apparently.'

'Ugh!'

'Quite. Anyway, I made the point to Beth that we don't have a monopoly on gruesome remains hoiked out of the river, even the ones found near our flat.'

'Course not, Marnie. I suppose I just thought it was a strange …'

'Coincidence?' Marnie suggested.

'Yeah, that sort of thing. That was all I meant. Oh, gotta dash. I'll be late for my human anatomy class.'

'How ironic,' said Marnie.

After she disconnected, Marnie sat thinking about Beth and Anne, the body of Roland Haddow and now those ghastly remains in the river by Tower Bridge. Frantic phone calls and human anatomy seemed to be the order of the day. Chewing the end of her ball-point, she wondered if coincidence and synchronicity were basically the same thing.

ooo0ooo

The evening followed its customary pattern with one exception. After supper Anne was about to withdraw to her attic room to study when she noticed Ralph's tennis team photograph on the floor. She stooped to pick it up.

'What's this?'

'Oh, Ralph must've dropped it. It's a photo of his tennis team from college.'

'Impressive trophy. Did they win that?' She raised the photo so that it was almost on the end of her nose and pointed. 'That's not you, is it, Ralph?'

Ralph smiled. 'It was a long time ago.'

'How old were you?'

'Oh, about twenty-two, perhaps, thereabouts.'

'It's really nice … too nice to drop on the floor.'

'I found it at the back of a drawer in my desk when I was looking for an envelope.' Ralph's tone was matter-of-fact, off-hand. 'Haven't seen it for years.'

'Don't you want to keep it somewhere safe?' Anne asked.

71

'Not especially.'

'Pity.'

Ralph could take a hint. 'You can have it, if you want.'

'Great! Thanks, Ralph. I'll treasure it.'

Anne went off happily, while Marnie and Ralph moved to the sitting room. As Marnie poured coffee, Ralph pushed a log into the wood-burner. They took their first sips, watching the flames licking round the log, listening to the gentle crackling of the wood, enjoying the warmth radiating from the stove.

'That was nice of you,' said Marnie.

Ralph shrugged. 'It was just an old photo, not important. I hadn't seen it in years.'

'Even so. And of course there was another thing. In that photo you must have been about the same age as Donovan when she first met him a couple of years ago.'

'Marnie, I have the impression that you're avoiding something.'

'I don't know what you mean.' Marnie hoped she sounded convincing.

Ralph said, 'You've got something on your mind. D'you want to talk about it?'

Marnie chuckled. 'How well you know me.'

'What is it? Tell me.'

'I had a call from Beth today. Did you know more remains have been pulled out of the Thames by Tower Bridge?'

Ralph stared into the flames, his expression serious. 'No.'

'Anne phoned, too, to tell me about it.'

'Why?'

Marnie shrugged. 'I suppose because of the Roland Haddow business.'

There was a gap of several seconds before Ralph spoke again.

'That's it, isn't it? That's how the proverbial mud sticks. Something happens, you get associated with it and then it seems to become part of you. You can't shake it off. The body was found at Tower Bridge, you said?'

'Yes. Only it wasn't a whole body, just a torso, apparently.'

It was Ralph's turn to chuckle, mirthlessly. 'Well, I suppose I should look on the bright side.'

Marnie gazed across at him. 'There's a bright side?'

'Of course,' Ralph said. 'At least this time I won't be asked to identify the body. The police won't be able to link me with this one.'

In under twelve hours he was proved to be wrong.

Chapter 11

THURSDAY

Thursday was to be the Day of the Great Move. Over breakfast that morning Marnie rehearsed the plans for taking *Sally Ann* up to the Stoke Bruerne locks, the first stage in relocating the boat to its new temporary base. Anne brought her notepad to the table and checked her understanding of the programme with Marnie's and Ralph's versions. Pleased that they all seemed to be on the same page – literally in Anne's case – they finished breakfast, and Anne set off for college with her usual haste.

After Anne left, Marnie stood and began to gather up the breakfast things. Ralph remained in his seat and raised a hand. Marnie stopped what she was doing and sat down.

'What is it?' she said.

'I went to see the Master yesterday.'

'How did you get on?'

'I didn't. It happened … again.'

'What did happen?' said Marnie.

'His secretary said he was unavailable.'

'He is a busy man,' Marnie observed, 'but that isn't why you're telling me this, is it?'

'No. There was that strange atmosphere again in the office. I had the impression that all was not as it seemed. The two secretaries looked at me in an odd way.'

'You think they were fobbing you off, that the Master is avoiding you because of the accusation of plagiarism against you?'

'Frankly, Marnie, I'd find that hard to believe. I've always got on so well with the Master. Until now I'd have said we were friends.'

'I know things are different in the academic world, Ralph, but I've sometimes wondered why you always refer to him – and address him – as the *Master*, especially as you regard him as a friend.'

Ralph shrugged. 'It's just a tradition, Marnie. All Saints was founded in 1500 by Henry VII. From the beginning, the head of the college has apparently always been addressed only by his title. It's the same for the present incumbent, Vivian Parry-Jones. That's Oxford for you, and I'm happy to go along with the custom. I suppose I quite like it, but in reality I don't even think about it.'

'And he addresses you as Ralph. Also a custom, presumably.'

Ralph nodded. 'Except at college dinners. There I'm always addressed as *professor*.'

Marnie smiled. 'Where would we be in Britain without traditions?'

'Quite.' Ralph hesitated, and Marnie knew that more was coming. 'There was something else,' he added.

'Oh yes?'

'I left a message that I'd be in touch when I next came in to college ... next week.'

Marnie looked at Ralph quizzically. 'I know. You told me that, but surely you'll be going in today.'

Ralph looked down at the hands in his lap. 'This accusation has brought it all back to me, Marnie, the way I felt when I first met you, when everyone seemed to have turned against me. I felt completely alone, abandoned, discredited.'

Marnie walked round the table and knelt beside him, taking his hands in her own. She spoke quietly but firmly.

'Well you're not alone now, Ralph. You've got me and Anne and Donovan. You're loved and respected – *revered* – as one of the most eminent people in your field in the whole world. We're going to get through this together. And you know we will.'

Ralph looked deep into her eyes. 'I hold on to that thought and it sustains me. But it's not going to be easy. You should have seen them.'

'Who?'

'The secretaries. They looked so relieved at the thought that they wouldn't see me again till next week.'

Marnie said, 'Then I know what you'll be doing today.'

'Two one-hour tutorials with second year postgrads,' said Ralph casually.

Marnie stood up. 'Before that, you'll breeze into the secretaries' office and remind them cheerfully that you expect to see the Master when you return next week. Yes?'

Ralph struggled to smile. 'If you say so.'

'I do. Now help me clear away. I have a journey to make, and you have tutorials to conduct. But first … those secretaries.'

Together they began to clear away the breakfast things. Ralph was stooping to open the dishwasher when he stopped and turned to face Marnie.

'I meant to tell you. I noticed something odd for the first time.'

'Are we back with the secretaries?' Marnie said.

'No, something quite different. I was tidying away some papers in my study on *Thyrsis* when I came across Jay's letter. You read it. Did anything strike you about it?'

Marnie paused to reflect. 'About Rhiannon, you mean?'

'No, about the letter itself. I meant to mention it earlier when I wrote on the envelope to post it. Jay's address is just given as a PO Box in Bicester. That strikes me as odd.'

ooo0ooo

Ralph stood beside the accommodation bridge over the canal and signalled back to Marnie that the way ahead was clear. Together they had checked that *Sally Ann* was well provisioned for Anne's first stint at the marina, that the water tank was full to the brim and that she had diesel a-plenty. Ralph had then walked the fifty yards or so to the bridge to check for oncoming traffic. After waving Marnie on, he watched while she pushed away from the bank and climbed aboard *Sally Ann* to start her journey to Stoke Bruerne. Marnie looked in her element as she lined the boat up for the bridge hole and glided past with a broad smile and a blown kiss.

Ralph too was smiling, pleased to see faint puffs of pale grey smoke issuing from the exhaust. He knew that Marnie was sensing how *Sally Ann* was running, listening to every sound from the engine below her feet, feeling the response of the tiller tucked under her arm. Marnie had travelled a hundred yards when she turned for one last wave and settled in for the journey. She was wrapped up from head to toe in warm clothing, relishing the crisp autumn air, breathing in deeply the scents of the countryside and the waterway.

Ralph's feeling of contentment and well-being lasted until he turned to head back towards *Thyrsis* and spotted the two detectives standing beside the boat, waiting for him. He had known DS Ted Marriner and DC Cathy Lamb for a few years, and they had shared some experiences together. Even so, Ralph judged that it was never wise to make too many assumptions where the police were concerned, especially officers of the CID. They didn't just happen to drop by.

'Good morning. What can I do for you?'

'We need to talk to you, professor. Have you got a minute?'

Ralph understood that a *minute* meant a conversation, and the use of his title probably signified an interview of some official kind.

'Of course,' he replied. 'We can go on board *Thyrsis*, but probably better to use Marnie's office … more spacious. Or we can go to the farmhouse. What do you think?'

ooo0ooo

Sally Ann was running smoothly and everything felt right. Marnie had learnt early in her life as a boatwoman that narrowboats possessed a character. It was difficult to explain it to people with no experience on the waterways, and she knew that such people received that kind of statement with a degree of scepticism. A boat to them was an inanimate machine made of steel, an inert piece of engineering, mechanical equipment, nothing more.

But there was nothing fey or fanciful about it, though Marnie was sensible enough to realise that the feeling of a boat was largely in the mind of the beholder. Like so much in life, it involved two-way traffic, a partnership. And Marnie often felt – or at least hoped – that when handling fourteen tonnes of narrowboat in all weathers and in all situations, it was a partnership of equals.

Marnie had put on a dark blue woolly hat before departure, but now she tugged it off and shook out her hair. The day, though overcast, was proving to be warmer than expected, and she enjoyed feeling the pleasantly cool air round her head.

Holding the tiller firmly under her right arm, Marnie unscrewed her Thermos flask and poured herself a mug of coffee. It smelled wonderful, and she took an inordinate delight in the steam rising from it. Much as she loved Ralph and Anne and Donovan and her job as an interior designer, she was always happy to indulge in the simple pleasure of solitude on the waterways in the company of *Sally Ann*.

ooo0ooo

Marriner and Lamb declined coffee but accepted chairs in Marnie's office. Ralph drew up another chair and looked at them expectantly.

'You asked if I had a minute, so what can I do for you? Please bear in mind that I have to leave very soon for tutorials in Oxford.'

'Fair enough,' said Marriner. 'You've probably heard that another body has been found in the Thames not far from your flat.'

'No,' Ralph said firmly.

Marriner continued. 'Then I should inform you –'

'Sorry to interrupt, sergeant, but you referred to a *body*. My understanding was that it was no more than a torso.'

'Er, well … yes, that is strictly speaking the case.'

'Surely it's entirely the case,' Ralph observed amiably. 'And, sorry again, but I'm not sure why you've come to tell me about this.'

'We have reason to believe,' Marriner began slowly, 'that you may have some knowledge of it.'

'Yes.' Another firm response from Ralph.

'You do?' Marriner quickly glanced at Lamb who was trying hard not to appear to be enjoying Ralph's reactions.

'Certainly. I heard that it was on the news yesterday.' Ralph checked his watch. 'I'm still intrigued to know what has prompted you to come here to discuss it with me.'

'I can't go into that, sir.'

Ralph stood up so quickly that both detectives were taken by surprise. His expression was friendly. Any onlooker would think he was saying goodbye to guests after a dinner party.

'Well, thank you for coming. I really ought to be getting along. Time, tide and postgrad tutorials wait for no man, as the saying goes.'

Ralph stuck out his hand and Marriner rose to shake it. Not for the first time, Lamb realised, her DS had been taken off-guard by Ralph's confident, firm, yet courteous manner.

'We had a phone call,' Marriner began.

'From?' Ralph asked.

'That's just it, sir. The caller gave no name.'

'But said something that led you to me, presumably. Perhaps now you've reached this stage you can give me some idea what was said?'

Marriner cleared his throat. 'The message was simply that, in relation to the … er, torso, we should contact you about it.'

'Gosh.' Ralph looked intrigued. 'That would count as an anonymous tip-off. I thought they only existed in crime stories. How interesting. But now, unless you have something else to ask me, I really must make a move. Always a pleasure to see you. Sorry I can't be more helpful.'

oooOooo

Marnie felt the mobile vibrating in the back pocket of her jeans and was just able to make out the ringing tone over the clanking of *Sally Ann*'s engine. She was travelling along a straight stretch of the canal under a cloudy sky, enjoying the autumn colours on the trees lining the waterway. The caller display showed Ralph's name and he outlined his conversation with Marriner and Lamb. Marnie was pleased to hear him sounding so positive, despite the odd nature of the visit by the police. She hoped her pep-talk after breakfast may have cheered him up.

'So how did you leave it?' she asked.

'We didn't. They obviously came to see if I'd react in any way, and of course I couldn't, so they left. I'm just on my way round to get the car and set off to Oxford.'

'You've locked the office?'

'Yes, and I even made sure the answerphone was switched on. I think I'm becoming a new man … tech-savvy and all that.'

'I always knew you'd get there in the end. I knew you had it in –'

'Damn!'

Marnie was alarmed. 'What's happened, Ralph?'

'I can't find my car keys … must've left them in the house. I'd better go back.'

'Have a safe journey, darling.' Marnie hoped he wouldn't notice the smirk in her voice. She was glad Ralph couldn't see her expression as she disconnected.

oooOooo

Marnie's words were ringing in Ralph's ears as he slotted the Jaguar into his reserved parking space at All Saints' College. With resolution in every step, he strode down the corridor towards the Master's office, knocked briskly twice and threw open the door. Clare Goodall was standing by a filing cabinet withdrawing a folder. Rosemary Martin was ending a phone call, replacing the receiver on its base.

'Good morning Clare, good morning Rosemary. Nice to see you.'

They both looked taken aback by Ralph's cheerful countenance. Together they muttered a muted reply. Before either could say another word, Ralph piped up.

'I have tutorials this morning, but I've just looked in to remind you to tell the Master that I expect to see him when I'm back in college next week. Have a good day!'

The secretaries were staring at him open-mouthed as he turned to close the door behind him. At the last moment, he looked back over his shoulder and smiled.

'Don't forget!'

With that, he was gone, leaving the two women to gaze at each other with puzzled expressions.

ooo0ooo

Later that day Operation Great Move stepped up a gear. In west London Donovan pulled on his driving gloves and Ray-Bans, turned the starter key of the Beetle and pointed it towards the North Circular Road in the direction of the M40 motorway. Soon afterwards Anne emerged from her last class of the morning, climbed into the Mini and set off towards Duke's Cut. At about the same time Ralph reversed the Jaguar out of its parking slot, threaded his way along the narrow lane leading from All Saints' College to the Oxford one-way system and followed signs northbound out of the city.

Meanwhile Marnie and *Sally Ann* were making good progress, better than expected. Within sight of the bottom lock of the flight leading up to Stoke Bruerne, Marnie checked her watch and made a rapid calculation. She could see that the gate into the first lock was gaping slightly open; it was in her favour. Marnie acted decisively. She would change plans and tackle the whole flight, aiming to reach the centre of Stoke Bruerne in good time, if luck was on her side.

It was one of those days when fortune smiled on the bold. To tackle the five locks of the Stoke Bruerne flight single-handed was demanding and tiring, but left Marnie feeling exhilarated, if slightly breathless. On arrival in the village she found a mooring a short way along the canal from the Waterways Museum. A brief call from her mobile alerted Ralph to the slight change of plan, and they agreed to rendez-vous in the museum car park.

The changing-of-the-watch on *Sally Ann* was accomplished without delay and with a little amusement. Marnie had noticed two packs of sandwiches that Anne had prepared in advance as lunch-on-the-move for Donovan and herself. Nothing had been left to chance. Typical Anne.

As Ralph and Marnie drove out of the car park for the short journey home to Glebe Farm, Anne was already pushing the boat away from the bank. While Donovan took the tiller, Anne dived inside the cabin and switched on every light, in readiness for the passage through Blisworth tunnel. With the thump of the engine echoing around them, they huddled together on the stern deck under a huge golf umbrella – protection against the inevitable downpours from the ventilation shafts.

Half an hour or so later they emerged into daylight. Anne unpacked the sandwiches while the kettle hummed on the gas-ring. They had before them a long pound leading some hours away to the next major events: the Wilton Locks and the Braunston tunnel. Anne placed the sandwiches and mugs of coffee on a tray and quickly checked the itinerary in her notepad. The plan was to go as far as they could that day, ready to tackle the locks and the tunnel as early as possible in the morning. They would stop for supper at a canalside pub. Anne was pleased with her planning. A few more ticks on the list.

oooOooo

'Things went pretty smoothly today,' Ralph said, pouring coffee after supper in the kitchen at Glebe Farm. 'You did well to get *Sally* right up to the centre of Stoke Bruerne.'

'Everything was in my favour,' said Marnie. 'Hardly saw another boat travelling all morning. No queues, no hold-ups.'

She was studying a cruising guide, running a finger along the line of the Grand Union Canal. Ralph placed a mug of coffee in front of her and took his seat at the table.

'With any luck the same will hold true for Anne and Donovan,' he said.

'Well, they're both competent boaters,' said Marnie. 'No reason why they shouldn't make good time. Once they've cleared the locks either side of Braunston tunnel, they've got a clear run to beyond Napton. Then it's probably a two-day run down to the marina near Duke's Cut?'

Ralph agreed. 'That sounds right. They should arrive not too late on Sunday evening, ready for Anne to go into college on Monday.'

oooOooo

And that was how it went. Anne and Donovan made excellent time and arrived at their destination earlier than anticipated on Sunday. Even the weather cooperated, and they were able to don lighter clothing for a pre-supper stroll along the canal after mooring *Sally Ann* at the marina. Anne had put on a brief pair of shorts and black tights with her blouson jacket, while Donovan sported a dark grey sweatshirt and black jeans. Holding hands, they chatted quietly as they sauntered past the other boats, and *Sally Ann* settled into her new temporary home.

Neither Anne nor Donovan noticed the curtain twitch on a nearby boat. Neither of them realised they were being observed that evening as the dusk began slowly to descend over Duke's Cut. It was on their way back to the boat, where the prospect of a pizza supper awaited them, that it happened.

They slowed at the sound of an unfamiliar voice behind them. It was preceded by what seemed to be a low whistle.

'Nice *legs*,' it said appreciatively. Then, after a pause, 'What time do they open?'

Anne was inclining towards Donovan to tell him to ignore the remark when she realised that she was alone. She was turning her head in the other direction when she heard a loud splash and felt the gentle pressure of Donovan's hand on her back.

'Come on,' he said. 'Let's get back to the boat. We don't want the pizza to dry out in the oven.'

'What did you –'

'Nothing,' Donovan said. 'It's all taken care of. Don't give it another thought.'

Neither of them spoke until they were on board *Sally Ann*. Donovan checked the pizza in the oven while Anne set about lighting the two oil lamps. She was frowning and touched Donovan on the arm as he began laying the table.

'Did you see who it was who said that?' she asked.

'Just briefly. He was about our age, long hair, dark. He made the mistake of advancing towards me. I took it as a menacing act.'

'What did you do?'

'Not much, just pushed him back … quite firmly.'

'And he ended up in the canal,' Anne added.

'Yes, he did.' Donovan spoke as if it was the first time he'd noticed what had happened. 'I spotted that.'

'You *spotted* it?' Anne repeated. 'What if he couldn't swim?'

Donovan gave her an old-fashioned look. 'Anne, the canal would be little more than two feet deep at the edge. He'd only have to stand up. The water would barely cover his knees.'

Anne tried to look disapproving at Donovan's apparent violent reaction to the assault on her virtue. Instead, despite herself, she laughed.

'Pizza, anyone?' Donovan said with a neutral expression, reaching for a spatula.

Chapter 12

Marnie was sorting the post on Monday morning when she heard the sound of tyres rolling to a halt on the gravel drive between the office barn and the farmhouse. Her first thought was that the post van had returned with some overlooked mail. It had happened before. Glancing over her shoulder she saw two familiar figures on their way to the office door. She stood up to receive DS Marriner and DC Lamb.

'Good morning,' she said. 'I'm guessing that you haven't popped in hoping for a cup of Anne's excellent coffee. She's away at college this morning, by the way.'

'It's your husband we've come to see, Mrs Walker. Is he about?'

Marnie reached for the phone and rang Ralph in his study on *Thyrsis*. She had registered the use of 'your husband' and the use of 'Mrs Walker'.

'He'll be with you directly. May I offer you something or will this be a short visit?'

'Better keep it formal, I think,' Marriner said.

'That sounds serious, even ominous.' Marnie gestured to the visitors' chairs. 'But can you at least take a seat?'

'Thanks. Perhaps we'll wait till your husband gets here.'

They didn't have long to wait. Ralph arrived a minute later with his customary friendly greeting and outstretched hand.

'I wasn't expecting to see you again so soon,' he said. 'So how can I assist you?'

Marriner cleared his throat. 'Our SIO, DCI Bartlett, wants us to talk to you again, mainly about the, er ... torso recently found in the Thames by Tower Bridge.'

'Really?' said Ralph. 'I thought we'd already established that I wouldn't be asked to try to identify that one.'

Marriner looked uncomfortable. 'Professor ... Ralph ...'

'The anonymous tip-off. That's what's bothering you, isn't it?' said Ralph.

'We do have to take such things seriously, you know.'

Ralph sighed. 'Well, what can I do? I obviously know nothing about your torso.' He smiled at Cathy Lamb. 'Sorry, perhaps I should rephrase that. Seriously though, I'm rather at a loss to know how I can help you.'

'Do you know the publication *Economics Review*?' Marriner asked.

The sudden change of direction caused Ralph to frown. 'Well, yes, of course. I contribute articles to it from time to time. I have done for some years.'

'Would you describe it as a reputable journal?'

'May I refer you to my previous answer, sergeant?'

'It comes out every month, doesn't it?'

'Yes, it does,' said Ralph hesitantly. He was becoming baffled by this line of questioning.

'And have you seen the latest edition?'

'Certainly. In fact I had an article in it comparing and contrasting the economies of the Far East with the so-called *Celtic Tiger* economy of Ireland.'

'That was last month's edition, I believe, professor.'

Ralph nodded. 'The latest edition, as you said.'

'I was referring to the newest edition.'

Marnie looked on, unaccustomed to seeing Ralph on the back foot like that. He stroked his chin, which she recognised as a sign of confusion.

'Sergeant,' he said, 'I wonder if we're talking about the same journal. *Economics Review* isn't due out for another week or so.'

It was the turn of DS Marriner to look confused. 'I see. Do you have an article in that edition?'

'No. My contributions are rather spasmodic.'

'Would it surprise you to know that you feature quite prominently in it?'

'It certainly would,' Ralph said. 'Can you be more specific?'

'We understand that it contains an article about the accusation of plagiarism in one of your books.'

Ralph stared at Marnie. She had never seen him so shocked.

'Can I ask a question?' Marnie said.

'Strictly speaking –'

'I'm going to ask it anyway, sergeant, and it's a rather obvious question,' she persisted. 'How do you know what is apparently included in the journal when it hasn't even been published?'

Across the office DC Cathy Lamb made a questioning murmur. Marriner turned his head to gaze at her. Before he could reply, Marnie pressed on.

'Would this by any chance be another anonymous tip-off? Can I take it that you've checked your facts?'

Marriner did his best to rally. 'There's no reason to believe the information is incorrect.'

'That doesn't really answer my question,' Marnie said firmly.

Ralph added, 'Is this supposed to refer to my book, *We're Going Wrong*? I thought we'd established that no such accusation had been made, let alone substantiated.'

Marriner turned to DC Lamb again. 'Cathy?'

She consulted her notepad and said, 'It's about a book called *Public Need versus Corporate Greed*.'

'Sergeant, this is *absurd*,' Ralph said. 'That book raised issues about which I was threatened with court proceedings by two multinational companies. The views expressed in it were controversial and entirely my own. No question of plagiarism ever arose. It's nonsense.'

'Were you in fact sued?' Marriner asked.

'No. The companies in question tried to buy me off.'

'So you made a lot of money out of it?'

'Absolutely not ... at least not like that.'

'What do you mean?'

'The companies backed down and the media moved on to other things. The country was experiencing turbulence around the Exchange Rate Mechanism at that time.'

'So how did you come out of it?'

'The book was a worldwide best-seller in the sphere of economics and the royalties I received were quite substantial.'

'And no one accused you of plagiarism at the time?'

Ralph shook his head emphatically. 'Quite the opposite. People tried to distance themselves from my views which were considered too radical, *definitely* original.'

Marnie joined in again. 'Sergeant, do you know who made the allegation about that book?'

Marriner turned to Lamb again. This time, she didn't even bother to check her notes. She simply shook her head.

Ralph stood up. 'Unless you have any other accusations up your sleeve, sergeant, I think we've gone as far as we can this morning.'

There was no shaking of hands when the detectives took their leave. Marnie and Ralph stood together in the doorway of the office barn and watched as Cathy Lamb manoeuvred the car and drove off up the field track.

'It's all very peculiar,' Marnie said as they closed the door and went back into the office. 'The whole thing seems quite unreal.'

'I think it's quite clear, though,' said Ralph. 'Someone is out to destroy my reputation … in other words, to destroy me.'

ooo0ooo

That evening after supper Anne had a phone call from Marnie.

'How are things going?' she asked. 'Have you settled in okay?'

'It's fine, very comfortable, very convenient. How about you?'

'We had a visit from our favourite local detectives this morning.'

'What is it this time? They're not still banging on about the plagiarism thing, are they?'

'Same thing, different day, different book.'

'You're kidding!'

Marnie outlined the questioning from DS Marriner while Anne muttered outrage from her end of the line.

'I don't get it,' said Anne. 'How do the police know about something that hasn't even been published?'

'Good question, Anne. It seems to be our old friend Mr Anonymous.'

'Donovan phones just before bedtime. Is it okay if I tell him about it?'

'Sure. Meanwhile, we're going to look into this. I'll keep you posted.'

Anne was mulling over the latest development on the plagiarism front when she heard a tentative knock on the stern doors. Only one person in the area knew she was on board. That was Harry, the owner of the marina, and he'd be long gone by now. It was almost eight o'clock. Anne was not of a nervous disposition or given to visions of axe-murderers or flesh-eating zombies, but she knew it was wise to be cautious.

She walked through the boat and stopped at the foot of the steps before the doors.

'Who is it?' she called out.

'Lucas,' came the reply, followed by, 'I'm a neighbour. My boat's called *Dandelion*.'

The name rang a bell. Anne had noticed *Dandelion* on her first visit. It was a rather scruffy forty-foot Springer in need of a lick of paint. She reasoned that no one on such a shabby craft – and a Springer called *Dandelion* to boot – could be a serious threat.

'Hang on,' she said. 'I'll open up.'

Pulling on the bolts, she pushed the door open to find a young man with long dark hair in jeans and a denim jacket standing on the stern deck. Anne knew at once who he was, though she'd never actually seen him properly before. In one hand he was holding a bunch of tulips; in the other he was clutching a bottle of wine.

'I thought I ought to give you a proper welcome to the moorings,' he said. 'And an apology.'

'It was you,' said Anne.

He nodded, shamefaced. 'It was me, and I'm really sorry.'

He was illuminated only by the light spilling out from *Sally Ann*, but even in the gloomy half-light of an autumn evening, Anne could see how contrite he looked. He held out both gifts towards her and in that moment she decided to be lenient towards him, such was his clear distress and discomfiture.

'D'you want to come in?' Anne asked.

'Only if you want me to,' Lucas replied in a quiet voice.

Anne sighed and stepped back. 'Come on.'

He slid back the hatch and stepped down into the cabin, turning to slide the hatch back into place and close the doors without bolting them. Anne had the impression he was on his best behaviour. He followed her into the saloon where she took the flowers from him and offered him a seat at the table. Once the flowers were installed in her only vase, she passed him a corkscrew and took two wine glasses from a cupboard. The visitor looked around him.

He took in the Liberty curtains on shiny brass rails, the deep blue carpet tiles and the Oriental rug. The interior of *Sally Ann* was warmed by central heating, and the oil lamps added just the right amount of cosy illumination.

'Nice boat,' Lucas said with feeling. 'Puts poor old *Dandelion* to shame. Talking of shame ...'

Anne placed the wine glasses on the table. 'What's the wine?' she asked.

Lucas stared at the label. 'It's supposed to be a dry white from Australia. I hung it in the water to keep it cold.'

He poured the wine and passed a glass to Anne.

'Thanks. My name's Anne, by the way, Anne Price.'

'Anne, I really do apologise for my ... unfortunate remark.'

'I think it was more than that,' Anne said evenly. 'It was downright crude and insulting.'

Lucas hung his head and murmured, 'I know. I deserved what happened.' He looked over his shoulder. 'Is your friend still around?'

'You're safe for the moment,' Anne said. 'Cheers.'

They both sipped the wine. It was cool and refreshing, though not quite chilled enough to do it justice.

'Look, Anne, I really and truly am –'

'I know. You don't have to keep saying it.'

'You see, I'd had too much to drink and I'd smoked a spliff. It sort of messed up my judgment. I said what I said before I realised it, if that makes any sense at all.'

Anne said, 'I appreciate you coming to apologise. Let's just put it behind us.'

'Thank you.' He pointed at the glass. 'This is my first drink today ... and it'll be the last.'

Lucas spoke quietly with no trace of regional accent. He had what would be regarded by many as an educated voice, and it was accompanied by a diffident manner. Anne gradually set aside her initial wariness about him and increasingly felt that he was basically harmless.

'Are you a student?' she asked.

'I was, but that was before ...'

'It's okay. You don't have to go into personal details.'

Lucas took a deep breath. 'I was a drama student here in Oxford and I'm hoping to go back. For the past six or seven months I've been in rehab ... a drink and drugs problem.'

Anne pointed at his glass of wine. 'Should you really be –'

'Oh, no. I'm not an alcoholic.'

'You said you'd been drinking and smoking weed when you made your ... *unfortunate remark*,' Anne pointed out.

'Yeah. That was a mistake ... a *big* mistake. I thought I could handle it ... wanted to test myself. I failed, like at so much in my life.'

Anne was keen to change the subject. 'So if you're not currently a student, what do you do?'

'For now I'm working in a restaurant in Oxford ... washing up. Monday's my night off.'

'And Sunday?' Anne asked.

'I wasn't working yesterday. I called in sick. It was my own fault. I bought some grass from a bloke and thought I'd give it a try. It got out of hand and ... well, you know the rest.'

Anne sipped her wine. 'Yeah. Will you go back to work tomorrow?'

'That's the plan, if they'll have me.'

'Do you think they will?' said Anne.

'The owner's pretty decent. He had to be to take me on in the first place. Do you know the restaurants in Oxford?'

Anne shrugged. 'Not very well.'

'It's the Golden Madras near the castle.'

'Okay.'

'It's pretty good, actually.'

'Where was your rehab?' Anne asked, adding, 'if you don't mind talking about it.'

Lucas hesitated, and Anne thought she might have trespassed on territory that was best avoided. She was wondering how to change the subject when Lucas replied.

'It was a sort of clinic just outside Brackley. D'you know where that is?'

'I know where Brackley is. In fact I know a drop-in centre, a sort of hostel, right in the middle of the town.'

Lucas perked up. 'You know Magdalene House?' Anne nodded. Lucas continued. 'They were really good to me there. I stayed there for a few nights after I'd been sleeping rough, and the guy who runs it got them to take me in at the rehab clinic. It was the first step in trying to get my life back on track.'

'Where does *Dandelion* figure in all this?' Anne asked.

'It's complicated.' Lucas stared down at his hands. Anne was just thinking again that she'd strayed too far when he said, 'The boat belonged to a guy I'd met. He pushed drugs. He let me stay on it for a couple of weeks after I dropped out of college. Then he got busted and sent down for five years. No one knew about the boat or about me being on board, so I just stayed.'

'Harry told me he's not keen on drugs round here,' said Anne.

'He's not. But he said I could stay on the mooring if I cleaned up the needles and stuff on the bank. I got rid of everything, and he kept his side of the bargain.'

'Moorings don't come cheap, Lucas.'

'Paid for till the spring, Harry said. I just pay the electric. Can I ask you something?'

'Go on.'

'How come you know about Magdalene House? Have you ever stayed there?' He looked around the cabin. 'Only you don't look as if you've dropped out of anything.'

'I'm a student and I've not dropped out, but other than that, I don't want to talk about my life.'

'No, okay, sorry.' Lucas drained the wine and stood up. 'I'd better be going. Thanks for letting me explain. And sorry again for … you know.'

Anne rose from her seat. 'Sure.'

Lucas nodded towards the wine glasses. 'Shall I wash up?' He smiled a sad smile. 'I'm an expert, you know.'

It's okay,' said Anne. 'It's your night off.'

Chapter 13

TUESDAY

On Tuesday morning Marnie stepped out of the office barn to meet the van from the local garden centre. They were delivering trees and plants for the walled garden behind the farmhouse. She spent some time explaining in detail to the gardening contractors precisely how her design should be turned into reality. Satisfied that all was clear and understood, she realised that it was past ten o'clock and Ralph hadn't appeared for coffee.

Her first thought was to ring him from the office, but it was a fine morning and she was enjoying the open air. She set off through the spinney, half expecting to meet him on the way. But he didn't appear, nor was there any sign of him on *Thyrsis* when she looked through the window of his study. She glanced across at *Sally Ann*'s docking area, now vacant, and spotted Ralph leaning on the parapet at the top of the accommodation bridge. He seemed lost to the world, gazing down at the canal. Marnie waved but he failed to see her.

She wondered if she should approach him, anxious not to disturb his thoughts. After a moment's reflection she decided that her presence would only remind him that he had her love and her support. She set off at a brisk pace, and he caught sight of her when she drew nearer. He smiled.

'Ready for coffee?' Marnie called out.

Ralph looked at his watch. 'That time already? I'll be with you directly.'

'The gardening people are here. I'll get the kettle on. See you in the office.'

But that was not how things turned out.

A few minutes later, as soon as Ralph came out of the spinney and turned to enter the office barn, he found Marnie standing on the gravel drive talking to two people. Neither of them were gardening contractors. Further back on the drive, behind the garden centre van he spotted a familiar grey Vauxhall Cavalier, an unmarked police car. The two people on the drive with Marnie were also familiar. Ralph guessed correctly that DS Marriner and DC Lamb had come to see him.

Ralph heard Marnie say, 'Won't you come in for coffee, or perhaps you'd prefer tea?'

He knew it was a good sign when they accepted and walked with Marnie to the office barn. Ralph joined them. Once they were all seated with mugs of steaming German coffee from Donovan's supply, Ralph detected a more relaxed atmosphere compared with the detectives' previous visit.

He said, 'I take it you've not come to cart me off in chains, sergeant. Or are we surrounded by the Armed Response Unit?'

Marriner permitted himself a smile, albeit a faint one.

'Actually,' he said, 'I'm pleased to be able to inform you that the torso recently discussed with you has been identified.'

Marnie and Ralph sat up abruptly in their chairs. 'How?' they said in unison.

Marriner turned towards Lamb. 'Cathy?'

She read from her notepad. 'There is evidence of a tattoo having been removed from the left shoulder. The subject of the tattoo is not clear, but prison records lead us to believe that it represented a spider's web, in which case the deceased was likely to be Frederick 'Spider' Webb, a member of a notorious gang run by the Trentham Brothers. The cause of death has yet to be established.'

Marriner raised a hand. 'You should forget that last bit.'

Marnie grimaced. 'The lack of a head might be a clue.'

Ralph chuckled. Marriner gave Marnie an old-fashioned look.

'Sorry,' she said. 'A case of flippancy covering up relief.'

'What's this so-called notorious gang notorious for?' Ralph asked.

'Oh, the usual. They operate in parts of east London: protection, drugs, prostitution … the kind of things you'd expect.'

'Not in my world,' said Ralph. 'I'm surprised you could ever have associated me with a naked torso.'

'Aren't you forgetting the phone call?' Marriner said. 'One question still remains: why did someone tip the Met off that you were involved?'

Ralph shook his head. 'I can think of another question: who tipped them off?'

'Well,' said Marriner, 'I don't know, and we'll probably never find out. But it is strange that with all these goings-on, your name keeps cropping up.'

Ralph added, 'And strange that the latest tip-off included mention of a journal that hasn't even been published.'

As if by a pre-arranged signal, they all sipped their coffee.

ooo0ooo

Marnie was surprised that Ralph remained in the office after the detectives had left. He moved to the rear of the space to sit at Anne's vacant desk, deep in thought. Marnie had the good sense to let him ponder without interruption. She was taking her seat at her own desk when Ralph spoke to her across the room.

'Can I run something past you, Marnie? This journal business doesn't make much sense.'

'Go on.'

'I've submitted articles to *Economics Review* for the past several years. I know Tim Buchan, the editor, very well.'

Marnie nodded. 'I've heard you speak of him.'

'That journal is read and respected around the world.'

'The academic world,' Marnie observed.

'Well, yes. You don't often see it on the Clapham omnibus.'

'Come to think of it, Ralph, we don't often see you on the –'

Ralph grinned. 'Okay, I take your point, but you take my meaning.'

'What are you getting at, Ralph?'

'I'm frankly astonished that Tim would even *consider* publishing an article about me without letting me know so that I could at least comment.'

'If that was in fact the case,' Marnie said.

Ralph stared at her. 'What do you …?' He sat back in the chair and folded his arms. 'Actually, Marnie, you have a point. Tim would *never* treat me like that. I'm sure of it.'

Marnie indicated the phone on Anne's desk. 'Be my guest.'

ooo0ooo

'He said *what*?!'

It was shortly before one o'clock, and Anne had phoned Marnie 'to touch base'.

'Marnie, do you really want me to repeat what Lucas said about my legs?'

'Well no, not really,' Marnie conceded into the phone. 'I suppose my question was just rhetorical. Did you say *Lucas*? How do you know his name?'

'He told me when he came on the boat.'

'He came on the *boat*?!'

'Marnie, is this going to be a conversation of purely rhetorical questions?'

'No. Sorry. It's just I can't imagine you actually allowing him on board *Sally Ann* after what he'd said.'

'He came to apologise with flowers and a bottle of wine.'

'Really?' Hastily Marnie added, 'I don't think that counts as rhetorical.'

'Fair enough. He seemed genuinely contrite and apologetic.'

'Okay.'

Anne gave an outline of her conversation with Lucas, his drink and drugs problem, and his trying to get his life in order, starting with a menial job as a washer-up in a restaurant.

'So you accepted his apology,' said Marnie.

'I took him at face value. I don't know if I'm a good judge of character, but he seemed ... you know ...'

'Well, you survived to tell the tale, so he can't have been all bad. Talking of bodies in water, we've had a visit from our friendly local cops this morning. They've definitely ruled out any connection between Ralph and the torso in the Thames by Tower Bridge. It's been identified.'

'Did they say whose torso it was?' Anne asked.

'Some gangster or other, apparently. They've got a name for him but don't know much more so far.'

'I could tell them something,' said Anne.

Marnie sighed. 'Go on.'

'They can probably rule out suicide.' Marnie groaned. Unabashed, Anne continued. 'There was one other thing I meant to tell you about Lucas. He'd stayed at Randall's drop-out centre in Brackley, and it was Randall who helped him make a new start.'

'How?' Marnie asked.

'He got him into some kind of clinic ... rehab, that sort of thing. Talking of which, I'd like to get Angela and Dorli to Autumn Lodge in Brackley at the weekend, so that Angela can see Randall and Frau Kreisler can see Dorli.'

'When do you have in mind, Anne?'

'I suppose it has to be Saturday. Vicars work on Sundays, don't they?'

'I've heard rumours to that effect,' Marnie said. 'I'll check with Angela about the weekend,'

Deadpan, Anne replied, 'I'm pretty sure you'll find they do work on Sundays. I think I read it somewhere.'

ooo0ooo

Twenty minutes later Ralph arrived in the farmhouse kitchen for a soup-and-sandwich lunch. He brought with him some news of his own.

'I had an interesting chat with Tim Buchan, the magazine editor. He phoned me back in reply to the message I left for him this morning.'

'About the scurrilous accusations about you in his journal?'

'That's right. Well, guess what ...' Ralph left a pause for dramatic effect while Marnie took a bite of her sandwich. '... there never was any such article.'

'What do you mean?' Marnie nearly choked on the sandwich.

'Just that. Tim denied that any such article existed. In any case he said he'd never print anything hostile, and would certainly never print anything about me at all without inviting me to comment beforehand.'

'So where did the idea come from? And how did the police hear about it? Don't tell me, Ralph. It was the anonymous tip-off.'

'Exactly. It was just a malicious call designed to get me rattled.'

'Which it hasn't done,' said Marnie.

After a moment's hesitation Ralph said, 'No. But it does make me wonder who is at the back of all this. It's obvious what they're trying to do.'

Marnie could think of any number of reasons for the attempts to damage Ralph's reputation. The constant drip-feeding of slurs against his integrity could lead to irreparable harm to his standing in the academic world and could, if left unchallenged and unsubstantiated, have a negative impact on his entire career. For Ralph, that would be the worst outcome imaginable.

While musing along these lines, another thought occurred to Marnie. Where would it all end? So far attempts had been made to discredit Ralph in the eyes of his peers. There was a vindictive edge to the accusations, a spiteful and malevolent tone that sought to attack Ralph in the heart of his professional environment. But where might it lead? Whoever was behind these attacks was familiar with Ralph's world, understood how to inflict damage on him in ways that would cause him distress and hurt. Yet there was a clear pattern of escalation becoming apparent. What if the next step was to cause him actual *bodily* harm? What if the perpetrator felt compelled to attack Ralph *physically*?

Marnie observed Ralph over the rim of her mug of soup. Had the same ideas occurred to him? If so, what did he propose to do about it? What *could* he do about it?

As they mulled over the possibilities they had no idea that the next assault would come quickly and from a totally unexpected quarter.

Chapter 14

THURSDAY

On Thursday morning Marnie's thoughts had turned to the pleasant prospect of Anne returning for the weekend later that afternoon. She was writing a note on her pad to remember to buy a posy of flowers to put beside the bed in Anne's attic room when Ralph came into the office. Marnie knew at once that all was not well.

'You okay, Ralph?'

'I've just had a phone call from Langley at Cranmer College. Lowell Rathbone has died. Heart attack, apparently.'

'Lowell Rathbone?' Marnie repeated uncertainly. 'Have I met him?'

'No. Rathbone was at Cranmer, Warburg professor of economic history, senior fellow in the college.'

'I don't think I've ever heard you mention him before, Ralph. Was he a friend?'

'Not exactly. In fact, not at all. He denounced *We're going Wrong* as 'fanciful twaddle' when it was first published and wrote a diatribe against *Public Need versus Corporate Greed* in one of the national dailies.'

'So not a fan, then.'

Ralph shook his head. It was one of those occasions when Marnie felt at a loss to find the right words, when she recognised her inadequacy to participate in Ralph's world on anything resembling equal terms. Rather than mouth something trite and inappropriate, she chose to remain silent. She was rescued from her dilemma by the sound of a car pulling up on the gravel drive across the way. Ralph turned his head towards the plate glass window.

'Probably the morning's post,' Marnie said. 'He's a little earlier than usual.'

But it was not the morning post. Marnie and Ralph both frowned when they saw their visitors approaching the door. They had become accustomed to occasional visits by DS Marriner and DC Lamb, but the sight of Detective Chief Inspector Bartlett caused them some concern. Marnie stood up as Bartlett and Marriner entered the office.

'Ah, Professor Lombard,' Bartlett said without preamble. 'Just the man I wanted to see.'

'What can I do for you?' said Ralph, without offering his hand.

'Do you know a Professor Lowell Rathbone, sir?'

'Of course. He was an eminent economic historian at Cranmer College, Oxford.'

Bartlett narrowed his eyes. 'You used the word *was*, professor.'

'Yes. I learnt this morning that he'd died.'

'How did you know that?'

'I had a phone call from a colleague at Cranmer ... T. J. Langley. He rang to inform me of Lowell's death about half an hour ago.'

'Would you mind telling me where you were at the time of his death?'

Ralph reflected. 'I don't think the time was mentioned. Can I ask you something?'

Bartlett nodded.

Ralph said, 'Would you mind telling me why you are here asking these questions?'

'I can't go into that at the moment, I'm afraid.'

'Then I think our conversation is at an end, chief inspector.'

With the atmosphere cooling from cold to icy, Marnie decided to intervene.

'Can I say something, Mr Bartlett? We've learnt that Professor Rathbone died of a heart attack. Is that right?'

'Yes.' Bartlett's tone was wary.

'As Ralph's colleague phoned here with the news this morning, I'm assuming that the professor died ... some time yesterday?'

'Why do you assume that, Mrs Walker?'

'Well, someone would hardly take the trouble to telephone at eight in the morning to say that a colleague had died a week or two ago, would they? And anyway, Ralph would've already heard on the university grapevine if that had been the case. You take my point?'

'I can see the logic of that,' Bartlett said slowly.

'But you can't tell us why you're asking these questions before nine in the morning?'

Bartlett eyed Marnie without speaking. She continued.

'From seeing detectives on television I've heard them say the first hours of an investigation are critical. Also the *chief inspector* – as senior investigating officer – usually comes out of the office only at the start of an investigation to get the feel of it.'

'What's your point, Mrs Walker?'

'I'm guessing that Professor Rathbone died yesterday and something has prompted you to connect Ralph with that. You also seem to be treating it as a suspicious death, which is logical, as you are a senior detective. You wouldn't be here for just a heart attack … what you would call natural causes.'

Another silence from Bartlett. Marnie looked pointedly at DS Marriner and continued in a weary tone.

'Are we looking at yet another anonymous tip-off?'

Marriner cleared his throat and stared down at his notepad.

Marnie looked again at Bartlett. 'You're wasting your time, you know, as well as ours.'

'Can you elaborate on that, Mrs Walker?'

'Sure. I think you have to make up your mind whether my husband is virtually a serial killer or someone is yanking your chain with these so-called tip-offs. Are you *seriously* entertaining the notion that for some *inexplicable* reason my husband, professor of economics and fellow of an Oxford college, has suddenly turned into a mass murderer with connections to the underworld of organised crime? Really, Mr Bartlett, whatever next?'

'Mrs Walker, you know as well as I do that we have to follow up every avenue in our investigations.'

'You also have to exercise some judgment when deciding on the priorities for spending your time. Do you have *any* reason to believe that Professor Rathbone died of anything other than natural causes … apart from some spurious anonymous tip-off?'

'I can't discuss such things, Mrs Walker. I think you know that.'

Before Marnie could reply, Ralph intervened. 'Lowell Rathbone was a coronary waiting to happen. I'm sorry to say this, but it's true. He was overweight, had a penchant for rich cuisine, smoked and drank heavily and never took exercise. We had our differences, yes of course. That's the academic world for you, but I would never wish him ill.'

Bartlett looked across at Marriner. 'We must be going, Ted.' To Ralph and Marnie he said, 'Thank you for your time.'

As the detectives closed the door behind them, Ralph said quietly, 'What the hell is going on?'

Marnie shrugged. 'Someone is trying to harm your reputation. We know that.'

'They could do that by challenging my books and views … as Lowell Rathbone did in the past. A lot of academics have rivals and critics. This is different, Marnie. This is rather more than malicious gossip. It has a sting in the tail.'

Marnie knew Ralph was right. She wondered where it would all end, but said nothing.

oooOooo

Donovan arrived that afternoon in his old but sprightly VW Beetle as dusk was descending on Glebe Farm. Marnie heard the distinctive rumble of his engine, shortly followed by a glimpse of him through the plate-glass window of the office barn as he advanced on the front door of the farmhouse. She saw that he was carrying a large cardboard box and guessed that any plans she may have had for supper that evening were now history.

Anne returned from Oxford soon afterwards and announced to Marnie that she had arranged to visit Frau Kreisler with Dorli at Autumn Lodge on Saturday morning. She would drop Angela off on the way at Randall's vicarage.

Opening the door as she set off to see Donovan in the farmhouse, Anne stopped and turned to Marnie with a further announcement.

'With Frau Kreisler and Dorli – not to mention Angela and Randall – I reckon it's going to be a slobbering weekend!'

With that, she laughed and was gone. At her desk, Marnie smiled, shook her head and muttered, *that girl.*

oooOooo

Ralph arrived in the office barn just before seven o'clock that evening. It was the customary time for the end of the working day. Anne had returned to the office from greeting Donovan, but had left half an hour earlier than usual, and Marnie had a fair idea why that was so. When Marnie closed the front door of the farmhouse behind them, Ralph was sniffing the air. A mixture of interesting smells was issuing from the kitchen.

'Ah …' Ralph observed. 'I take it that Donovan is here and has taken over the Aga.'

'A brilliant deduction, Watson,' Marnie muttered and led the way forward.

When they entered the kitchen, Donovan announced that supper would be ready in about ten minutes. The meal was predictably German and hearty, with Frankfurter sausages (including the vegetarian variety for Anne), sauerkraut, mashed potato and onion gravy. For dessert Donovan had bought *Apfelstrudel* from his local Austrian delicatessen, which would be served with whipped cream. Anne had just finished laying the table, on which she was lighting two chunky candles.

Ralph made a further deduction that he would not need to choose a wine for the meal, as beer glasses had been positioned at each place setting.

Within a few minutes Anne was passing round bottles of Beck's beer from the fridge while Donovan was fielding compliments for the food. Over the meal Ralph brought him up to date with the latest news on what had become known as the plot to damage Ralph's reputation.

Donovan said, 'Could this Professor Rathbone have been part of the plot, Ralph?'

'How could he be?' said Marnie. 'He's dead.'

Donovan shrugged. 'The plot could've involved other people. Someone might have seen his death as something to exploit.'

Ralph replied without hesitation. 'The academic world is full of rivalries, and some people can be particularly vindictive. For Rathbone it was all about politics, of course. He was a severe critic of my work, there's no denying it. On the other hand, I can't honestly see him using any underhand tactics. His criticisms were made openly in public. I had no problem with that.'

'Can you really not think who might be behind it all?' Donovan asked.

Ralph reflected. 'Frankly, I'm at a loss. With modern communications it could be anyone, anywhere in the world.'

'And you have a worldwide reputation,' Marnie observed.

Donovan took a mouthful of beer. 'I've been thinking. I'm not sure about this worldwide thing. Of course, Ralph has a tremendous reputation ...'

'When he's not being vilified,' Marnie added.

'Sure. But it seems to me,' Donovan continued, 'that whoever is behind this plot must be someone in the academic world nearer to home. In fact, the more I've thought about it, the more I've convinced myself that it must be someone based at Oxford, at the university.'

'Are you serious?' Anne said.

'All the indications are that it must be an insider, someone who knows intimately what's going on in the university at any given time.'

'I think you've got a point there,' said Ralph. 'And frankly it doesn't give me much comfort. On the other hand, I don't suppose things can get any worse.'

Marnie and Anne seemed encouraged by Ralph's point of view. But Donovan viewed him appraisingly and without comment over the rim of his glass. As he drained his beer he was mentally crossing his fingers.

Chapter 15

SATURDAY

By the standards of that autumn the rest of the week passed without excitement. There were no bodies in the Thames, no unexpected fatal heart attacks, no anonymous tip-offs, not even a headless limbless torso waiting to be claimed. Marnie and Ralph were almost wondering if life was returning to something approaching normality, though both wondered privately how long it might last. Friday found the residents of Glebe Farm absorbed in their respective mundane tasks of work, study and research.

On Saturday morning Donovan and Anne picked up Angela, with Dorli in her carrying basket, and they set off for Brackley in Donovan's Beetle. The first stop was the vicarage of Randall Hughes. A suitably restrained embrace between Randall and Angela took place on the doorstep, though Anne tried to imagine something more enthusiastic taking place between them once the front door was closed. The brief exchange of glances that she shared with Donovan gave her cause to reflect that such a notion might not be far-fetched.

Autumn Lodge was a pleasant surprise. Formerly a rather grand manor house, it was set back from the road on the outskirts of Brackley at the end of a long paved drive. The house, now tastefully converted to a home for the elderly of significant means, dominated a walled site of several acres. The landscaped grounds suggested the care and attention of a team of gardeners.

It came as no surprise to Anne that Frau Kreisler emerged swiftly from the house as soon as Donovan parked the car. The old Austrian lady may have been advanced in years, but as soon as she spotted the pet carrier she advanced with haste across the forecourt of the house, keeping up a rapid stream of German all the way. Her smile lit up the morning as she threw her arms round Anne before turning her attention to her beloved Dorli.

'*Ach, Schätzchen,*' she cried, *Oh my darling*, as she poked a finger through the grill of the carrier and stroked behind the ears of her adored pet.

Donovan, ever practical, asked how they would manage the visit, given that animals were not allowed in the building. Frau Kreisler looked up at him with a twinkle in her eye.

'I have spoken with the ...' She searched for the word. '... *die Hausmutter.*'

'The duty manageress, perhaps?' Donovan suggested.

'*Ja, ja* ... that person. She says we can use the conservatory for your visit. And for Dorli too. It is very good, yes?'

'*Ja, sehr gut*, very good,' Donovan agreed.

Frau Kreisler led the way through the house, and Anne was pleasantly surprised how charming it was. With the typical outlook of a young person, she had expected it to smell of over-cooked Brussels sprouts and the mustiness she vaguely associated with *old people*. But no. Autumn Lodge felt like a country house with furnishings and décor to match. There was a hint of lavender in the air. Even the few residents that she saw were moving about, unencumbered with Zimmer frames, wheelchairs or the paraphernalia of infirmity. Frau Kreisler in particular had a spring in her step as she hastened them towards the conservatory.

Donovan was transporting the pet carrier with scrupulous care with one ear attuned to the constant, excited flow of German from their hostess. From time to time he inserted appropriate comments until they arrived at a pair of French windows. Frau Kreisler opened them both wide and gestured to her visitors to enter. The conservatory was spacious with comfortable upholstered seating and views across the landscaped grounds. Donovan set the pet carrier down on one of the armchairs as Frau Kreisler carefully closed the French windows behind them. She knelt on the ground beside her much-loved cat and cooed at Dorli quietly in German while Anne and Donovan took their seats and smiled at her. It was a touching reunion.

'You are so kind, Anna, to bring my lovely Dorli to see me.'

Anne had no problem with her name pronounced the German way. 'I'm sure she is very happy to see you again, Frau Kreisler,' she said.

Donovan rose to his feet. 'Shall I open the catches? They are rather fiddly.'

'Oh, thank you. That would be nice,' Frau Kreisler said and settled herself in an armchair.

They all looked on as the cat stepped cautiously out of the carrier and sniffed the air. For the next few minutes Dorli explored the conservatory, pushing her nose into every corner. To Frau Kreisler's absolute delight the cat walked decisively across the floor with tail held high and jumped up onto her lap. The old lady gently stroked the cat who snuggled down with eyes closed, purring softly. Frau Kreisler was not the only one present with a smile on her face.

Just then one of the French windows opened and a woman looked in. She was middle-aged and wearing a white nurse's outfit. Her eyebrows raised as she spotted Dorli.

'Oh, a cat.'

Frau Kreisler looked up anxiously at the newcomer. 'It is in order,' she said. 'Mrs McKenzie has approved it.'

'Well, that's lovely. Always nice to have visitors. Can I get you all some tea?'

ooo0ooo

On the way home, Anne, Donovan and Angela agreed that the visit had been a success, and Dorli seemed to be relaxed in her pet carrier. It was a satisfactory day from every point of view. Frau Kreisler in particular seemed enchanted both with Dorli – who had quickly related to her – and with the opportunity to speak some German with Donovan.

'How did your get-together with Randall go, Angela?' Anne asked.

'Very well. In fact he said he was rather disappointed that we had to leave so soon. He would have liked to take me for a pub lunch. I told him we had to make allowance for Frau Kreisler's lunchtime at the home.'

'Perhaps next time we come we could arrive at mid-day and visit Frau Kreisler in the afternoon,' Anne suggested. 'Then you could do your pub lunch with Randall.'

'That could work,' Donovan agreed.

'What about your visit?' Angela asked. 'How was that?'

'No probs,' said Anne. 'Dorli was pleased to see Frau Kreisler, and we even got a cup of tea from one of the staff.'

Angela chuckled. 'Randall told me the place was run by a Scottish dragon called Fiona McKenzie. You must have got on the right side of her if she gave you tea.'

Anne said, 'I think the person we met was a Mrs Albright. Definitely English, I thought.'

'That's the dragon's deputy,' said Angela. 'She's new.'

Donovan spoke over his shoulder. 'That's her. She said she only joined the staff a month or two ago.'

'That sounds about right. Randall said she came from another residential place.'

'Would that be The Grange?' Anne asked. 'The vicar before you … Toni Petrie … she used to do pastoral visits there.'

Mention of Toni Petrie's name always produced a few moments of silence as they thought of their friend who had been killed in the church soon after taking up her post.

'It's possible, Anne. The Grange is also an old people's home, and I do visits there. I don't think I've ever come across a Mrs Albright, though.'

Chapter 16

I t had been a calm weekend, though on Monday morning Marnie did find herself wondering if the police would be back with more questions, more hints about anonymous tip-offs and more probing questions about Ralph's movements. It seemed to be the default setting for their lives at that time.

Alone in the office barn, with Ralph on *Thyrsis*, Anne and Donovan away at their universities and only Dolly for company, Marnie had half an ear tuned to the sound of any vehicle crunching over the gravel drive. It was a sad sign of the times that she could recognise the authoritative arrival of a police car, compared with the more sedate parking of the postman's van.

Marnie reckoned to have peace and quiet in the office before nine o'clock, so it came as a surprise when the phone rang soon after eight. Her stomach turned over as she reached for the receiver and checked the caller ID. She didn't recognise the number, though the first digits seemed familiar.

'Walker and Co, good morning.'

'Walker?' A man's voice, confused and uncertain.

'This is Marnie Walker. Can I help you?'

'I thought this was the number for Ralph Lombard.' The tone had changed and was now bordering on indignant, edging towards confrontational.

'If you'd like to leave a message, I can ask Ralph to ring you back.' Marnie was doing her best to conceal her irritation.

'Are you his secretary? Do you keep his diary?'

Marnie fought the temptation to slam the phone down.

'I'm the principal of Walker and Co, interior design consultants.' Marnie spoke slowly and clearly through clenched teeth. 'I can pass on a message to Ralph if that would be helpful.'

There was silence on the line. Marnie was leaning forward to replace the receiver when the voice returned.

'Could you ask Professor Lombard to phone me as soon as possible.'

'That might be difficult.'

'Why?'

'Mainly because you haven't told me who you are, and also because you haven't given me your number.'

There followed a few seconds of bluster. 'It's, it's … er … Dr Greville Rickman. He has my number.'

Marnie reached for a pen while listening to dialling tone.

ooo0ooo

When Ralph arrived in the office barn at coffee time, he was carrying his driving jacket and briefcase.

'Sorry about Greville,' he said. 'I think you caught him off-guard. No excuse for him being so rude.'

Marnie smiled sweetly. 'No, sir. Shall I carry your briefcase to the car when I go to retrieve it from valet parking? Let me pour you coffee.'

Ralph slumped on the visitor's chair with a sigh. 'Oh God, Marnie.'

Still maintaining her sing-song voice, Marnie added, 'Walker and Co, secretarial services, are always happy to oblige.'

Ralph held up his mug while Marnie poured coffee. 'If you hear on the news today that an Oxford don has been hideously battered to death in his rooms at All Saints' College, you know nothing, okay Marnie?'

Resorting to her normal voice Marnie replied, 'Do I take it I might also have to provide you with an alibi?'

'That would be appreciated. Thank you.' He raised his mug. 'Cheers.'

ooo0ooo

It was shortly before eleven that morning when Ralph steered into his parking space at All Saints' College. As usual, he glanced over towards the college's main entrance. The Master's Saab occupied its reserved space, but Ralph noticed something that hadn't struck him before. Its surfaces were littered with fallen leaves, resting on a light coating of dust. The car had not been moved for a while.

He was musing on the significance of that as he made his way along the corridor to the rooms of Dr Greville Rickman, fellow, senior lecturer in Aristotelian Philosophy and Vice Dean

108

of the college. They had agreed to meet at eleven o'clock. Ralph checked his watch; perfect timing. He knocked and entered.

'I'm sorry, Greville, I didn't realise you had a meeting. I'll come back later.'

'No, Ralph, do come in. I've invited a few colleagues to join us, well just two, in fact.'

The other men rose and they all shook hands. Rickman made introductions.

'I'm sure you know Harry, officially of course Henry Boulter, professor of Hispanic Studies.'

The tone was chummy and false. It grated on Ralph but he concealed his feelings.

'Of course.' They exchanged nods.

'And this, Ralph, is Oliver Ringstead. Oliver's field is pure maths. He joined us last term from Cranmer. Shall we sit?'

Rickman's rooms were comfortably furnished with a mixed clutter of elderly sofas and button-back leather armchairs. Ralph settled on one of the latter. He sensed that some discussion had already been taking place between his colleagues and waited for Greville Rickman to speak.

'It's good of you to come, Ralph, at such short notice.'

Ralph crossed his legs, outwardly entirely relaxed, but internally wary.

'That's okay, though I wasn't expecting a delegation. What do you have in mind, Greville?'

Rickman looked uncomfortable. 'Not exactly a delegation, Ralph, just …'

'Yes?'

'A group of colleagues … friends … who have the good name of the college at heart.'

'A concern that I naturally share,' said Ralph.

'Quite.'

Rickman glanced quickly at the other two dons. Neither spoke.

'So was that it?' Ralph asked. He uncrossed his legs.

'Not entirely. You see, Ralph, we have become rather concerned at the recent allegations made against you, together with the enquiries being made by the police into your … shall we say, activities. We wondered if it might be desirable for you to withdraw from the college for a time.'

Ralph said nothing.

Dr Ringstead added, 'Perhaps just until the scandal around the accusations has died down.' He smiled in what he hoped was a friendly fashion, adding, 'You are in any case rather *off-shore*.'

Ralph's expression remained calm and unruffled. 'I'm rather bewildered by what you mean. What are these allegations? What have the police to do with anything?'

'We understand that you have been accused of certain things,' Rickman said slowly.

'Things?' Ralph prompted.

'An article in a journal is accusing you of plagiarism, I understand.'

'No, Greville. There is no such article.'

'But I –'

'Have you checked your facts? The journal in question is the *Economics Review*. I heard of such a rumour and spoke with Tim Buchan, the editor. He was astonished and flatly denied knowledge of any such article.'

'What about the police and their enquiries, Ralph?' It was Professor Boulter who spoke.

'Ah, yes, Harry. That's another matter.'

'So they have been in touch with you?'

Ralph nodded. 'I'm afraid so … a very distasteful affair.'

'Can you enlighten us?'

Ralph paused. The three dons exchanged glances.

'I was asked to identify a body pulled from the Thames a short while ago. The police had believed the corpse to be … me.'

The effect of Ralph's statement on all three men was instant. They sat bolt upright in their seats, their expressions startled.

Boulter said, 'You were asked to identify a dead person they believed to be yourself?'

Ralph could not suppress a smile. 'Not quite, Harry. Think about it.'

The Luis Gonzales Professor of Spanish language and literature stammered in an untypical fashion, clearly confused. 'I … well … I, er … I …'

Ralph came to his rescue. 'It appears they'd received an anonymous phone call. When they checked their *facts* they discovered it wasn't true.' Ralph got up from his chair. 'I'm sure we'd all agree that was sound academic practice, wouldn't we?'

Ralph walked to the door. He was turning the handle when Greville Rickman spoke again.

'I'm sure we take your point, Ralph, but perhaps we should be mindful of that old saying, *there's no smoke without fire*.'

Ralph stared back at him. 'And I'm equally sure, Greville, that we would be mindful of the principle of not speaking in clichés, especially when they do nothing but distort the truth.'

As he went out, Ralph closed the door quietly behind him.

ooo0ooo

There was laughter that evening over supper at Glebe Farm. Marnie chuckled as Ralph recounted Professor Boulter's discomfiture when he inadvertently asked if Ralph had been invited to identify his own dead body.

Marnie said, 'Sorry, Ralph. I know it's not funny, but I'd like to have seen his face when you picked him up on what he'd said.'

'He was in a state of shock. The three of them were. Most of all, Greville Rickman obviously felt like a fool. He'd got a little band together with the aim of getting me out, at least until things had died down. Then it backfired on him.'

'Well I for one don't have any sympathy for him, Ralph. What on earth was he thinking? Did he seriously believe such nonsense about you?'

Ralph finished his wine before replying. 'There's a lot of jealousy in the academic world, Marnie. When you first met me I was at my lowest ebb, and I really did think my career – even my life – was at an end. Then I bounced back – you played a major role in my recovery – and some people found it hard to stomach that I continued with my work and was even awarded a personal chair. These days I'm regarded as some kind of eccentric, working on a canalboat. And there are quite a few who envy my combining the role of visiting professor with – let's face it – a lucrative programme of lecturing and consulting around the world.'

'You've worked your way back, Ralph. You've done that by your own efforts.'

'What I've done has been with your support, Marnie ... and Anne's. That meeting may have had its amusing side, but let's not forget that Greville had received an anonymous letter mentioning that non-existent article in *Economics Review* and my contacts with the police.'

'You managed to fend off the accusations quite easily,' said Marnie.

Ralph looked thoughtful. 'Be that as it may, it's clear that the campaign to harm me is still rolling on. And the more I think of it, the more certain I am that Donovan was right. Whoever is

111

pursuing me is an insider. It's someone in the university, possibly even in my own college. And I'm wondering where it will all end.'

Marnie stood and began clearing away their plates. 'I'd no idea university life could be so unpleasant. The colleges are so beautiful, I just assumed ...'

'Actually,' said Ralph, 'the academic world can have its redeeming side.'

'Presumably you chose it because it attracted you once upon a time.'

'You're right, and it's a fact that in that world everyone has opinions, and you can never be quite sure what they might be.'

'What do you mean?'

'As I left Greville's rooms I bumped into another colleague, no less a person than Professor Sir Reginald Barton.'

'I've heard you speak of him before,' Marnie said.

'Oh yes. He's one serious player, a real heavy-hitter.'

'In economics?'

'His field is Government. His books are the standard works on the British Constitution, and he's played a big part in constructing the constitutions of a number of Commonwealth countries.'

Marnie said, 'I'm guessing he's not a card-carrying member of the Politburo.'

'And your guess would be correct.'

'I'm also guessing that he's probably not your biggest fan.'

'Well spotted, Marnie. When we passed in the corridor he asked if I had a minute. *Hey ho*, I thought. *Here we go again.* He invited me into his study, sat me down and offered me a brandy.'

'At that time of the morning?' Marnie said.

'The words *gift horse* and *mouth* floated before my eyes, and I accepted.'

Marnie was frowning. 'I'm not sure I like where this is heading.'

'Sir Reginald – you can't even *think* of him as *Reg* – said he'd heard rumours about accusations of plagiarism and also that the police had been interviewing me. I didn't ask how. I just sipped my brandy – a very fine old cognac – and waited for the onslaught.'

Marnie was now frowning and sitting forward in her chair.

'Did you say anything?' she asked.

Ralph shook his head. 'Nothing. It's difficult to spar with someone as eminent as Barton. I just let him do the talking.'

'And?'

'He looked me in the eye and reminded me that we stood on opposite sides of the political divide. He said he'd never quite accepted my interpretation of certain areas of economic policy, but he would never believe me guilty of using anyone else's ideas. In short, he dismissed the accusations of plagiarism as nothing more than malicious gossip – his exact words – and said he'd make his views known in all quarters of the university and beyond.'

'Blimey!'

'That's what I thought, Marnie, though of course I didn't say it out loud.'

Marnie smiled at Ralph across the table, but all the while she was thinking that it was time someone took the gloves off. It was all very well having gentlemanly exchanges in the privileged rooms of an elite academic institution. The time had come for a serious assault on the perpetrator of the attacks on Ralph's good name, before they turned into something more physical. And Marnie was becoming convinced that actual violence could be just around the corner.

Chapter 17

TUESDAY

Tuesday morning found Ralph back at All Saints' College, and it proved to be a day of contrasts. The Master's car was in its usual place near the college entrance, its bodywork now free of leaves and dust. Shiny and clean, it looked as if it had been through the car-wash. Ralph braced himself mentally for his meeting with the Master. Normally that would be an enjoyable experience. Ralph had known Vivian Parry-Jones for several years. He liked and admired him, and they had always got on well together. But these days something had changed, and Ralph had no idea what was going on. He decided to settle in to his office before the encounter with the Master's personal secretary.

That encounter happened much earlier than Ralph expected. He had no sooner walked into the entrance than Clare Goodall materialised beside him.

'Professor, good morning.'

'Clare, are you lying in wait for me? Is everything all right? You seem rather agitated.'

'Sorry. It's er …'

'Yes?'

She glanced down the corridor. 'Could we speak? Have you a moment?'

'Of course. Would you like to come to my office?'

'Please.'

Ralph was convinced she was about to give an excuse for why the Master couldn't see him that day. He was wrong. As Ralph hung up his driving jacket, he gestured Clare to a seat then drew up another chair to face her.

'What can I do for you, Clare?' he asked.

'It's delicate,' she said. 'And you'll probably think I have no right to even speak to you like this, professor.'

'Look, Clare, why don't you just tell me what's on your mind? And why don't we drop the titles? Just call me Ralph. What is it?'

'Well … Ralph …' She looked down at her hands. 'This is so difficult.'

'Is it about me seeing the Master?'

Her head jerked up. 'No. Well, not directly. You see, there are rumours going around …' Her voice tailed off.

'About me.' Ralph's tone was firm. She nodded. Ralph said, 'You mean about me stealing other people's ideas and claiming them as my own?'

'That kind of thing.' Clare's embarrassment was palpable.

'And you're wondering if they're true?'

'No, no, not at all,' she said hastily. 'I don't know how to put this.'

'Just say it, Clare. Whatever it is, I'm not going to fly off the handle.'

Clare took a few moments to gather herself together, then looked Ralph in the eye.

'I was here a few years ago when there was a kind of campaign against you, Ralph. Forgive me saying this, but I know you suffered a lot at that time. Some people tried to get you condemned for your views. I know I'm only a secretary, but I could see what was going on. You pulled through then, and I know you'll pull through now. I don't see how you can be attacked for stating opinions that put you at odds with conventional thinking, then attacked for pinching other people's ideas. It doesn't seem logical to me.'

Clare was surprised by Ralph's reaction. He grinned broadly.

'You know, Clare, I don't think I could have put it better myself.'

Clare looked relieved. 'Thank you for taking it like that, prof … Ralph. Please don't tell anyone I mentioned this to you. People will say I was speaking out of turn, but I couldn't let it pass without commenting. It all seemed so unfair.'

'Clare, there's something I want to ask you.'

'Yes, Ralph, I was lying in wait, as you put it.'

'But not only to tell me about your concerns, presumably. You were there on behalf of the Master?'

'Yes.'

Ralph was convinced that Clare was about to fob him off as on his previous attempts to speak with the Master.

Instead she said, 'The Master wonders if you would be free to join him for coffee at eleven o'clock.'

Ralph was momentarily speechless. 'I shall certainly be free at that time. Thank you, Clare. Please tell the Master that I'll be delighted.'

They stood and crossed to the door. Ralph held it open for her. She smiled.

'Back to normal once I step outside? Is that all right?' she said.

'Of course, if you wish. Thank you for coming, Clare.'

'Thank you, professor.'

With the click-clack of Clare's shoes echoing in the corridor, Ralph closed the door to his office and walked quickly across the room to his desk. Before anything else he had to re-arrange the commitments in the diary for that day. There was no way he would turn down the invitation from the Master.

ooo0ooo

'Professor Lombard to see you, Master.'

'Excellent. Thank you, Clare.' Professor Vivian Parry-Jones, Master of All Saints' College, rose from behind his desk to welcome Ralph. He was smiling broadly.

Not a tall man, he had a slightly fleshy face with strong features and piercing dark eyes under heavy brows. Ralph liked him immensely, and he knew that the feeling was mutual. As the Master extended a hand, somewhere in a distant corner of the college a clock was striking eleven.

'Good morning, Master. Good to see you.'

'Come in, come in. You must think I've been avoiding you, Ralph.' The accent was a gentle, educated Welsh. 'Take a seat. I think Clare will be bringing us coffee in a moment. So how are things? You've been having a difficult time of late, I hear.'

'If you had been avoiding me, Master, I could hardly blame you. Rumours of my *alleged* misdeeds have been rife these past few weeks.'

'Total nonsense, of course.' With an owlish countenance and a thick crop of grey hair, turning to white, the Master had an inquisitive expression and often, as now, a twinkle in the eye. 'The idea of you purloining anyone else's ideas is completely absurd.' The Master chuckled. 'You're the last person who would need to borrow the views of another to find yourself in hot water.'

'Thank you, Master.' Ralph paused to reflect. 'At least, I think that's the appropriate reply.'

Both men were grinning as the door to the study opened and Clare Goodall entered carrying a tray. The Master gestured to a low table and moved from his desk chair to take a seat opposite Ralph.

'If you'd like to leave the tray, Clare, we'll help ourselves.'

After his secretary left the room, the Master took charge of coffee pot and milk jug and served his guest and himself.

'Just a little milk for you, Ralph, and no sugar, if my memory serves me well.'

'Exactly right, Master.'

Another twinkle in the eye. 'I should know after all these years, Ralph.'

When they were both settled with coffee Ralph said, 'Did you ask me to see you for an explanation of what's been happening around me?'

The Master looked momentarily confused. 'Not at all. I gather you've been along to see me on at least two occasions while I've been absent. It's rather for me to offer you an explanation, Ralph.'

Ralph shook his head. 'Quite unnecessary, Master. When I came hoping for a word with you, I only wanted to assure you that there was no truth in the reports of plagiarism. We all have the interests of the college at heart and for my part I –'

Ralph stopped as the Master raised a hand. His expression was now more serious. 'Ralph, there is no question of my paying heed to any such allegations. You have a personal chair here, and the use of the term *visiting* in your title only reflects the fact that you are in such demand in the wider world. The aim of the governors is to give you the freedom to operate to your best advantage. Do I really have to spell out that your role here enhances the reputation of our college?'

Ralph was almost overwhelmed by the Master's words. Frowning, he sipped his coffee. 'Master, I ... I really don't know ... what to ...'

'There's nothing for you to say, Ralph. And I didn't mean to embarrass you. There is something you can do.'

'I could try ending a sentence,' Ralph muttered.

The Master smiled. 'Well, apart from that.' He looked over at the wall of books lining his study as he gathered his thoughts. 'I think perhaps this is a *Vivian* moment.'

Ralph smiled. 'I've always been happy to call you by your title, Master.'

'Entirely as you wish, my old friend. But as I was saying, there is something you could do. I read your recent article in *The Times*. You're clearly convinced that the Japanese economy may be heading for a period of stagnation. You seem to be unique in holding that view, as far as I can judge. I'd be very glad to know more about your latest thinking on the situation in the Far East as a whole.'

Ralph leaned forward in his seat, steepled his fingers and cocked his head on one side. 'Well, Master, as I see it ...'

ooo0ooo

After taking leave of the Master, Ralph rounded off his morning with a postgrad tutorial with one of his brightest students, an ambitious young woman of firm views who had the title Future Merchant Banker written all over her carefully-groomed persona. She had taken a first in PPE – Philosophy, Politics and Economics – at Balliol College and was now homing in on a lucrative career in the City of London like a heat-seeking guided missile. When Ralph had asked if they could possibly put back their meeting till eleven-thirty, she had immediately acquiesced, and would no doubt have spent the extra half hour studiously engaged in the library.

Punctually at one o'clock Ralph took his seat in the Bistro Lebon, a short walk from All Saints' College. Having rearranged his programme for the rest of that day, he was pleased that he had arrived on time and in advance of his colleague, Professor Waldo Forrest. Forrest was spending a year at Oxford as part of an exchange programme with American universities. He was a New Yorker, a colourful, exuberant character who occasionally crossed swords with Ralph on policy matters, but always with a smile on his face.

However, on that day, arriving in the restaurant in a rush and slightly late, he was definitely not smiling. Ralph raised a hand as soon as he saw him enter, and he watched his colleague negotiating a pathway between the tables, looking uncharacteristically red-faced and flustered.

A waiter quickly came forward and pulled back the chair opposite Ralph. Forrest gratefully sank onto it as the waiter asked if he would like to order a drink.

'I could sure use something,' Forrest growled. 'Can I get a Scotch on the rocks?'

It was unusual for Forrest to drink more than a single glass of wine at lunchtime, and Ralph could tell that something had disconcerted his friend.

'Are you all right, Waldo? What's the matter?'

Forrest took a few calming breaths before speaking.

'I had a phone call just before leaving the house. Some guy asked if I'd recovered.'

'From what?' Ralph asked.

'That was my question.'

'Who was this ... guy?'

'No idea, Ralph. He didn't give a name or, if he did, I didn't catch it. I asked what he meant. He said he'd heard I'd had a nasty experience.'

At that moment the waiter returned and placed a whisky on the table beside Forrest. Ralph waited while Forrest downed half the glass. When he replaced it, his next utterance took Ralph by surprise.

'What car do you drive, Ralph?'

'Car?'

'Is it a Jaguar?' He pronounced it the American way, like Jag-wahr.

'Er ... yes, it is.'

'What colour?'

Ralph was bemused by this sudden apparent change of subject. Before he could reply, Forrest spoke again.

'Is it grey, dark grey, with metallic paintwork?'

'Well, yes Waldo, as a matter of fact, it is. Why are you asking about my car?'

'The guy on the phone said he was surprised to be talking to me. He'd phoned to express his concern to my wife. He'd heard I'd nearly been run down by some crazy driver on my walk into town. He was driving a Jaguar, dark grey, with metallic paintwork.'

'Waldo, I'm not really following this. Were you talking to this person just a short while ago?'

'In the last fifteen minutes.' Forrest took another sip of whisky and put the glass down.

'And had you been out of the house before then?'

Forrest shook his head. 'No, Ralph. You changed the time of our meeting, so I didn't need to leave home till just now. I've gotta ask –'

'No, Waldo, my car hasn't been out of the car park at All Saints since I arrived earlier this morning. I changed my schedule to see the Master at eleven, after which I had a tutorial with Janie Gawcott, then I walked here, passing my car in the car park as I did so. I got here at one o'clock exactly.'

A waiter was hovering, so for a few moments the two men perused the menu before making their choices. The waiter murmured something indistinct and withdrew. Ralph picked up where he left off.

'Waldo, you said someone phoned your place and you spoke to him. You've really no idea who it was?'

'Like I said, he may have given a name but to be honest I was so stunned by what he said ...'

'And you didn't recognise the voice?'

Forrest raised both palms by way of reply. 'You've got an idea who it might've been, Ralph?'

Ralph looked blank. 'Not at all, but one thing seems certain.'

'Yeah?'

'Whoever it was, he must have been an insider. Only someone within the university could have such detailed knowledge of our plans and movements.'

ooo0ooo

'I don't get it.' Marnie sipped her coffee that evening with a puzzled frown.

She and Ralph were sitting side by side on a sofa in the drawing room of the farmhouse after supper. Logs were crackling in the wood-burner, and in the background guitar music by Acoustic Alchemy was providing a soft accompaniment to the relaxing atmosphere.

Ralph said, 'It's really quite straightforward. Someone knew that Waldo would be joining me for lunch in the Bistro Lebon at twelve-thirty and planned to put a rumour around that a car identical to mine had tried to run him over. By postponing the time of our lunch by half an hour, the plot failed.'

'Yes, I understand all that,' said Marnie. 'What defeats me is why anyone should devise such a bizarre scheme.'

'It fits in with all the other strange goings-on,' Ralph observed. 'I suppose we should be grateful that nobody got hurt this time.'

'It's a pretty odd way of blackening your character, all the same ... strangely premeditated and contrived.'

Ralph turned his head to face Marnie, his expression curious.

'What is it?' Marnie said.

'I'm not sure you're right about that, Marnie.'

'You don't think it's odd?'

Ralph shook his head. 'It's not that. It's whether it was premeditated. I've no problem with it being contrived, but there's something opportunistic about it, don't you think?'

'Go on.'

'It strikes me that someone might have heard that Waldo and I were meeting for lunch and hastily came up with a plan to put me in the wrong.'

'But almost running him down in the street, Ralph? He's your friend. It's inconceivable.'

'A friend, yes, certainly. On the other hand there are quite a few areas in which we don't see eye to eye. Waldo is more of a free market capitalist than I am.' Ralph shrugged. 'Not really surprising. He is American, after all, with all that country's faith in the power and value of the free market.'

'But I take it, you and he don't actually come to blows,' said Marnie.

Ralph's reply was in an accent and tone worthy of a Chicago mobster. It was almost a growl. 'He's one o' the good guys, babe. You gotta believe it.'

ooo0ooo

That night the phone rang at ten o'clock. Marnie checked the caller ID on the tiny screen. It was Anne touching base as usual. They chatted for a few minutes about Anne's course, her new friends at art school and the project she was currently undertaking. When Anne asked for any 'news from home' Marnie told her about the latest round in the Ralph-plagiarism-denigration saga.

'I don't get it,' said Anne.

Marnie replied with, 'That was my line.'

To this Anne retorted, 'We can still share it, can't we?'

Marnie knew that Anne's logic was irrefutable. 'Okay,' she said.

'Then can you explain in simple language what was going on, please? I'm confused.'

Marnie took a breath and began. 'It seems that Ralph had arranged to meet this other man, Waldo Forrest, for lunch at twelve-thirty. Because of his meeting for coffee with the Master, he had to change the lunch to one o'clock. That was to take account of altering the time of a tutorial with one of his students. Professor Forrest arrived in a hurry because he'd had a phone call from someone expecting to talk to his wife about him, Forrest, almost being run down by a car that sounded – or rather looked – like Ralph's Jaguar. But it wasn't Ralph's car at all and in fact it wasn't any car. The whole thing seems to have just been made up to make it appear that Ralph had tried to run

Forrest down because Ralph and Forrest had had policy disagreements in the past. They are actually good friends despite not always agreeing about economics.'

Silence.

Marnie said, 'Anne? Are you there?'

'I'm here, and I have a question.'

'Go ahead.'

'Did you actually take a breath during all that?'

Marnie chuckled. 'It was rather long, I suppose. But that is what happened.'

'Well,' said Anne, 'I'm glad I didn't ask for the unedited version.'

'Sorry about that, Anne. Tell me, were you able to make sense of any of it?'

'I'm not sure I'd go that far, but there is something that bothers me.'

'Is this a wind-up?' Marnie sounded suspicious.

'No, I'm serious. How did anyone know about the original lunch arrangement between Ralph and his friend – I mean before he changed it? Or did I miss that part? I dozed off for a while in the middle.'

'Good question, Anne. I'm only sorry I don't have a good answer.'

They kicked that thought around for a few minutes before hanging up. After replacing the receiver, Marnie sat thinking things through before joining Ralph upstairs in the bedroom. She was assailed on all sides by questions. About one thing she was convinced: Donovan and Ralph had been right when they surmised that whoever was behind the plot against him was surely someone on the inside of college life. But who could it be? How could the perpetrator have such detailed access to Ralph's movements, his activities, his life?

Above all, two questions bothered Marnie. What might happen next? And what would become of Ralph?

Chapter 18

WEDNESDAY

It was a week for playing catch-up. Ralph was back in college the next morning, seated at the desk in his study, going through correspondence, when the phone rang.

'Professor Lombard, Ralph Lombard?' It was a man's voice, slightly distorted; obviously a poor line.

'Yes. Who is this, please?'

'I'm speaking from the Oxford University Press. Dr Gareth Kempson wonders if you'd be free to join him this afternoon at three o'clock.'

Ralph looked down at his timetable and saw that he had only one postgrad tutorial after lunch. A brisk walk through the city would be more than welcome.

'Yes. That should be all right. I can be there. Did Dr Kempson say –'

Too late. With a brief reply of, 'Thank you, professor' he was gone. Ralph had no time to dwell on the matter as, at that moment, there came a knock on the door and the first student of the day looked in. Back-to-back tutorials occupied the rest of the morning and into the early afternoon, leaving just half an hour to record two letters on the Dictaphone and grab a quick sandwich for lunch.

ooo0ooo

For Marnie, it was a day of fulfilment. She spent all morning working on scheme designs for clients who, as usual, wanted top quality materials at low prices and, preferably, within a very short timescale. By coffee time she was wondering if she should have taken up a career as a magician. She voiced that opinion to Ralph when he phoned from college while eating his sandwich.

'I thought you already were one,' he replied.

'Thank you, kind sir. And how is your day progressing?'

'That's why I'm phoning. I may be back a little later than planned. A meeting has come up at the OUP.'

'Something interesting, no doubt?' said Marnie.

'I expect so, but in fact I didn't get to find out the purpose of the meeting, but when the Oxford University Press calls, it's likely to be worthwhile.'

'Who are you seeing?'

'Kempson. He's one of the top people in business and management publications.'

'You've mentioned him before, but I don't think we've met.'

Ralph paused for a moment. 'Odd, that.'

'Not really. I don't know all your colleagues and contacts.'

'No. I mean it's odd that the person who rang to fix up our meeting called him *Gareth* Kempson. I'm sure of it.'

'So?'

'He's actually called *Garth*.'

Marnie let it go without comment. 'What time are you seeing him?'

'At three, so I may be held up by traffic on the ring road. You know what it's like.'

'All the Cheslea tractors and people-carriers on the school run,' Marnie commented.

'Exactly. So I'll see you when I see you.'

ooo0ooo

Anne rang Marnie at lunchtime. It had become a habit for them to chat in the middle of the day in the middle of the week, and Marnie suspected that Anne was troubled by her conscience. Desperate to become a fully qualified interior designer, she fretted from time to time that she was not pulling her weight in the company these days. Marnie did her best to reassure her and tried to change the subject when Anne criticised herself for spending time away from what she called the *coal face*.

'Ralph phoned a little while ago. He's going to be held up by a meeting at the OUP.'

'You see, Marnie? Everyone's deserting you and leaving you to battle on all by yourself. It's not fair.'

Marnie reminded Anne that Ralph didn't in fact work as an interior designer. As an afterthought she mentioned the apparent mispronunciation of Garth Kempson's name by the man on the phone. Like Marnie, Anne let the remark go without comment.

ooo0ooo

Anne was in the college refectory and had just finished lunch when the mobile began vibrating in the pocket of her jeans.

'Hi, Donovan. Are we still on for tomorrow at the marina?'

'Sure, though I may be a bit later than last week.'

'What's up?'

'My supervisor wants to go over my dissertation.'

'You've handed it in already?'

'Yeah, and it's important that I see him … it's a big chunk of marks towards the degree.'

'Good luck! I'll even forgive you for coming late if you win a prize.'

'Let's not get carried away.'

'It seems to be the season for being late.'

'What d'you mean?'

Anne explained about Ralph's call to Marnie and his meeting at the OUP. Inconsequentially she added what Marnie had said about the man from the office getting Kempson's first name wrong.

Donovan's reaction surprised her. 'What did you say?' His tone was serious.

'Oh, it's nothing, I expect. The man was probably new to the job.'

The line went quiet. Anne could almost hear Donovan's brain working.

Eventually, he said, 'Maybe, but anything unexpected where Ralph's concerned ought to be taken seriously these days. What time is he due there?'

'Marnie said three o'clock.'

'How would he be going?'

'Dunno. Knowing Ralph, he'll probably walk. The traffic in Oxford can be murder.' Anne regretted it as soon as she'd spoken. 'Unfortunate choice of words.'

Donovan said, 'He'll probably be setting off some time soon. Have you got his number?'

'Why?'

'Something's not right … the mispronouncing of that name.'

'Donovan, it was just a slip of the tongue.'

'Ring him straight away and tell him to be careful. Keep me posted. Do it now.'

Donovan hung up without another word.

ooo0ooo

Anne was in a dilemma. Donovan's instincts were usually good, but she sometimes felt he exaggerated small details and elevated them to a greater status than they merited. What to do for the best? Without hesitating further, she began pressing familiar buttons on the mobile.

'Walker and Co, good afternoon.'

'Marnie, it's me.'

Anne outlined her conversation with Donovan.

Marnie said, 'How did he react when you said it was a slip of the tongue?'

'He said to ring Ralph straight away, Marnie. He sounded quite bothered.' She added casually, 'I expect there's nothing to it.'

Marnie tended to agree with Anne about this, but she had faith in Donovan's judgment and knew he was rarely off-target.

'I'll give Ralph a ring,' she said. 'Can't do any harm. Just a quick word.'

But it didn't turn out that way. Marnie's call went straight to voicemail. She guessed that Ralph hadn't switched on his mobile. Marnie sighed – *typical*! Next stop was the college switchboard.

'No reply from his office, caller. I can try the common room.'

'Thanks. Yes, please.'

The phone rang three times before it was picked up. The voice at the other end was familiar, but not Ralph's.

'Who is this?' the voice said. Marnie announced herself. 'Ah, yes. This is Greville Rickman. We spoke the other day.'

Marnie's heart sank. Of all the people who might have answered the common room phone, this was the last one she would have chosen, the man who only recently had tried to humiliate Ralph, and had organised others against him. On the other hand what else could she do, but explain that she needed to be in touch with Ralph?

'You've just missed him, I'm afraid. He left a few minutes ago. I think he was off to a meeting, but I thought he was mistaken.'

'Sorry. I don't follow.'

'Well, I thought I heard him say he was going to see Garth Kempson at the OUP.'

'That's right. He is.'

'That's not possible. I know for a fact that Garth is away at a conference in Colombo, Sri Lanka. He won't be back till next week.'

Marnie was stunned. What the hell was going on? It seemed that Donovan had been right to be suspicious. Marnie became aware that Rickman was speaking.

'… anything I can do to help.'

Huh! Marnie was about to dismiss the idea when her misgivings about a possible escalation to violence came to the fore. She wished that Donovan could appear like magic. He would leap into action without a second thought. But Rickman? How could a middle-aged academic do anything, especially one whose antagonism towards Ralph was undeniable? Even so …

'Thanks for offering, but I wanted to stop Ralph going to the OUP. I think he could be in danger.'

'*Danger* … at the OUP?'

'No, of course not, but someone might be plotting to do him harm. I know you think he's guilty of –'

Rickman ignored what she was saying, and was now muttering to himself. 'No point trying to drive there …too much traffic. Got it! I'll take my bicycle. Sorry, Miss … Mrs, er … I must dash.'

With that, he was gone.

oooOooo

Ralph was glad he'd decided to walk to the OUP. The traffic in the centre of Oxford was crawling and, even if it was moving faster than a pedestrian, he knew he could spend an age trying to find a parking space at the other end. A slot in the visitors' car park at such short notice would be out of the question. He'd calculated that by keeping up a steady pace, he could arrive precisely on time, perhaps even with a minute or two to spare. By the time he reached Walton Street the traffic had thinned considerably. He was making good time when a remarkable thing happened. In fact, three things happened almost at once.

The first was the clattering sound of a bicycle falling to the ground somewhere behind him. This was not unusual in Oxford and scarcely merited Ralph's attention. He hardly gave it a moment's thought. But the second thing almost literally took his breath away. A man cannoned into him and thrust him across the pavement. The two of them crashed violently into the boundary wall of the Jericho Health Centre. At that very moment a car that had mounted the pavement roared past them at considerable speed, making no attempt to stop. They felt its pressure wave as it swept by within inches of them both.

Ralph was about to exclaim, 'What the hell d'you think you're ...' when he found himself staring into the face of the man who had plucked him out of harm's way, someone he would never have expected to come to his aid, and in such a dramatic fashion.

'Greville? How on earth ...'

But no other words came at that time. Ralph and Greville Rickman stood up against the wall as if locked in a warm embrace. The two were gasping for breath as they turned their gaze on the bicycle lying at the kerbside. Both its wheels were mangled by the impact of the vehicle that had come close to hitting the pair of them. Simultaneously they turned their eyes in the direction of the car in time to see it turn at speed into Great Clarendon Street, a hundred yards or so away.

Pedestrians on either side of the street had stopped in their tracks to witness the aftermath of the spectacle. The nearest passer-by lifted the bicycle by its handlebars, noted the extent of the damage and lowered it gently back down to the ground. Ralph and Rickman released each other from their grasp and stared into each other's faces.

Eventually Ralph said, 'I think we could both use a brandy. What do you say?' Rickman nodded without speaking. Ralph added, 'There's a pub just down the road. Come on. It's the least I can do ...'

He took Rickman by the arm and guided him along the pavement. They made slow progress, and Ralph could feel Rickman trembling beneath his jacket. At that time of day it was easy to find an empty table, and Ralph settled his colleague before going to the bar. He returned after a minute with two large brandies and placed one in front of Greville Rickman who still had a glazed expression on his face. Ralph pushed the brandy glass closer.

'Here. Take a sip. It'll help you feel better.' Ralph checked his watch. 'I'm going to leave you just for a minute or two. I need to find a phone to tell Kempson I've been delayed.'

Ralph was making to stand up when Rickman took hold of his arm.

'No need, Ralph.' The words came out as a meaningless croak. He cleared his throat and repeated himself.

'Well, I think I should at least let –'

Rickman shook his head. 'Kempson isn't here.'

'What do you mean? I'm on my way to see him.'

'No, Ralph. He's away ... conference ... Sri Lanka.'

128

Ralph relaxed in his seat. 'I think you'd better tell me what's going on, Greville. Are you up to it?'

Rickman momentarily closed his eyes, took some deep breaths, sipped his brandy and explained everything he knew, since receiving the phone call to the senior common room from Marnie. When he finished, ending with the dramatic rugby tackle and the near-miss from the car, he sat back and finished the brandy.

Ralph listened without comment or interruption, sipped his brandy and said, 'Greville, one thing is clear: I owe you my life. I can only offer you my sincere thanks.'

Rickman shook his head again. 'Not just one thing, Ralph. It's equally clear that you are the victim of a wicked plot, and I can only offer you my sincere apologies for misjudging you so badly.'

ooo0ooo

That evening Ralph's return home to Glebe Farm was later than planned. Sitting in his office at All Saints' College, he'd realised that he felt too agitated to drive. He suspected that his body was flooded with adrenaline after the close encounter with the homicidal car driver followed by his dramatic rescue by Greville Rickman. He'd phoned Marnie to tell her he'd been delayed and hoped she had not picked up on his disturbed state of mind. He was wrong.

Eventually, as soon as he drove into his space in the garage barn, Marnie appeared beside him. No words were necessary. She took his arm and walked him to the farmhouse where she settled him in a comfortable chair at the kitchen table, close to the gentle warmth radiating from the Aga.

'Are you ready to eat something?' she asked quietly.

'Not just yet.'

'Do you want to tell me about it?'

After a few moments' hesitation, Ralph told his story from the time he received the phoned invitation to the OUP to his conversation with Greville Rickman in the pub and their subsequent return by taxi to the college.

'So the call was a decoy,' Marnie said. 'It was planned to lure you out.'

'I know, I know. Greville told me you'd rung the SCR to contact me. What prompted you to do that, Marnie?'

'It was something Donovan said to Anne. You know how suspicious he is.'

'Well he was certainly right this time.'

'I can't help thinking …' Marnie looked puzzled.

'Thinking what?' Ralph prompted.

'This … incident, or whatever we can call it, reminds me of that business with Waldo Forrest.'

'The *hit-and-run* that never was, you mean?'

Marnie nodded. 'What nearly happened to you was a kind of mirror-image of all that. Instead of him being the target …' There was no need to finish the sentence.

'I could use another brandy,' Ralph muttered. 'This whole thing is getting beyond a joke.'

Marnie stood to fetch the bottle. Looking down at Ralph she said, 'It never was a joke.'

Chapter 19

THURSDAY

Marnie had a surprise call from Donovan on Thursday morning. He had spoken with Anne on the phone as usual the previous night, and she had relayed the story of Ralph's incident in Oxford. Now he was ringing for an update.

'So what did the police do?' he asked.

'The police?'

'When you reported it,' Donovan added helpfully. 'You did report it, presumably?'

'Er ...'

'Surely you did?'

'Actually, Donovan, Ralph was so shocked – as I was – by the whole event that I don't think either of us has been thinking clearly.'

'It's understandable, Marnie. We're so used to avoiding the police that we tend not to factor them into our thinking. But this is one time when they need to be informed, especially with all the other things that have happened.'

'I suppose you're right. I'll mention it to Ralph when he comes for coffee.'

'No. Don't do that.'

'You've changed your mind?'

'No. I mean he should contact them straight away. It'll look odd if he leaves it any longer.'

After disconnecting, Marnie sat thinking about Donovan's advice. Was it a good idea to contact the police? What might the consequences be? In Marnie's experience the police had a way of interpreting things in ways that could be difficult. She wondered if it might make them probe ever deeper into Ralph's life in such a way that his career could suffer. Wasn't it Greville Rickman who had tried to force Ralph out of the college on the grounds that even being questioned by the police was a reason for suspicion?

And yet, Donovan surely had a point. Two men were almost run down on the pavement in Oxford in broad daylight. The mangled remains of Rickman's bicycle were clear evidence of what could so easily have become a serious, even fatal, hit-and-run incident. And there must have been witnesses. Even if no one came forward with an eye-witness account of what happened, there were several who saw the immediate aftermath. And there was Rickman himself. He would almost certainly have reported the incident to the police.

Donovan was right. Ralph had to call them. Marnie reached for the phone and dialled Ralph's number on *Thyrsis*. Engaged. She was on the brink of leaving a message when she had a better idea. She grabbed her jacket, switched on the answerphone and headed out.

ooo0ooo

At about the same time, Donovan was cycling home to Uxbridge from Brunel University in west London. He had taken an executive decision. After returning some books to the library, his only timetable commitment that morning was a final tutorial on his dissertation. As it had already been submitted and approved, he was free for the rest of the week.

Arriving home, he packed his bags for the weekend, filled the Beetle's fuel tank and called in at the Austrian delicatessen for a selection of goodies to take to Glebe Farm.

ooo0ooo

Marnie strode out of the spinney to find Ralph closing the side doors on *Thyrsis*. Catching sight of Marnie, he looked at his watch.

'It can't be coffee time already,' he said.

Marnie replied, 'Are you off somewhere? I thought you were working from home today. I've been trying to phone you, but your line was engaged.'

'Greville Rickman phoned. I'm meeting him in Oxford. Then we're going to the police together to report the incident.'

'That's good. He seems to have become your newest bestest friend. Or does he want to report the damage to his bike? He'll need a crime number to claim on his insurance.'

Ralph grinned. 'O cynical one! I must dash. I have to change, then meet Greville in college an hour from now.'

oOo0ooo

Lucas was lying in wait. There was no other way of putting it. His determination had been growing steadily, and it was matched so far only by his patience. But even that was running out, and he was desperately trying to devise a plan for achieving his goal. The more he thought about it, the less certain he was about what his ultimate goal really was. On that day and in that place he had resolved to make a decisive move that would bring matters to a head.

He checked his watch, knowing that his target adhered to a regular timetable. But it was at that same moment that things started to go wrong.

oOo0ooo

Ralph was lining up the car to slot it into its regular parking place when he caught sight of movement near the college entrance. To his considerable surprise, Greville Rickman was waving and hurrying in his direction. Ralph switched off the engine and waited as Rickman ran to the passenger door and climbed in.

'Good timing, Ralph. I suggest we go straight to the police station. I've told them we're on our way. Good to see you. Journey okay?'

Ralph was astonished. It was a far cry from the naked hostility shown by Rickman and his cronies at the start of the week. Greville was positively showering him with bonhomie. *We should get run down more often*, Ralph thought, but he bit his tongue. His reply was much more mundane.

'Hello, Greville.' He gunned the engine and began reversing the Jaguar out of its slot. 'Er … where are we going, exactly?'

'The copshop's in St Aldates, further down and on the same side as the House.' He was using the common university shorthand for Christ Church, one of the largest colleges. 'It's right opposite the Crown Court. We can probably park in the side street. I doubt they'll keep us for more than an hour.' *You'll know more about police procedures than I do*, Greville thought, but he didn't say it out loud.

Greville Rickman's change of attitude was now so marked that Ralph could scarcely believe it. Greville even made small talk as they drove on.

'Didn't you use to have a rather ancient Volvo, Ralph?'

133

'I swopped it for this car a year or so ago. It was left behind by a former tenant of Marnie's. I bought it from them. It's rather like yours, isn't it, Greville?'

'Same make – Jaguar – same colour, certainly, and same model, though this is an earlier version than my one.'

Greville's background could be described as comfortable, decidedly privileged, even relatively wealthy, and he was known to like the finer things in life.

Ralph began threading his way south through the mid-morning traffic while Greville extolled the virtues of Jaguar cars. Ralph listened with only half an ear. These days he was aware – even wary – of his surroundings and remained constantly vigilant. It took no more than fifteen minutes to reach the Thames Valley Police headquarters, during which time Greville moved on to a continuous narrative on how he had phoned the police, informed them of the 'near-miss hit-and-run', as he described it, and arranged for Ralph and him to give their formal statements that morning. They parked in the street beside the building and went in. Ralph left it to Greville to do the talking.

ooo0ooo

Lucas had spent the past half hour watching out for Anne to return to the marina in her bright red Mini. His heart sank when a black VW Beetle rolled into the car park and out climbed his nemesis, the last person he wanted to see. Dressed in a black bomber jacket and dark grey jeans was the man who had pushed him into the canal. There and then, Lucas's plan to confront Anne and tell her of his feelings took its own dive into the canal.

Lucas looked on as the young man scanned the car park, presumably checking to see if Anne's Mini was there, before heading in the direction of the marina office. He was returning to the Beetle when the Mini drove in. Lucas had to endure the sight of Anne's obvious pleasure at seeing the nemesis and rushing forward to embrace him warmly.

A minute later Donovan moved the Beetle to the far end of the car park. Harry wanted to make space for one of the marina's regular users. By that time Lucas had withdrawn from the window to sit moodily in his cabin where he tried and intermittently failed to concentrate on a textbook for his course at drama school. The book described the development of the genre known as the 'revenge tragedy'. In a moment of lucidity, Lucas recognised that the subject matched his mood rather well.

Meanwhile, unbeknown to Lucas, Anne and Donovan were chatting amiably as they walked hand-in-hand to *Sally Ann*. There they closed the doors, drew the curtains and disappeared for the rest of the afternoon.

ooo0ooo

It was early evening when Anne and Donovan decided that they would travel the next morning to Knightly St John to spend the weekend at Glebe Farm. After their languorous if energetic afternoon on the boat, they preferred to take it easy for the rest of the day. When Anne raised the question of what to have for supper, Donovan remembered the box of goodies that he had left in the car. It included Frankfurter sausages (veggie variety for Anne) and a tub of German-style potato salad, an ideal light supper. Donovan went off to collect them from the Beetle, leaving Anne to lay the table in the saloon.

A few minutes later, hearing footfall on the stern deck, she called out to Donovan.

'Come through. Nearly ready. Hope you've brought some beer.'

But it was not Donovan who stepped down into the cabin and walked through to the galley and saloon. Anne had a surprise when she glanced round to find Lucas standing a few feet away. He smiled tentatively.

'Not beer, actually, but I've brought a bottle of wine.'

'Oh ...' Anne realised that her reply was not the warmest of welcomes. 'I was, er ...'

'You weren't expecting to see me ... obviously. You thought I was someone else.'

'Me.'

The single word was spoken in a quiet tone of voice, but the effect on Lucas was electric. His head shot round, and he stared at Donovan, who had entered soundlessly behind him and now stood innocently clutching a cardboard box in his arms.

'Jesus ...' Lucas muttered at the sight of his nemesis.

'Donovan actually,' Donovan said calmly. 'It's okay, don't worry. I'm not going to throw you into the canal this time ... at least not immediately.'

'Is that a promise?' Lucas hoped he sounded more relaxed than he felt.

'Of course. I wouldn't want to break a window on a friend's boat and, anyway, my box of provisions might get damaged.'

Lucas looked as if he didn't find Donovan's reply totally reassuring. Anne decided to come to his rescue.

'Were you wanting something, Lucas?'

Lucas looked down at the bottle he was holding. 'Well, er ...'

In the hiatus that followed, Donovan said, 'Can I put this box down?'

Lucas stepped swiftly aside, and Donovan laid the box on the table. He looked appraisingly at Lucas and then at the bottle that he was holding.

To Anne, Donovan said, 'Were you expecting a visitor?'

'Not really. This is Lucas. He lives on a boat along from here.'

'I believe we've met,' said Donovan, adding, 'briefly.'

'I'm really sorry about what I said that time,' Lucas mumbled. 'I've already apologised to Anne about it.'

Donovan nodded. 'So, is that all right?'

Anne said, 'I suppose.'

'We're going to have supper,' Donovan said evenly.

'Okay, well, I'd better be –'

'You can stay if you want, if that's all right with Anne. We've got plenty.'

Lucas looked confused. 'Er, I wouldn't want to –'

'You've come bearing gifts.' Donovan inclined his head in the direction of the bottle.

Lucas shrugged. 'It's a fairly cheap plonk.'

Donovan shrugged. 'It's a fairly modest supper. That Aussie red would go quite well with what we've got.'

Lucas hovered on the brink of uncertainty, so Anne intervened.

'Why don't you open it while we start getting the meal ready?'

ooo0ooo

At Glebe Farm that evening, Ralph described his visit to the police with Greville Rickman. It had proved to be a remarkable turnaround from the antagonism shown to Ralph only a few days earlier. Both men had given their statements verbally and separately while a police officer took notes. After a short interval they had received the typed statements for checking, agreed and signed them and were on their way in not much more than an hour. Ralph had been astonished when Rickman suggested lunch together.

'What had your relationship with Greville been before ...' Marnie asked. '... I mean before this whole plagiarism business arose?'

Ralph gave the question a few moments' thought. 'I saw him around college, knew who he was. Can't say we were great buddies, but we'd greet each other cordially enough in passing.'

'So not a close colleague.'

'Not as such. Philosophy is his field. We'd run into each other from time to time.'

Marnie grinned. 'Unfortunate choice of words, Ralph.'

Ralph smiled ruefully. 'Well at least that experience brought us together – if you see what I mean – and it has the advantage that Greville is Vice Dean of the college. Nice not to have him badmouthing me around the place.'

'And you've got the Master on your side, too,' Marnie said.

Ralph agreed. 'Yes. I can't see anyone turning him against me.'

Marnie made no reply, but mentally crossed her fingers.

ooo0ooo

If Donovan had any qualms about Lucas's intentions towards Anne, he didn't show it. Lucas, on the other hand, continuously glanced in Donovan's direction while laying the table for supper that evening. He observed the easy-going familiarity between Donovan and Anne preparing the meal, side by side at the galley workbench, passing each other bowls, pans and implements with the minimum of words. He deduced that theirs was a relationship based on intimacy and mutual understanding, and his heart sank.

Donovan had described the 'simple' evening meal as *Siedewürstchen mit Kartoffelsalat*, Frankfurters with potato salad. As predicted, it went well in the company of the red Australian shiraz wine that Lucas had brought. When Donovan voiced that opinion, Lucas had for a brief moment felt pleased with himself.

'Are you a student as well, Donovan?' he asked.

Donovan nodded. 'Media and Communication, Brunel, final year.'

'Media Studies,' Lucas said quietly. 'Isn't that supposed to be ...?'

Donovan deduced correctly that Lucas hesitated to denounce his course as *a cushy number*, an *easy option*, or even *a non-subject*. 'It's formal title is Multimedia Technology

137

and Design,' Donovan said, 'but most of us, like you, use Media Studies as a kind of shorthand. You?'

'Er ... well, Drama here in Oxford.' He chewed and swallowed. 'Actually, I sort of dropped out in the first year, but they've let me start again.'

'Me too,' said Donovan. 'I started a degree in electrical engineering at another place, but soon realised it wasn't for me, so I decided to take a year off and think things over. The course at Brunel looked good, and they said they'd have me. So ...'

'Tell us about your course, Lucas,' said Anne. 'Do you study method acting?'

Lucas shook his head. 'There isn't much of an emphasis on that these days. It can take a toll on your mental health, apparently. I couldn't really use that as an excuse, could I?'

Donovan looked quizzically at him. 'So what kind of programme do you follow on your course?'

'Oh, you know, basic stuff: body conditioning, movement, stage combat. We study texts of plays quite closely, line by line ... try to understand the inner motives of the characters.'

'You're aiming to become a professional actor, then?' Anne hoped she'd kept the scepticism out of her voice.

Lucas reflected. 'The drama schools turn out loads of actors every year. I get the impression there's a lot of luck involved.'

Donovan took a sip of the shiraz but said nothing.

ooo0ooo

Lucas left soon after they finished supper. His offer to help with the dishes was politely declined, and he pleaded the need to do some reading for his course. There was a brief hesitation before he shook hands with Donovan when taking his leave.

After everything was cleared away, Anne and Donovan sat in the saloon for a chat before bedtime.

'I was surprised when you invited Lucas to stay for supper,' said Anne.

Donovan grimaced but made no other reply.

Anne persisted. 'Are you regretting it now?'

'No, it's just ...'

'What?'

Another grimace. 'I kind of felt sorry for him.'

'After pushing him in the canal that time?' Anne fluttered her eyelids and tried to look like a Victorian damsel in distress. 'You were after all defending my honour.'

Donovan chuckled. 'Not so much that, but … it's hard to say. He looked so nervous and pathetic. He was coming across as a loser, and that's just one step away from seeing himself as a victim. Not good for the psyche.'

Anne nodded. 'I know what you mean. What he said to me that time was really crude, and he probably deserved what you did, but I don't think he's really such a bad person. I do agree with you, though, about him being a loser. It's hard to imagine him making a career as an actor.'

A smile flitted briefly across Donovan's features.

'What is it?' Anne asked.

'I suppose I shouldn't say it, but I got the impression that if he auditioned for *Hamlet*, he'd be up for the part of …'

'The leading role, the part of Hamlet?' Anne failed to keep the incredulity out of her voice.

'I was thinking more of the role of … Yorick.'

Anne laughed. 'That's wicked, Donovan! You know as well as I do that Yorick is just a skull dug out of the ground.'

Donovan shrugged. 'I reckon he'd be in with a chance of getting the part … of his understudy.'

'Donovan!' Mock indignation. 'I think it's time for bed.'

Donovan smiled. 'Now you're talking.'

'Unlike Yorick,' Anne said with a twinkle in her eye.

Chapter 20

FRIDAY

Friday was a day of mixed fortunes. During the morning, Anne phoned to say that she and Donovan would arrive in the afternoon. That suited Marnie and Ralph well, allowing both of them to work without interruption on their projects. The day turned out rather differently from what any of them expected.

At around five o'clock Anne and Donovan appeared in the office barn. Marnie suspected that their arrival at the time of the usual tea-break was no coincidence. Neither was she surprised that Donovan was carrying a substantial cardboard box. She guessed correctly that it was filled with goodies from Donovan's local Austrian-run delicatessen.

'No Ralph?' said Anne, looking at the wall clock. 'He's usually here by now.'

As if on cue Ralph walked in. It was obvious that something was bothering him.

'Everything all right?' Marnie said.

Ralph shook his head. 'I think I need more than tea.'

'What's happened?'

'The Master has had an anonymous letter accusing me of plagiarism. He phoned just after two to ask if I could look in on him on Monday.'

'Well,' said Marnie, 'he's not exactly treating it as urgent, is he?'

'I did ask him if he'd like me to come today ... told him I was willing to go to Oxford straight away.'

'And?' Marnie prompted.

'It's odd. He said he had a meeting that would last all afternoon.'

'Sounds reasonable.'

Ralph's expression was troubled. 'Not sure. There was something cagey about the way he said it. It was as if he was hiding something.'

'You don't think you could've imagined that, do you, Ralph?'

Ralph shook his head and sighed. 'I've become paranoid lately.'

'I think we all have,' Marnie agreed.

At that moment they heard a car pull up on the gravel drive.

'That'll be Angela Hemingway,' said Marnie. 'She said she might pop round to talk about a visit to Randall in Brackley over the weekend.'

But Marnie was wrong. Two people swept past the window, not one. There came a perfunctory knock on the door and in walked Detective Sergeant Ted Marriner and Detective Constable Cathy Lamb. Their expressions were grim, and Marnie guessed that they would not be accepting tea.

'I'm glad you're all here.' Marriner wasted no time on greetings. 'It's mainly you I've come to see, professor, but I was hoping to talk to you all.'

Anne and Donovan drew up visitors' chairs, and Marnie invited the detectives to take a seat. After a moment's hesitation they accepted.

'Is it appropriate to offer you refreshments?' Marnie asked tentatively. 'We all have tea at this time of day.'

'Not today, thanks,' said Marriner.

'So what can I do for you?' Ralph said in an amiable tone.

'You've been to Oxford this week, I understand.'

'That's correct. Quite a lot, in fact. I was in college on Monday and Wednesday. You'll doubtless know that I also went in yesterday to give a statement at the police station concerning a hit-and-run incident on Wednesday. I went there with my colleague Dr Greville Rickman.'

Marriner looked down at his notepad. 'Quite so. How long were you in college on Wednesday?'

Ralph thought back. 'I went in first thing to catch up on correspondence, then had an invitation to the OUP – that's the Oxford University Press. It turned out to be a hoax, or rather a trap. You probably know what happened.'

Marriner nodded. 'You chose not to take your car to this, er … OUP meeting. Is that right?'

'It is. I reasoned that there was little to be gained by driving. The traffic can hold you up in the city centre, and parking can be a headache. Anyway, I'm a fast walker. It's not far from All Saints to the OUP.'

'Do you know the car belonging to Professor Parry-Jones?'

Ralph looked surprised. 'The Master? Yes, of course.'

'Can you describe it?'

'Certainly. It's a Saab. He's had it for a few years. I'm not sure of the model, but its paintwork is metallic silver. The Master has his own reserved parking space close to the main entrance.'

'Did you know he's received a letter about you, alleging that you've used somebody else's ideas in at least one of your books?'

'I did.'

'Does that bother you?'

'Not in the slightest. I have a very good relationship with the Master.'

'I notice you don't refer to him by name.'

'No one does. It's a custom in the college to use his title. Everyone uses it.'

'Did you know his car exploded this afternoon and was completely destroyed in a fireball?'

The abrupt change of direction brought gasps from everyone in the room, apart from Cathy Lamb.

'Good God!' Ralph exclaimed. 'Is the Master all right?'

Marriner stared at Ralph for some seconds before replying. 'Yes. He wasn't in the car at the time.'

Ralph breathed out audibly. 'How did it happen?' Some sort of mechanical fault?'

'It appears that an explosive device was attached under the fuel tank and set off probably remotely by someone using a mobile phone.'

Ralph sat back in his chair and stared at Marriner who looked down at his notes.

'Do you have a mobile phone, professor?'

As Ralph looked quizzically at Marriner a sound was heard in the room. It was something between a snort and a chuckle. Marriner looked sharply at Donovan.

'Do you find it amusing that a car was blown up in Oxford in broad daylight?'

Donovan regarded the detective without blinking. 'No, of course I don't. But I find it ludicrous that anyone should suspect that *Ralph* would be capable of carrying out such a crime.'

'And why is that, might I ask?'

Anne leaned towards Marnie and whispered, 'I bet there'll be two reasons. There always are with Donovan.'

In an even tone, Donovan said, 'For two reasons.'

Anne suppressed a snigger; Marnie gave her a diluted version of the heavy eyelids and murmured, 'Smartarse.'

'Go on,' Marriner urged.

'The first is that Ralph and the Master have been close friends for several years. Ralph is the last person who'd wish him any harm. Ralph would probably not be a professor without the full support of the Master.'

Ralph made no comment, but noticed that Cathy Lamb was taking rapid notes. Donovan continued.

'The second, and more importantly, Ralph is a brilliant man, a world authority in his field, but I doubt if he even knows how to download an app on his mobile phone, let alone use one to set off a bomb.'

Ralph, still in a state of shock, nodded. He turned his head towards Donovan and said, 'I'm not sure if that's entirely complimentary.'

'But it's true,' Donovan said.

Ralph nodded again. 'I suppose so. Anne usually installs one of those … things for me, if I need one. I don't recall her installing one for setting off bombs.'

Donovan fixed Marriner with a stare. 'You know Ralph had nothing to do with what happened, Mr Marriner, so I'm wondering why you pursued that line.'

Marriner looked momentarily discomfited. 'It's important to explore every line of enquiry. I think you know that's how we work. I seem to recall that you've been investigated yourself.'

'And no evidence of any kind was found, as you well know, sergeant,' Donovan said calmly.

Marriner was rising from his seat when the sound of a car was heard on the gravel drive. Ralph hurried to open the door for the detectives. Marriner said nothing and made no eye contact as he went out, while Cathy Lamb mouthed silent thanks and smiled. Ralph kept the door open as Angela Hemingway breezed in.

'Tea, vicar?' Anne asked with an impish grin.

Angela smiled back and accepted the offer of tea and also a chair from Donovan. 'So,' she said, 'you've had a grilling from the forces of law and order … again. I'm surprised you haven't given them their own reserved parking space.'

'We thought about it,' said Marnie, 'while discussing which mug to print your name on.'

Angela's admiration of Glebe Farm beverages was well known. She gave a wry smile. 'Seriously,' she said, 'is everything all right?'

Marnie said, 'The Master of Ralph's college. His car has been blown up by a bomb.'

'Oh, my dear Lord!' Angela exclaimed. 'Is he –'

'He's fine. He wasn't in it, apparently.'

'Thank goodness. But why are the police –'

'Fishing, Angela. They wanted to know if Ralph had any ideas on the subject.'

Angela accepted a mug of tea from Anne. 'Has this something to do with that plagiarism nonsense?' she asked.

Ralph replied, 'The police seem to think so.'

'Do you, Ralph?'

'On the whole, yes, I do.'

'Well, one thing seems clear.'

'What does, Angela?' Marnie said.

'Whoever is behind this, it must be … what's the term? … an inside job. Only someone in the college could get access to the Master's car. Only someone like that would know what was going on internally at any given time.'

All eyes turned towards Ralph.

He said quietly, 'We'd rather come to that regrettable conclusion ourselves.'

Chapter 21

Sunday came and with it, surprisingly to Marnie, came Angela Hemingway. It had become a good-natured private joke between them that Angela, as vicar, worked on one day each week. But on that particular Sunday Angela had agreed to accompany Anne and Donovan on a visit to Brackley. A curate, undergoing pre-ordination training, was entrusted with that afternoon's evensong. They would leave soon after morning service and set off to arrive in time for Angela to go out to lunch with Randall. Anne and Donovan would take Dorli the cat on to Autumn Lodge to see Frau Kreisler.

The morning was bright and crisp, and Donovan's VW Beetle ate up the miles in light traffic to the accompaniment of intermittent protests from Dorli in her travelling basket. She shared the back seat with Angela. Anne had been amused to note that for once Angela had dispensed with her usual clerical grey dress and dog collar in favour of a pink sweatshirt and navy slacks. When they arrived at Randall's rectory they were met by the Rural Dean of Brackley wearing a white Aran sweater, blue chinos and tan loafers. Casual was the order of the day for the two clerics.

This visit followed the same pattern as the first, with Frau Kreisler almost overcome at the sight of her dearly-beloved cat. Anne's previous forecast of a 'slobbering weekend' was re-enacted, which came as no surprise.

They were welcomed, as before, by Mrs Albright the assistant manager, who escorted them through the building and offered tea. The 'no pets' rule was being conveniently disregarded. Dorli was allowed out of her basket and given the freedom of the conservatory which, as on her first visit, she proceeded to explore, investigating every nook and cranny. Frau Kreisler was enraptured and gave a running commentary on Dorli's actions in a gushing staccato blend of emotional German and English.

'Lovely markings, your cat,' Mrs Albright observed, pouring tea from a Brown Betty teapot.

'Oh yes,' Frau Kreisler crooned. 'She was a most beautiful kitten. Und jetzt, dass sie groß geworden ist ... Oh, sorry. I must use my English. Dorli has grown to be a fine ... how do you say? ... cat lady?'

The 'cat lady' stared quizzically at the humans on hearing their outburst of laughter.

'It's nice of you to let us bring Dorli, Mrs Albright,' said Anne, accepting a cup of tea.

Mrs Albright smiled. 'Well, she's no trouble, is she? And she means such a lot to Mrs Kreisler.'

'I think you are well known for your kindness,' said Anne.

Mrs Albright looked questioningly at Anne. 'Why do you say that, dear?'

'I've met someone who speaks very highly of you. In fact, he asked me to give you his regards.'

'And who would that be?'

'His name is Lucas. I don't know his surname. He says he knew you at Magdalene House, and you were very kind to him.'

'Lucas?' Mrs Albright reflected. 'That would be Lucas Fellowes. You've met him, you say?'

Anne nodded. 'He lives on a canal boat near Duke's Cut.'

'How's he keeping?'

'He's okay, back at college, studying. I'll tell him I passed on his good wishes. He'll be pleased.'

'I'm glad. I've always thought he was one of our success stories. It would be nice to see him some time.'

Chapter 22

MONDAY

On Monday morning Ralph set off for Oxford straight after breakfast. He had arranged to see the Master, and hurried along to his office as soon as he arrived at All Saints' College. When parking the Jaguar, he automatically glanced towards the main entrance and noticed an ominous gap where the Master's Saab was usually to be seen. Something else seemed not right, but Ralph was unable to put his finger on it as he hastened into the building.

Once again there was a strained atmosphere in the secretaries' office, but on this occasion Ralph suspected that it was neither in his imagination nor relating to the accusations levelled against him. A soon as Ralph entered the secretariat, Clare Goodall stood and knocked on the door of the Master's office. She gave Ralph a brief smile as she held the door open to let him pass.

Ralph advanced quickly across the floor as the Master rose from his seat, and the two men shook hands. Ralph was alarmed but not really surprised to see how disturbed the Master seemed. They sat.

'A dreadful business,' said Ralph. 'How are you, Master?'

'Well, Ralph, I've discovered – if in fact there was ever any doubt it – that I'm no James Bond. To be honest, I feel definitely shaken and stirred.'

'It's hardly surprising.' At that moment, Ralph realised what had struck him as odd when he arrived. 'Master, there doesn't seem to be any sign of damage to the building. Were any other cars caught up in the explosion?'

'It didn't happen here, Ralph. It was in the station car park. The cars on both sides of mine were virtually destroyed in the fireball. It's a miracle that no one was hurt … or worse.'

'And you yourself, Master?'

'I was already on the train when I witnessed the blast. I'd just taken my seat, and the train was pulling out of the station when it happened. Everything just became a blur when I realised that it was my car. I'd been driving it only minutes earlier.'

'You saw the explosion?'

'Quite clearly. I'd driven to the station to catch a train to London for a meeting. It was quite a sudden change of plan. I had been due to see the Vice-Chancellor, but I was ... er, summoned to ... er, this other meeting at short notice.'

'I see.' For the second time that morning something odd occurred to Ralph, though it didn't register with him at the time. 'Well, Master, I'm delighted that you weren't injured.'

'Yes. Gwynedd keeps telling me how fortunate I was not to be in the car when it happened.'

'And there's no question that it was an act of sabotage?' said Ralph. 'No possibility of some sort of mechanical or electrical fault?'

'None whatever, as far as the police are concerned. Apparently some sort of device had been attached directly under the fuel tank ... hence the fireball.'

'And how is your wife?' Ralph asked.

'Gwynedd is as shaken up as I am, I can tell you.'

Ralph shook his head. 'I can only say how greatly relieved I am that you're unharmed.'

'It's very kind of you, Ralph. And good of you to come in early like this.'

'You said you'd received an anonymous letter, Master.'

'Oh, yes.' He picked it up from the desk with a dismissive gesture and handed it to Ralph. 'You'll see it repeats this ludicrous accusation that you plagiarised someone else's ideas for at least one of your books. No mention of any name or any other details ... totally baseless and unfounded, obviously.'

Ralph read it rapidly, shaking his head all the while.

'Is this how it arrived, Master? It's clearly a photocopy.'

'No. The police took the original for forensic examination ... fingerprints and the like.'

Ralph reflected. 'So they think there's a potential link between the accusations and the bombing of your car?'

'It would seem so. Don't you?'

ooo0ooo

Ralph spent the rest of the morning dealing with routine college correspondence, followed by a light lunch in the refectory before driving back to Glebe Farm. He was barely out of the car when he heard a call and turned to find Marnie hurrying to greet him.

148

Seconds later he was wrapped in her arms as she hugged him tight.

'I must go to college for an early meeting more often,' he muttered when he regained the ability to breathe.

'Come on,' said Marnie. 'I'm giving you a large brandy, and you can tell me how you got on. How's the Master? Why didn't you phone to keep me in the picture? What's the state of the Master's car?'

'Marnie, you are allowed to draw breath, you know. The brandy's a good idea. As for your questions, the answers are: putting on a brave face; I wanted to get my office work up to date; and totally destroyed. In that order ... I think.'

Linking arms, Marnie led Ralph into the farmhouse and installed him in a chair by the Aga. We've been through this routine before, she reflected, while she poured him a generous measure of brandy. He swallowed a good part of it and took a deep breath. At Marnie's prompting, he related the conversation with the Master while she listened patiently.

Ralph concluded with, 'The Master's been badly shaken by this episode.'

'That's hardly surprising,' said Marnie.

'I think, for him, the worst aspect is knowing beyond any doubt that the perpetrator is one of his own colleagues. It's bad enough having slanders directed at *me*, but a deliberate attempt on his life ... that's something else and altogether more sinister.'

'If that's what it was,' Marnie said quietly.

'What do you mean?'

Marnie stood up and walked to the window. She turned and spoke.

'You said the Master had changed his plans. Instead of calling on the Vice-Chancellor, he took the car to the station. That's right, isn't it?'

Ralph nodded and replied slowly. 'Yes. So without the change of plan, he wouldn't be anywhere near the car when it blew up.'

Marnie said, 'He had a narrow escape, but perhaps the bomb wasn't meant to kill or injure him, or possibly anyone else. Have you thought of that?'

'Then why plant it at all?' Ralph said.

'The Master receiving that letter wasn't a coincidence, was it? I think the two are linked together.'

'One reinforcing the other,' Ralph nodded. 'The Master thought the same.'

'Exactly. I may be completely off-target, but the anonymous letter and the bomb could be intended to show that everything connected with you, Ralph, leads to disaster.'

'Assuming that the person who sent the anonymous letter also planted the bomb.'

'Or is that all too far-fetched?' said Marnie.

After a pause, Ralph said, 'Not necessarily. As I said, the Master made the same connection. The letter and the bomb lead to the same end result: Everything to do with me becomes toxic.' Ralph imagined the explosion in the station car park. In his mind he saw the fireball and clouds of black smoke billowing from not one but three burning wrecks. He added, 'Inevitably, some people are going to think there's no smoke without fire.'

ooo0ooo

That evening Marnie phoned Anne and asked how the visit to Brackley had gone. She made all the appropriate noises while Anne described Frau Kreisler's enraptured reunion with her pet. For her part, Anne muttered indignantly about the anonymous letter sent to the Master. She gasped and spluttered when Marnie told her of the explosion that had wrecked the Master's car. The incident had featured on the evening's TV news programmes, but Anne had missed them.

Marnie had debated with herself about whether she should mention the incident to Anne. It had always been her policy to shield Anne from anything unpleasant, but on this occasion she reasoned that Anne should be aware of the growing menace confronting Ralph and those around him. Above all, Marnie wanted Anne to be on her guard, though she was fairly certain that Anne was not directly in any personal danger.

Minutes after they disconnected, Anne's mobile warbled again; the nightly call from Donovan.

'All quiet at Duke's Cut, I trust. How are things, Anne?'

'Yes, all quiet up here,' she replied casually. 'On the other hand, the Master of Ralph's college did receive an anonymous letter accusing Ralph of plagiarism.'

'How did he react?'

'Marnie said he rejected it as nonsense and told Ralph so.'

'That's good.'

'Yes,' Anne agreed. 'That's the good news.'

'Something tells me we're into a *good-news-bad-news* scenario,' said Donovan suspiciously. He too had evidently missed the news bulletins.

'Well ... the Master's car was blown up and totally destroyed in a fireball.'

'*Bloody hell!* What about the Master?'

'Nowhere near it at the time, and no one was hurt, so not sure how that qualifies.'

Donovan reflected for a moment, then, 'Oh, I'm fairly sure that qualifies in the bad news camp.'

'Me too,' Anne agreed, 'but it could so easily have been an unexpected disaster.'

'What does that mean ... an *unexpected disaster*?'

'Marnie thinks the Master shouldn't have been anywhere near the car when the bomb went off.'

'You're losing me, Anne. It was his car, and presumably he drives it.'

'Apparently, the Master was supposed to be meeting the University Vice-Chancellor in Oxford, but got summoned to London at the last minute, so took the car to the station. That's where it exploded. If he'd not changed his plans he wouldn't have been using the car at all.' Anne found herself listening to silence. 'Donovan?'

'London? Why did he have to go there?'

'I dunno. He just did. He sometimes has meetings there, I think.' More silence. 'Donovan?'

'Something strange is going on.'

'Obviously. It's not every day a bomb goes –'

'No. I mean there are two possibilities.'

'There's a surprise!'

'Seriously, Anne. If the call was a hoax, it might've been a trap to get the Master in the car to blow him up with it.'

'You mean like the call that lured Ralph to that non-existent meeting at the OUP?'

'Exactly. But if it wasn't a trap, but a genuine call to go to London ...'

'What are you getting at?'

'Well, a meeting with the V-C is quite a big deal, isn't it? Even for the head of a college, it would be pretty important. After all, the V-C is the top person of the whole university, not the kind of person you put off just like that.'

'So?'

'So what's going on that's so important that it trumps the Vice-Chancellor?'

'I hadn't thought of it before,' said Anne. 'Good question.'

oooOooo

That night in the bedroom at Glebe Farm, Marnie and Ralph were having a very similar conversation. Marnie was sitting on the corner of the bed, towelling her hair dry from the shower, while Ralph was sitting up in bed, checking the synopsis for a new book.

'One thing is fairly clear,' Ralph said.

Marnie briefly stopped towelling. 'I know. It's an inside job. I think we all agree on that.'

'Yes, but it's clear that the insider isn't one of the secretaries … unless, of course, the Master really *was* the target for the bombing.'

'How do you mean?'

'I'm just trying to think who would have detailed knowledge of the Master's movements.'

'But surely you don't think the secretaries –'

Ralph shook his head. 'No, not possible. I'm sure we can definitely rule them out. I've known them for years; they're beyond suspicion. Anyway, they wouldn't have the clout to get the Master to change his plans and miss the Vice-Chancellor to go to a fictitious meeting in London.'

'You're sure there was a real meeting, Ralph?'

'Ye-e-s.'

'You don't sound very sure.'

'It's odd. I asked the Master what that meeting in London was about. He was vague to the point of being cagey, though I put it down to the general state of shock he was in and I didn't pursue it.'

'Now you're not so sure?'

'Marnie, do you remember the times I told you the secretaries were acting strangely?'

'Of course.'

'Well, it was like that. There's something going on in the background, though I don't know what it might be. It's obviously important for the Master.'

'What's his subject, Ralph? I don't think you've ever mentioned it.'

'Applied maths is his field.'

'So, for example, he wasn't invited to Downing Street to advise on a political matter, like government policy.'

'Probably not.' He murmured reflectively, 'It doesn't add up,' and was surprised when Marnie laughed and threw her towel at his head.

Chapter 23

TUESDAY

The next day, Ralph set off for college after breakfast for a tutorial with a postgrad student. Traffic was heavy at that time of the morning, and conditions were made worse by a lorry having broken down on the dual carriageway between Bicester and the junction with the M40 motorway. On arrival, Ralph only had time to gather up that day's post and drop it into his briefcase before a knock on the door signalled the arrival of the student. For the next ninety minutes Ralph's concentration was entirely focused on the contribution of viticulture to the economic development of Chile and Argentina.

By mid-morning he was in need of some liquid sustenance of his own, and he made his way to the senior common room. There, he found himself standing beside Greville Rickman while serving himself from the coffee-pot.

'How are things with you, Ralph?' Rickman asked.

'Fine.' Ralph held up the coffee-pot and raised an inquisitive eyebrow. Rickman nodded and held out a cup for Ralph to pour. 'And you, Greville? How goes it?'

'Still somewhat shaky, to tell you the truth.'

'The hit-and-run business, you mean?'

'Yes. It keeps coming back to me.'

'It seems to be the season of near-misses,' Ralph remarked.

'God, yes!' Rickman exclaimed. 'Quite a shocker for the Master. He seems to be bearing up very well.'

The phrase *putting on a brave face* floated through Ralph's mind, but he refrained from comment. While Rickman droned on about nightmares, headaches and sweating palms, Ralph surreptitiously observed the members of staff in the common room. Could he rule out Rickman? On balance, he thought he probably could, though he did wonder if Rickman's near-miss hit-and-run performance could have been just that, a performance, a kind of bluff, to throw Ralph off the scent. With a sense of shock, Ralph realised the implication of that line of enquiry:

Rickman would have had to have an accomplice. Presumably that would be Jay Harper. Was there really such an elaborate conspiracy against him, arising from a brief encounter with a young woman some twenty years past?

'Could I trouble you for the milk, Ralph?' Rickman's tone was hesitant as he pointed at the jug, standing beside the coffee-maker.

'The ...? Oh, yes. Sorry. My thoughts were elsewhere.' Ralph passed the jug to Rickman, who had a slight tremor in his hand as he poured a little milk into his cup.

In his mind, Ralph heard the voice of the Master: *I'm no James Bond.* Glancing at Rickman's troubled features, Ralph reached the conclusion that here too was another non-candidate for the role of 007, secret agent.

Casually scanning the common room, Ralph was fairly certain that one of the staff members was behind the plagiarism campaign against him and, more recently, its development into out-and-out violence. In particular, his eyes were drawn to Henry Boulter and Oliver Ringstead, Greville Rickman's erstwhile ... Ralph searched his mind for a suitable term to describe them. He dismissed calling them *conspirators* and wondered about *allies*, before settling on *confederates*. Yes, confederates. Ralph smiled inwardly at the thought that the American Civil War didn't turn out very well for that faction.

ooo0ooo

Marnie's concentration that morning was focused on a sadly-neglected country house in the Northamptonshire Uplands, that was crying out for a complete renovation. It was now in the ownership of a self-made millionaire who had accumulated a fortune in merchant banking in the United States and now wished to return to Britain to live the life of a country squire. He had heard about Marnie on the county-set grapevine and given her to understand that no expense would be spared.

Marnie liked that kind of contract.

She was consulting a catalogue of the latest range of chalk paints when the phone rang. It was Ralph, and he sounded disturbed.

'Are you okay, Ralph?'

'I was.'

'Until?' Silence. 'What's happened? Speak to me.'

'I've had another letter from Jay Harper.'

'And?' Marnie could sense anxiety vibes coming down the line. She decided not to press Ralph further, but let him speak in his own good time.

'Rhiannon's funeral is due to take place the day after tomorrow.'

'The day after ...?' Marnie repeated. 'That's rather short notice.'

Automatically, Marnie found herself pressing buttons to bring Ralph's diary up on the computer. As far as she could tell, he had no commitments that day.

'In his letter he says he's just found out ... something to do with the coroner releasing her body after a post mortem.'

'Will you be attending the funeral?' Marnie asked.

'I'm wondering what to do for the best.'

'Do you want to go?'

'I don't know. What do you think, Marnie? Obviously, if I went, I wouldn't expect you to go with me.'

'Is Jay's letter an invitation?'

'He just writes that it's taking place at Hobb Hill crematorium between Banbury and Bloxham. He gives the address and the time: eleven o'clock. That's it.'

'I think only you can decide, Ralph.'

Ralph paused. 'Do I have any choice?'

ooo0ooo

Anne had a visitor on *Sally Ann* that evening. She was using her laptop, typing up notes from a lecture on Augustus Pugin and the Gothic Revival in the nineteenth century, when there came a tentative knock on the stern doors. She guessed at once who might be calling; the reticent style was unmistakable. Sighing, she pressed the Save key on the computer and padded to the door.

'Lucas ... what a surprise!'

'Hope I'm not interrupting your work.' He grimaced. 'Just thought I'd pop along and ... you know.'

Anne stood aside to let him enter. 'Come in ... aboard ... below ... or whatever's the right term on a narrowboat. Only you can't stay long. I've got work to do for tomorrow.'

He stepped down and followed Anne through to the saloon. She indicated a chair and sat opposite, while Lucas stared around him as if he had never seen the inside of the boat before. A thin plume of smoke was rising from a joss stick beside a candle burning in a ceramic holder. The air was scented with jasmine – though Lucas didn't recognise it as such – and a cassette of acoustic guitar music was playing softly in the background. The only lighting was provided by a reading lamp and two oil lamps, which bathed the interior in a warm glow. It picked out the muted colours of the Liberty print curtains – cream and red and blue – and the Oriental rug on the floor.

'Wow, Anne! You've made it really nice in here.'

Anne shrugged. 'It's the same as it was when you've been here before. And I am supposed to be training as an interior designer, after all.'

'I know, but ...' he gestured over the table. '... the incense, the candle, the music and all that.'

'It's meant to be conducive to working.' Anne didn't want to appear inhospitable, but she hoped he might take the hint. 'Don't you try to make your boat cosy when you're studying for college?'

Lucas frowned. 'Maybe that's what I was trying to do back then, in a weird sort of way, when I used to smoke weed in the evenings.'

'Well, how can I put this without causing offence?' Anne reflected. 'What I try to do with designing my workspace isn't exactly going to fry my brain. Or is that too blunt?'

Lucas cleared his throat and spoke quietly. 'Anne, I came to tell you that I ... I really like you.'

Anne felt guilty at being exasperated, but she just didn't need that kind of conversation when she was trying to assess the reasons for Ruskin's hostility to Pugin as an architect.

'Lucas ... I ... I really ... I seem to be finding it difficult to finish a sentence right now.

'Sorry, Anne.'

'Look, this is tricky. You know I have a boyfriend. You've met Donovan.'

'I suppose ...'

'You can hardly overlook someone who pushed you into the canal.'

'No, I hadn't forgotten that little episode. Actually, Anne, when I met him properly he seemed like a nice kind of guy.'

'He is and, to make myself clear, he's *my* nice kind of guy. I'm sure you take my meaning.'

'Yeah ... yeah.' Lucas made to get up, but Anne spoke again, and he remained in place.

'I ought to mention that we saw Mrs Albright again at Autumn Lodge.'

'Why do you go there? Doesn't seem like your sort of place.'

'I think I told you about it before. We visit an old lady and take her cat to see her.'

'Oh, yes. I'd be glad to see Mrs Albright again. She helped me a lot when I was in Magdalene House … helped get me into rehab.'

'She told us – Donovan and me – that she'd be glad to see you again, too.'

'That's good.'

'Okay, well we'll see if we can take you with us next time we go.'

Chapter 24

THURSDAY

The letter that Ralph had received from Jay Harper requested a reply to a PO Box return address if Ralph wished to attend the funeral. He had therefore written a hasty note with a first class stamp to confirm attendance and dropped it in at the porter's lodge to go out in that afternoon's post.

Thus it was that on Thursday morning Ralph set off in the direction of Banbury shortly after breakfast. He wore a charcoal grey suit with a white shirt and black tie. On setting off, he had called in at the local garage, topped up with fuel and taken the Jaguar through the car wash. Its dark grey metallic paintwork gleamed like new in pale autumn sun as he pointed the car across country, content that its restrained colour showed due respect to someone whose life had touched his, albeit briefly, all those years ago.

The mid-morning traffic was light, and Ralph made good time to reach the Banbury to Bloxham road, aware that the sky was gradually turning grey. He found himself humming an old favourite song – *'California Dreamin'* – that he had first heard in his student days, when a sudden downpour descended, drowning the road like a flash flood. The windscreen wipers could barely fend off the deluge, even at their highest setting. Instinctively Ralph slowed, anxious to avoid running into another car or being rammed from behind. Visibility was appalling as Ralph turned on the headlights and flicked the switch for the rear foglight. Speed was down to not much more than twenty, and Ralph strained to see anything ahead of him, conscious that the road ran through open country, with a ditch on either side.

Ralph was concentrating hard when something caught his eye in the rear-view mirror; a sudden flash of light distracted him for a split second. It disappeared as quickly as it had come, but Ralph was horrified to discover that a car had raced alongside him and begun to swing across towards him. He braked firmly, praying that there was no lorry coming up behind. In that moment, the other car swerved into his lane, narrowly failing to make contact. Ralph knew that if he hadn't hit the brakes when he did, they would have collided and careered off the road into a ditch.

The other car skidded, but the driver retained control and accelerated away at a reckless pace. With so much spray being thrown up from the road, coupled with the pouring rain, there was no chance of identifying the dangerous car or its dangerous driver.

An absurd thought crossed Ralph's mind. He wondered fleetingly if the other driver was going to the funeral and feared arriving late. Ralph dismissed the idea as the product of his shock at what had happened. He thought that driving so badly, the other driver could soon be on the way to his own funeral.

Then it struck him. He had not just witnessed an example of really poor driving. That driver had deliberately tried to force him off the road, with probable dire consequences. The rain was now easing off, but only to the extent that Ralph could see a short way ahead. A sign came up indicating a lay-by half a mile distant, but the hostile car was out of sight. Ralph's only impression was that the car was dark, possibly black, grey or navy blue. He became extra vigilant, wary in case that car was waiting for him in the lay-by. But as he approached, he could see that it was empty.

Ralph signalled and pulled off the carriageway to come to a halt at the lay-by's furthest point. He switched off the engine and for the first time realised that he was breathing heavily and his hands were shaking. He leaned back against the head-rest and closed his eyes until his breathing subsided to normal. The gentle rhythm of the rain falling on the car's roof helped Ralph to get himself under control, but a vague notion was nagging at him. He knew it had something to do with the near-miss, but at that moment he couldn't pin it down.

ooo0ooo

'Walker and Co, good morning.'

Marnie was wrestling with a decision about the choice of colours for carpets in the rundown country house in the Northamptonshire Uplands. She hoped that the phone call wouldn't distract her for long. As soon as Ralph spoke she knew something was wrong, and she refocused all her attention.

'Don't be alarmed, Marnie, but I've been involved in a sort of … incident.'

'Incident? What does that mean? An accident? What's happened? Are you all right?'

It was a typical Marnie response. Her barrage of questions felt comforting and reassuring. Ralph even managed a smile and a chuckle.

'Yes, I'm all right. Some bloody lunatic almost ran me off the road.'

'*What?!* Where are you? What bloody lunatic?'

'I'm in a lay-by somewhere between Banbury and Bloxham. I don't know who it was. He took off at high speed and vanished in the murk.'

'He was driving a Mercedes?'

Ralph laughed nervously. 'Not that sort of Merc! Sorry, Marnie. I think I'm shell-shocked. I don't know what he was driving. I meant murk in the sense of *gloom* … poor visibility. There's been a downpour here.'

Marnie glanced at the window and saw that the sun was shining on Glebe Farm.

'It's bright and sunny here. You're sure you're okay?'

'Yes. I am now. But that car …'

'The non-Merc? What about it?'

'That's just it. I don't know … can't put my finger on it.'

'So what are you going to do, Ralph?'

'I've got bags of time before the funeral. I think I'll just sit here for a while and get my breath back.'

'Good idea. Make sure your mobile's switched on.'

Marnie's natural instinct was to phone Ralph back and tell him she would join him at the crematorium. She was aching with anxiety, worrying that the 'bloody lunatic' might go back and make another attempt on Ralph. She was musing along those lines when the phone rang again.

'It's me, Marnie.'

'Anne, listen, something's happened to Ralph.' Marnie explained about the 'incident with the bloody lunatic' and Anne listened without interruption.

'What are you going to do?' Anne said.

'I'm thinking of driving over there to be with him … moral support, at least.'

'That's what I thought you'd say. Look, Marnie, I'm nearer than you and I could … wait a minute.'

'What is it?'

'I was ringing to say that Donovan is on his way up here, and we'll be coming over later this afternoon. I could get him to divert to wherever this funeral is taking place. We could all converge there to be with Ralph. Shall I ring Donovan straight away?'

That became the agreed plan. Marnie was saving her work on the computer and reaching for her car keys when Anne rang back.

'Just spoken to Donovan. He asked if there really was a funeral. You know what a suspicious mind he –'

'Blimey! I hadn't thought of that.'

'He thinks it's worth checking at the crem.'

Marnie needed no further prompting. She logged on to the crematorium's website and found a phone number. She expected to hear a deep lugubrious male voice, but in fact her call was answered by a cheerful young woman.

'I'm phoning to enquire about a booking this morning. I have it in my diary for eleven o'clock. Can I check that's the right time with you?'

'Okey-dokey. Let me see. Ah yes, well try to get here a bit early, if you can. Parking may be tricky.'

'But do I have the right time? The name is ... sorry, what's that about parking? Are you expecting large numbers?'

'We are. Biker funerals are always huge, especially when it's the Hell's Angels. All those big motorbikes, you see. We sometimes get a few hundred.'

'What name do you have, may I ask?'

'It's ... er, let me see. Mr William Black. His mates wanted to bring a floral tribute in the name of *Big Willie*, but we're rather formal here. I'm sure you understand. Was he a close friend?'

Marnie brought the conversation to an end with as much solemnity as she could muster and straight away phoned Ralph. She was relieved that he was still recovering in the lay-by. He agreed to wait there until they all converged on him. After a quick call to Anne about the change of plan, Marnie set off in haste.

ooo0ooo

Marnie was the first to arrive in the lay-by and took up station immediately behind Ralph's Jaguar. They were joined a few minutes later by Anne in the Mini and Donovan in his VW Beetle. The rain had now given way to a cool, damp haze, and the group held a council of war in the lea of Marnie's Freelander. It was clear that there was no funeral arranged for Rhiannon Ellis that morning; it had been another hoax, a trap designed to involve Ralph in a serious crash. They listened while Marnie gave an account of her conversation with the cheerful crematorium lady.

'Bikers and Hell's Angels?' Anne said. '*Big Willie?* That's one of those words that makes everyone laugh ... like *knickers.*'

They all laughed. The laughter stopped abruptly as they remembered why they had driven as fast as they could to be with Ralph.

Marnie said, 'Have you had any further thoughts about who it might've been, Ralph?'

Ralph shook his head. 'I didn't even catch sight of him, not for a second. Everything happened so quickly, I was taken by surprise.'

'You said *him,*' Donovan said. 'You're sure it was a man driving?'

'I can't imagine it would be anyone other than a man, really. But I suppose that's just ...'

'And the car?'

'I've been thinking about that. Now, I can't be certain – I said everything happened very quickly – but I'm wondering if it was the same car that tried to run Greville and me down in the street in Oxford last week.'

'The one that mounted the pavement?' said Marnie. 'What made you think of it?'

'Not sure. All I know for certain is that it was dark ... black or navy blue or possibly grey. In fact, looking at Donovan's black VW makes me think my assailant's car was perhaps dark blue.'

'The same as last week's attempt at hit-and-run?' Marnie said.

'It's just a vague impression,' Ralph murmured.

'What about the make, or at least the shape?' Donovan asked. He pointed at the Beetle. 'Did it have rounded bodywork like mine, or was it more the style of your car?'

Ralph closed his eyes to think. Eventually, he said, 'It's only a fleeting impression, but I'm pretty sure it wasn't remotely like your car, Donovan.'

'Size?'

'Not large.'

'A saloon car like yours, or an SUV like mine?' Marnie asked.

'More low-slung than yours, so more like mine.'

'Performance?' Donovan again.

'Well, it took off at some speed.'

'Like the car in Oxford,' Marnie observed.

'I think probably so.' Ralph thought for a moment and added, 'But I couldn't swear to anything.'

'Who knew you'd be travelling on this road this morning?' said Marnie.

'Just you and me, I suppose.'

Marnie nodded. 'And whoever wrote the letter. Someone wanted to lure you into another trap.'

'Yes, and ... oh my God.'

'What, Ralph?'

'It came in the internal post.'

'So absolutely no doubt that it was sent by someone in college.'

'Absolutely none.'

ooo0ooo

A unanimous decision was taken to respond to the situation in accordance with British tradition. And so they headed back to Glebe Farm for a cup of tea.

Afterwards, while Anne cleared away the crockery, Ralph declared himself well enough to retire to his study on *Thyrsis* to continue proof-reading his latest chapter. Meanwhile, Donovan busied himself in the garage barn with cleaning the spark plugs on the Beetle. This left Marnie and Anne together in the office barn with time before lunch to review the rundown country house project.

It soon became clear to Marnie that Anne's thoughts were wandering elsewhere.

'You all right, Anne?'

Anne tried to look focused. 'Sure. Where were we?'

'We hadn't started.'

'Oh ...'

'Something's troubling you. Tell me. Are you worrying about Ralph?'

'No. Well, not in the way you mean, Marnie.'

'What then?'

Anne bit her lower lip. 'I don't quite know how to put it.' Marnie waited for Anne to continue. 'Do you remember that thing about Ralph's *wife* a while back?'

'You mean Laura? Sure. It's quite a few years now since she died.'

163

Anne shook her head. 'No, not her. I mean the woman who rang and *said* she was Ralph's wife ... the woman in the psychiatric home in Nottingham.'

'I remember. What about her?'

Anne said hesitantly, 'Is she the person who's died? I mean, the one who's funeral? ... or do I mean non-funeral? ... Ralph was supposed to be attending ... Oh dear, I seem to be muddled don't I?'

'If you mean was Rhiannon that woman, then I think the answer must be *no*. I seem to recall her name was Tricia.'

Anne frowned, mentally wrestling with thoughts she couldn't articulate and had no wish to share with Marnie.

'So Tricia ... definitely not Rhiannon. You're sure of that.'

Marnie said quietly, 'What is it that's bothering you, Anne?'

'I don't know how to put it into words. I don't want to face up to it.'

'Then let me try to help you. Are you wondering if Ralph might be some kind of serial womaniser, who might one day leave us to take up with somebody else?'

'*Us?*' said Anne, bewildered. 'I wasn't thinking it was about *us*, not in that way.'

'Anne, if Ralph was like that – and I can tell you that he absolutely isn't – then his leaving would impact on you as well as me, though in a very different way, obviously.'

'I think this is all beyond my experience, Marnie. I've always thought of Ralph as someone special, someone I'm really, really fond of ... not in the way that you are, naturally, but ...'

'He has a special place in your life. That's what you mean, isn't it?'

Anne's eyes filled with tears. 'I couldn't bear it if ...'

'Anne, I know what you mean. Let me try to explain things to you. Ralph is the kind of person that a lot of people find attractive. He's very compelling in all sorts of ways, and I can imagine that when he was a young man many young women were drawn to him. But I know him well enough to know that he didn't exploit that. He's mature enough to know what he wants from life. I'm a part of that for him, and you are, too, in your own way. Do you understand?'

While Marnie spoke, Anne was nodding. She wiped her eyes with the back of a hand.

'There's something else, Marnie.'

'Go on.'

'This Jay person really wants to harm Ralph, doesn't he?'

'So it seems.'

'At first it was just about Ralph's reputation. Now it's getting seriously dangerous. I worry about what he might do next, and where it will all end.'

'You're not alone there, Anne.'

'Why is he doing this? It seems so *extreme*.'

'Whatever the reason, it isn't because Ralph exploited some poor girl and dumped her, I'm certain of it.' Marnie reflected. 'I can't help feeling that there's more to it than that.'

oooOooo

The rest of that day was spent catching up with the work that had been missed as a result of the incident involving Ralph and the non-existent funeral.

While Anne and Donovan occupied themselves with college projects, Ralph was in his study on *Thyrsis*. In theory, he was checking a chapter in his next book. Marnie was at her desk in the office barn. In theory, she was finalising the scheme for rejuvenating the rundown Uplands house, but her thoughts kept turning to Ralph who had been uncharacteristically quiet since they returned home. She worried that he might be fretting about his near miss on the road, so she decided to go to see him and bring him a measure of comfort. What she found surprised her.

After draping a long navy blue cardigan over her shoulders, she strode briskly through the spinney and knocked on the side doors of *Thyrsis*. Ralph opened up and took her hand to steady her on the steps down into the boat.

'I'm glad you've come, Marnie. I've reached a decision and I want to run it past you.'

He led the way to his study and offered Marnie the sofa, while he swivelled his office chair to face her. Far from looking anxious, Ralph's demeanour was positive and determined.

'You've reached a decision?' Marnie prompted.

'I've had enough of being on the defensive. I'm going to take a leaf out of your book and tackle Jay Harper head on.'

Ralph's tone was forthright. Marnie's expression was puzzled.

'My book? In what sense?'

'You always act positively when faced with a problem. I've seen you in action many times, Marnie. You're always ... dynamic.'

Marnie tried not to look sceptical. This was a side of Ralph that she had rarely seen before. He was one of the most gifted people in his field in the country, probably in the world, yet she had never really imagined him as a man of action.

'So what do you intend to do?' she asked.

'We know with reasonable certainty that whoever is behind all this … hostility … is on the inside of All Saints' College. I'm going to confront my colleagues and get at the truth.'

'By …?'

'First, I'm going to speak to Greville Rickman. I'm pretty sure he has nothing to do with it, but he may well have insights into who does.'

'You're convinced that Dr Rickman isn't –'

'Gotta start somewhere, Marnie. I've already spoken to him. He has no lectures or tutorials tomorrow morning, so I'm seeing him in the common room for coffee at ten. What d'you think?'

Marnie thought about it and could come up with nothing better. 'Seems like a plan,' she said.

'Good. I'm going for it.'

ooo0ooo

Up in her attic room Anne closed her book and announced that she had a suggestion to make.

'Isn't it a little early?' said Donovan. 'We haven't even had supper yet.' He looked thoughtful. 'On the other hand …'

Anne flashed him the heavy eyelids. 'I'm being serious.'

'Fire away.'

The suggestion was to take Dorli to see Frau Kreisler and Angela to see Randall. Donovan agreed and arrangements were put in hand. He suggested Saturday for the visit, but Angela assured him that she and Randall could organise themselves again to meet on Sunday.

Chapter 25

FRIDAY

On Friday morning, prompt at ten o'clock, Ralph entered the senior common room at All Saints' College and found Greville Rickman already pouring coffee. He smiled at Ralph and handed him the cup. It was a friendly, uncomplicated smile, and Ralph took it at face value. He was almost totally convinced that Greville was not the plotter behind the plagiarism accusations or the violent attacks. Even so, he was alert to any hint of duplicity.

'Shall we sit over there, Ralph?' Greville nodded in the direction of two armchairs in the corner of the room. There, they would be able to talk in private.

'I hope I'm not interrupting your work,' Ralph said when they were settled.

'Nothing that won't keep. Aristotle and Plato can wait a while. I suspect there's something important you want to talk about, and I can probably guess what it is.'

Ralph replied without preamble. 'Someone tried to kill me yesterday.'

Greville sat bolt upright with a start that spilled coffee on his trousers. 'Good God! What happened?'

Ralph described the incident on the road to the crematorium, while Greville stared back open-mouthed. Horror was etched into his features; Ralph was sure Greville's shock was genuine. Ralph handed Greville a handkerchief to mop his trousers. Greville muttered quietly to himself, words that Ralph could neither hear properly nor understand.

'Who knew you were going to the funeral, Ralph?'

'Nobody, apart from Marnie and me ... plus the person who wrote to tell me about it. By the way, there was no funeral.'

'Just as there was no meeting arranged last week at the OUP?' said Greville.

'Exactly.'

'Presumably you were given a name – otherwise, why would you be attending?'

'It was supposed to be the funeral of Rhiannon Ellis.'

Greville made a face. 'Can't say I've ever heard of her … friend of yours?'

'Just someone I knew a long time ago.'

'Did you see who the driver was, Ralph?'

Ralph shook his head. 'But I'm sure it's an insider, and I think we both agree on that. Who else could it be?'

'What are you going to do about it?' Greville said eventually.

'I'm going to follow Marnie's motto.'

'Your wife has a motto?' Greville sounded dubious.

'The motto of the Royal Marines School of Management, she says.'

Greville frowned. 'Is there such a place?'

'Metaphorically. Marnie made it up, also the motto, which is: *seize the high ground*.'

'Which means?'

'Just what it says: take the initiative.'

'Of course … yes,' Greville murmured. 'Take arms upon a sea of troubles and, by opposing, end them.'

'I would hope for a better outcome than the fate that awaited Hamlet,' said Ralph.

Greville was now more composed. He replied, looking Ralph straight in the eyes. 'You're playing for high stakes, aren't you?'

'Do I have much choice, Greville? I can't sit around waiting for the next attack. He might have more luck next time.'

'So we come back to my original question. How are you going to seize the high ground?'

'It's why I'm here. This is where I start. I want you to think back to the day you confronted me in your study.'

'You think that I –'

'No. No, I don't. But you persuaded two colleagues to join you and face me that day.'

'At that time all we wanted was for you to keep out of the limelight for a while. No one present on that occasion wished you harm … myself included, but I think you know that.'

'In hindsight, Greville, you were all acting for the good of the college, not for my own good.'

'What are you getting at, Ralph?'

'I wonder if you got the impression that either Harry Boulter or Oliver Ringstead was particularly hostile towards me.'

Greville considered this for a long moment. When he shook his head, it was decisive. 'No, definitely not. I approached them, and they were both initially rather reluctant. And afterwards, when I told them that I thought I'd misjudged you, both seemed frankly relieved. You must know, Ralph, that you are held in high regard in the college as an original thinker. Just mentioning *plagiarism* in the same breath as your name seems utterly ridiculous.'

If Ralph had not been so concerned with the situation, he might have swept the compliment aside. Instead, he mentally removed Boulter and Ringstead from his list of potential suspects. By now other fellows were drifting into the common room, chatting quietly together and forming an orderly queue to serve themselves coffee.

Greville followed his gaze as Ralph observed the dons. Momentarily the two men exchanged glances. Ralph guessed that they were sharing the same thought: one of the innocuous-looking fellows of All Saints' College was quietly plotting Ralph's downfall and would stop at nothing to destroy him. What other possibility could there be?

Chapter 26

SATURDAY

By Saturday morning Ralph was no further forward with identifying which colleague at All Saints might be plotting his downfall, or what had prompted such violent hostility after all this time. That it concerned Rhiannon had never been in doubt, but their brief liaison ended twenty or more years ago, and there had been no contact between them in the intervening period. So why now?

From the other side of the breakfast table, Marnie pointed out the obvious. 'Well, it must be to do with her death, mustn't it?'

Ralph looked sceptical. 'I've been thinking about that. How do we even know she's died? We've no proof of it, apart from the letters from Jay. How reliable is that? There was no funeral, only a trick to get me on a certain route at a certain time.'

'Good point,' said Marnie. 'How can we check that she really has died? Her death would no doubt have to be registered somewhere. I suppose we'd need to know where she was living at the time, if we're to consult the local BMD registry – births, marriages and deaths. Any ideas?'

Ralph looked blank. 'None at all. Marnie, I've had no contact of any kind with Rhiannon since … I don't know when. It really was a very long time ago. It was before I even met Laura. She and I were engaged for over a year, then married for nearly eight years, and it's almost as long since she died.'

'So you haven't a clue about where Rhiannon lived.'

'None, and no way of knowing, unless …'

'Unless?' Marnie prompted.

Ralph shook his head. 'I was wondering if I could remember where she was living at the time of our …'

'*One night stand* is the term you're looking for, I think,' Marnie said helpfully.

Ralph groaned. Suddenly, Marnie sat upright. 'What is it?' said Ralph.

'Her college! You met her at an academic conference, you said. And you mentioned where she was studying ... wasn't she doing a master's degree somewhere? Perhaps they might have contact details for her. Where was it? Can you remind me?'

'It was ... wait a minute ... yes. She was doing an MBA at the Highgate Business School in London.'

'You have a friend there, don't you?'

'Graeme MacKinnon, yes; he's the principal.'

'Worth a try?'

'Anything's worth a try,' Ralph said with feeling. 'On the other hand, I'm not entirely sure what good might come of it.'

ooo0ooo

Anne and Donovan had left Marnie and Ralph at the breakfast table and taken themselves off for a walk by the canal. It had been obvious to them that Ralph was still fretting about Rhiannon, the attempts to injure him – or worse – and the whole plagiarism business, and they judged it fitting to give them some time together. Plus, they had plans of their own to make.

There had been a shower during the night, and Anne linked arms with Donovan as they stepped over puddles on the path as if taking part in a choreographed sequence. They walked for a time in comfortable silence until Anne spoke.

'I said we'd pick Angela and Dorli up at around eleven tomorrow. Shall we go in your car?'

'Sure.'

'You're very quiet today,' Anne observed. 'Are you OK?'

'Thinking about Ralph's dilemma. Do you know much about this Rhiannon person, who seems to be at the heart of it all?'

'Not much,' said Anne. 'I gather she was some old girlfriend of Ralph's, and this Jay character seems to be waging war on Ralph apparently because he dumped her.'

Donovan looked sceptical. 'There must be more to it than that. Otherwise it's way over the top.'

'I know what you mean. Have you any ideas about why Ralph's being targeted like this?'

Donovan stopped and turned to face Anne. 'Plagiarism seems to suggest professional jealousy, I would've thought.'

'Yes. Ralph thinks it's someone in his college who's attacking him. I heard him say that to Marnie.'

'A rival, you mean?'

'I suppose so. Who else could it be?'

'That makes obvious sense, but it doesn't really explain the Rhiannon connection.'

Feeling none the wiser, they turned back along the towpath.

oooOooo

Later that morning, Ralph managed to track down Graeme MacKinnon on the phone after a meeting of the planning committee of the board of governors of the Highgate Business School. There was something about MacKinnon's melodious Hebridean accent that Ralph found calm and soothing, but he knew his friend's brain was razor-sharp.

'You're lucky, Ralph. As a visiting professor you don't have to spend your Saturdays dealing with committees and the tribulations of the planning laws relating to listed buildings. Anyway, that's enough bleating. I expect you want to sound me out about something a wee bit more important. Go ahead.'

'Someone's trying to kill me.'

'Well, that got my attention! Even the planning committee members aren't out for my head on a plate ... at least not just yet. Are you serious?'

'There's more, Graeme.'

'I can hardly wait.'

'Whoever's doing it is also trying to destroy my reputation, my career. That amounts to the same thing.'

'Tell me about it and what you think I can do to help.'

Ralph gave as much detail as he thought necessary, while MacKinnon listened without interruption. At the end of Ralph's narrative, silence rolled along the line for several seconds between Highgate and Northamptonshire.

'It would obviously help if you could identify the car in question, Ralph, and ideally who was driving it.'

'When everything happens so quickly ...'

'Sure. I get the picture. So what can I do?'

'There's another dimension ... slightly embarrassing.'

'I think I can feel a *cherchez la femme* scenario coming on. Am I right?'

'Spot on. I'm afraid the whole situation certainly does me no credit.'

'I'm guessing we've all been there, Ralph, some time in our lives. Who is she?'

'Wrong tense, Graeme. She's dead, but she is the reason why I'm phoning you.'

'This is not quite what I expected when you rang.'

172

Ralph spared no details in narrating the sad story of the lovelorn Rhiannon and her recent demise.

'You think there's a link between this Rhiannon Ellis and the plot against you.'

'Exactly. There has to be.'

'And you need my help to ...?'

'I'm wondering if somewhere in the school's records you might have information about where she lived. I know you can't give her address, even if you had one, but I don't see anything unethical in letting me know the area in question, especially now that she's died.'

'That would enable you to track down a death certificate, you mean?'

'It's a long shot, I know, Graeme. Can you help?'

'If you can wait till Monday, I can get my secretary to go through our files.'

'Perfect.'

Chapter 27

SUNDAY

L ate on Sunday morning, Angela Hemingway dashed home after conducting the family service. She quickly changed from Sunday-best clerical garb to *smart casual* sweater and slacks, and was coaxing Dorli into her travelling basket when Donovan's Beetle pulled up outside the house.

Within two minutes they were setting off under an overcast, threatening sky, heading for the marina to pick up Lucas. When they made the arrangement to include him, they had forgotten how tortuous the journey would be from Knightly St John to Brackley with a detour to Duke's Cut near Oxford. While Angela occupied the back seat with Dorli, Anne was sitting up front with the road atlas on her lap calculating the best route. She had a furrowed brow.

'Sorry to be so slow, Donovan. Just head down towards Bicester then I'll let you have directions to the marina.'

'Okay.' His tone sounded vague.

Anne was going to remark on it, but she needed all her concentration to plot the best route using main roads only onto the A40 beyond Oxford's northern by-pass.

'Got it!' she said. 'Come off by the Pear Tree Park and Ride, follow signs to the centre, then turn right at the next roundabout, signposted A40, westbound.'

'Mm ...' Again Donovan sounded vague; again, Anne let it go.

Some miles later they hugged the left-hand lane at the Park and Ride sign, turned off the main road and headed towards Oxford.

'Go right at the next roundabout,' Anne said decisively. 'Look for signs, A40.'

No reply.

'Did you get that, Donovan?' Anne glanced sideways and saw that Donovan was staring intermittently at the rear-view mirror.

He said, 'If we head into town on Woodstock Road, what's the first turning on the right after this roundabout?'

'Why would we –'

'Just tell me. Please.'

Anne looked down at the map. 'First Turn.'

'Yeah.'

'That's what it's called: First Turn.'

'Good. After that, can you see how we get back to this roundabout?'

Anne ran a finger down the map.

'Easy. You just keep on that road – First Turn – and it curves round up to a main road ... er, Godstow Road. Turn right there, and you come back to the roundabout. The A40 is the first exit on the left. Can I ask my question now?'

'There's been a black car some way behind us ever since we left home. It turned off when we did. Don't look.'

From the back seat, Angela sounded nervous. 'You think it's following us?'

'Could be.'

'What make is it?' Anne asked.

'Too far back to tell. All I could see for sure was that it's black ... or it could be dark blue.'

'You mean like the car that –'

'Possibly. I don't want to lead it to where your boat is moored. The trouble is, this old VW is rather conspicuous. I couldn't easily throw him off – if he is following us – without it being too obvious.'

'If you were to speed up ...' Angela suggested.

'He'd know I spotted him. I've improved the Beetle in lots of ways, but there's no chance of out-running a modern car.'

At the roundabout Donovan took the exit for Oxford city centre and lined up to take the first turning on the right.

'Did he follow us?' said Anne.

'I hope he spotted our general direction, but not where we turned off.' Donovan accelerated along First Turn, but the road was not wide, and cars were parked along much of it. He needed every ounce of concentration on the road ahead, with scarcely a second to glance in the mirror. 'Angela can you see if anyone's behind us?'

She craned her neck. 'I don't think there is.'

As they wove their way back up to the main road, there was a tense atmosphere in the car. Even Dorli the cat seemed to be holding her breath. Donovan approached the roundabout with caution. He didn't want to find himself confronted by a pursuer. He needn't have worried; all was clear.

Now, their mood was lightened, and as Donovan accelerated firmly out of the northern suburbs, he felt relaxed enough to mutter in his best attempt at an American drawl, 'Hold onto your butts.'

Behind him, Angela grinned. It was not the kind of instruction normally given to lady vicars. And she was convinced that Dorli, in her travelling basket beside her, was totally baffled.

The rest of the journey passed without incident, though Donovan maintained his vigil with frequent glances in the rear-view mirror. In fact, the whole visit was a success. There had been the usual gushing from Frau Kreisler who showered Dorli with affection. The cat tolerated this with feline fortitude and resignation and certainly without complaint.

They had collected Lucas from the marina, and the other reunion – between Lucas and Mrs Allbright – passed off with less effusiveness, though they were obviously pleased to see each other again. Anne had been amused to notice that Angela now had her own key to Randall's house, and she smiled coquettishly towards Anne and Donovan as she let herself into the rectory.

ooo0ooo

Later that afternoon, Donovan remained vigilant as the Beetle chugged back towards Knightly St John to deliver Angela and Dorli to the vicarage. It was another circuitous route, but Anne and Lucas needed to be returned to the marina, where Donovan would stay with Anne before travelling down to London early on Monday morning. The mysterious dark-coloured car did not reappear behind them, so Donovan concluded that it had either been a product of his imagination or he had given it the slip.

Lucas and Angela sat either side of Dorli's travelling basket. Angela was happy to sit quietly with her private thoughts, and though Anne had a fairly good idea of what they involved, she kept her own thoughts to herself. Lucas, on the other hand, seemed oblivious to the reflective atmosphere in the car. He became relentlessly chatty, shuffling on the seat in the confined space.

'What's this?' he asked.

Anne glanced over her shoulder. 'Oh, it's my bag. Just chuck it on the floor if it's in the way.'

Lucas moved it onto his lap. 'So, Donovan, how's your course going?' he said.

'It's fine … soon coming to an end. How about yours?'

'I'm enjoying it. It's good to be back.'

'You've been away?'

Lucas hesitated. 'You mean Anne hasn't told you?'

'Told me what?'

Another hesitation. 'I … took some time off.'

'A gap year?'

'Two years nearly, in fact. You didn't know what I was doing?'

'Not really. I seem to recall you said you'd opted out for a spell.'

'I was … in rehab. I'd had a problem.'

'I see.'

'That's how I know Mrs Albright.'

'You were in rehab at Autumn Lodge?' Donovan sounded incredulous.

'She was at the rehab clinic before. She used to do regular visits at Magdalene House … health check-ups for the er …'

'Guests,' said Anne. 'Randall calls them *guests*.'

'Whatever,' Lucas said. 'She's a nurse, you know.'

'I didn't know there was a rehab clinic in Brackley,' said Donovan, 'though I know Randall's place, of course.'

'The rehab clinic is part of the Alberic psychiatric hospital near Brackley. It's a small unit for about a dozen … patients.'

'She seemed pleased to see you, Lucas.' Anne thought it was time to stress the positive.

'She's all right … Mrs Albright. In fact, that's what she was called – *All Right Albright* – by some of the inmates.'

'Patients,' Anne corrected him.

'Yeah. That's what I meant.'

They were surprised to hear a strong neo-German accent – or so it was intended – from the vicar on the back seat. 'Frau Albright is very nice person. I am very much liking her.'

It was an almost passable imitation of Frau Kreisler and was followed by a burst of laughter. For Angela it was a better response than her sermon had received in church that day.

ooo0ooo

The phone rang in the farmhouse that afternoon as Marnie and Ralph returned from a walk beside the canal. It was Greville Rickman. Marnie passed the phone to Ralph.

'Greville, hello. Everything all right?'

'Fine, Ralph, fine. Is it convenient to talk?'

177

'Certainly. Go ahead.'

'I've been thinking about what you said when we spoke yesterday. You thought that whoever was behind all this ... business, had to be an insider in college.'

'I thought you felt the same,' said Ralph. 'Am I wrong?'

'Probably not, but I've had an idea. In your position as visiting professor you're not in college as much as some of us, so perhaps you don't have the same perspectives, or at least not in quite the same way.'

'What do you have in mind, Greville?'

'Well, when you referred to an *insider*, I had the impression that you were thinking of those of us who are dons. But academics aren't the only people around the college.'

'Who else are you thinking of, Greville? You surely can't be thinking of the secretaries or the college servants.'

'Well, to be honest, Ralph, I've racked my brains and I can't think of any of the academic staff who'd ever accuse you of *anything*, certainly not plagiarism.'

'I'd hope not, but the nature of the accusation makes me feel that it's someone like an academic who might accuse me of something like that. A porter might be aware of our day-to-day comings and goings, but I couldn't imagine one of them actually levelling that sort of accusation against me. And then there's the loyalty aspect. Some of them have followed in the footsteps of their fathers and even grandfathers in the porter's lodge. They'd never do anything to harm the reputation of the college.'

Greville sighed. 'No, on reflection I'm sure you must be right. Frankly, I'm at a complete loss to know who's behind it all, but there's definitely something odd going on.'

Hollow laughter from Ralph. 'That much is fairly obvious, Greville.'

'No, I don't just mean the plagiarism business. I'm wondering what's going on with the Master.'

'The *Master*? You surely can't think –'

'No, no. I don't mean that. I don't know how much you might've noticed, but he never seems to be around these days. In the past, if I wanted to see him, I'd just pop along to his office for a quick word. *Now*, it's almost like seeking an audience with the Pope!'

'I know exactly what you mean, Greville.'

'Do you really?'

'Oh, yes. I've had much the same experience.'

'And have you any idea what's happening?'

'Not the foggiest. The Master seems to be turning into a man of mystery.'

oOo0ooo

Later that same day another 'man of mystery' – namely, Donovan – was popping open three small bottles of German lager in the saloon of the narrowboat *Sally Ann*. Having installed Lucas on a safari chair by the table, Anne was tipping cashews and olives into bowls. When they were all seated round the table, they began pouring their beer into glasses. Anne noticed that Donovan was watching Lucas, who was carefully pouring his lager slowly and at an angle so that no foam lay on the top.

'Do you always pour like that?' Donovan asked.

Lucas examined his glass, then turned his gaze towards Donovan whose beer had a layer of foam on top to a depth of about two centimetres. Lucas nodded.

Donovan said, 'If you did that in Germany they'd suspect there was grease on the glass and pour it down the sink.'

Lucas looked dismayed. Anne laughed. It was time to change the subject.

'Do you think we were being followed on our wat to Oxford this morning, Donovan?' she said.

'Hard to tell, but I have my suspicions.'

'Did you manage to get a look at the driver?' said Lucas.

Donovan shook his head and drank some beer. Time for another change of subject.

'So what's your course like?' Lucas asked.

Donovan swallowed. 'It's quite technical.'

'You mean cameras, microphones, lighting … that kind of stuff?'

Donovan nodded. 'That kind of stuff.'

'Are you aiming to be a film director?'

'I think I'm more interested in editing. Good editing can make average directing look good. Poor editing can make good directing look mediocre.'

'What about the actors?' Anne said. 'Can editing make them look good?'

Donovan smiled. 'I don't think the course has covered that aspect of the work.'

Anne knew that Donovan was in his final year and had already submitted his major project for assessment. She judged it wise to steer the conversation in a different direction, so they talked about canals and boating for half an hour till Lucas took himself off to his own boat.

As he rose from the table, he said, 'Can I visit Autumn Lodge with you some other time? It was nice seeing Mrs Albright again. Made a nice change to get out and about.'

'Sure,' said Anne. 'I'll let you know next time we're going.'

Donovan managed to contain his joy. He drained his beer in silence.

Chapter 28

MONDAY onwards

On Monday Marnie was concerned when Ralph once again failed to appear for mid-morning coffee. It had become their custom to discuss the programme for the week at that time and was almost sacrosanct. After a moment's reflection she picked up the phone and dialled Ralph's mobile. It was engaged and she decided not to leave a message on voicemail.

Twenty minutes later Ralph arrived somewhat breathlessly in the office barn.

'Sorry to be late, Marnie. Graeme phoned just as I was preparing to set off.'

'Graeme MacKinnon, Highgate Business School?' Marnie said.

Ralph nodded as he poured coffee into a mug 'If you remember, he was trying to find a recent address for Rhiannon so that I could check if she really had died.'

'And did he?'

Ralph planted himself on a visitors' chair. 'Interesting. Graeme said the only contact details for Rhiannon held at HBS were more than ten years old. It appears she was a long-term resident in a psychiatric care home.'

'That was your understanding, wasn't it, Ralph?'

'It would be in line with what Jay Harper wrote in his original letter. He said she was committed to a psychiatric home for – quote – most of her life.' Ralph looked downcast.

'How did the business school come to have that kind of address for her?' Marnie asked. 'She'd hardly still be studying there while living in a home like that, surely.'

'HBS sends out an annual report to former students. My guess is, someone returned it to the school with a forwarding address. But that's not what's interesting about it.'

'Go on.'

'The home was part of a psychiatric hospital not far from here. All these years Rhiannon was living not twenty miles away near Brackley.'

Marnie stood and went to kneel beside him. 'Ralph, please don't start regretting things. I know you think you could have treated her better, perhaps at least have visited her from time to time, but your life had moved on in a totally different direction. After all, you were married to Laura.'

Ralph was desolate. 'I can't escape the fact that I may well have ruined her life or at the very least contributed to her mental problems.'

Marnie took hold of one of Ralph's hands. She spoke quietly. 'I really don't want to sound heartless but plenty of people experience the break-up of relationships in their lives; not everyone collapses as a result. If that's what happened to Rhiannon, something in her own character probably led to it.'

'I know, Marnie. Even so ...'

'Ralph, from what little I know of Rhiannon she seems to have had a rather obsessive personality. I'm sorry to speak of her like this, but you can't hold yourself responsible for her behaviour, her actions, how she lived her life. We all have to make choices in our lives.'

Ralph shook himself mentally. 'Of course. You're right, Marnie. I'm being self-indulgent. I ought to focus on the positive.'

'Talking of which,' said Marnie, 'we normally spend this time on a Monday looking at what we have in store for the coming week.' She walked back to her seat and opened the diary on her computer. 'It's business as usual for me: two new design projects, a briefing meeting on Wednesday, and I'd rather like to take in an exhibition in Birmingham on Friday. Anne would like that too if she's back from college that day. What about you? How's your week looking?'

'I'm still working on the new book about developments in the Far East. Apart from that there's just a regional examiners' meeting on Thursday ... Warwick University. It's a fairly quiet week.'

Let's hope it stays that way, Marnie thought.

ooo0ooo

Ralph's prediction proved to be correct, at least for the first half of the week. Marnie was able to make progress with her design projects, and Anne and Donovan made plans to return to Glebe

Farm on Thursday evening with a view to visiting the exhibition in Birmingham the next day. But on Thursday everything changed.

It was already dark when Ralph eased the car into its slot in the garage barn and climbed out to be met by Marnie rushing anxiously towards him.

'Thank goodness you're all right!' She hugged him tight.

Surprised, he muttered, 'This is becoming a habit. Examiners' meetings aren't usually considered hazardous.'

As Marnie released her grip, Ralph realised that his flippant response was not really appropriate. He added, 'Has something happened?'

Marnie stared at him. 'We've just had a call from Miles Gooch.'

'Miles … in my department … the Research Fellow?'

'Yes. He said he was on his way back from the Warwick meeting when he saw what he took to be your car off the road in a ditch. He said it seemed to have crashed into a tree.'

Ralph raised a hand to his mouth. 'My God!'

Marnie took Ralph's arm and began walking him to the house. 'He said he pulled up and looked inside it, but there was nobody there. Dusk was coming down, but he said he was pretty sure it looked like your car.'

'A Jaguar?' Ralph said. 'Dark grey metallic?'

'That's how he recognised it.'

Well, it obviously wasn't my car, so I suppose …'

'What?' said Marnie.

The security lights came on as they turned towards the front door. Before Ralph could reply, they heard the phone ringing in the farmhouse. Ralph rushed through to the kitchen and picked up the receiver. It was Greville Rickman, and he spoke without greeting or preamble.

'Are you all right, Ralph?'

'Fine. More to the point, what about you? Have you been in an accident?'

'Yes. Well, strictly speaking, no. I was more or less pushed off the road not far from Leamington.'

'But you're okay?'

'Shaken and shocked, but otherwise okay. Good old airbags!'

'What happened, Greville?'

'I was driving back to Oxford on a small country road. The light was fading and I was going fairly slowly as I was approaching a bend. Suddenly, this lunatic appeared from behind me out of nowhere, overtook and swerved across the front of me.'

'Another car, you mean.'

'Yes. I had to brake and pull right over. I didn't realise there was a ditch by the roadside. Next thing I knew, I'd bounced into it and smacked into a tree.'

'What about the other car?'

'He roared off without stopping.'

'I'm going to ask a silly question,' said Ralph.

'No. No idea. I didn't get a good look at it. All I know is, it was dark in colour.'

'Well, there's a surprise! What happened next?'

'I rang nine-nine-nine and luckily there was a police car in the vicinity. He arrived in minutes, so at least I could report the incident. I was assuring the officer that I was unhurt and hadn't been drinking when Doug Longfellow came along, so he gave me a lift back to college.'

'And the car?'

'I've just arranged for it to be collected and taken to a garage. I expect it'll be a write-off. But listen. On the way back with Doug I suddenly thought that if the lunatic had a go at me, he might've tried to get you, given that our cars are so similar. That's why I thought I'd ring you.'

'Very good of you, Greville, but I'm okay.'

They chatted on for a few minutes while Marnie put a glass of brandy on the table in front of Ralph. After disconnecting, he swallowed it in one gulp and took a deep breath. He outlined the conversation to Marnie. Both of them conjured up a mental imagine of Greville's car in the ditch … a Jaguar with metallic dark grey paintwork … just like Ralph's.

ooo0ooo

At supper that evening Ralph was persuaded to relate the story of the *Greville's Jaguar incident* to Anne and Donovan. Predictably Anne was horrified and sat listening enthralled with her mouth open until Donovan closed it with a finger under her chin. For his part Donovan refrained from comment, or in fact any outwardly visible reaction at all. He sat lost in thought and frowning.

'Will you report it to the police?' Anne said.

Ralph shook his head. 'That's surely for Greville to deal with. In any case, he did actually speak to a police officer about it. I don't think there's anything I can add. Something along the lines of an *incident occurred when another car was mistaken from my own in poor light* isn't going to merit much investigating.'

'But that other driver tried to *kill* you, Ralph,' Anne protested, 'and not for the first time.'

'Or maybe not.'

All eyes turned towards Donovan after he spoke.

'What d'you mean?' said Anne. 'He ran Dr Rickman off the road and into a tree, thinking it was Ralph.'

Donovan shrugged with one shoulder.

'Go on,' Marnie urged him. 'What's your thinking?'

Donovan hesitated as he gathered his thoughts. 'Okay. Dr Rickman drives the same sort of car as Ralph ... same make, same colour. Light was fading, but still adequate to identify the car, more or less. Whoever came up behind the car knew that Ralph would be returning home from the Warwick meeting.'

'Isn't that fairly conclusive?' Anne said. 'A question of mistaken identity, but the intent was there.'

'Can we be sure about that?' said Donovan.

Ralph took a sip of wine. 'Go on. I'm intrigued.'

'You said that Dr Rickman told you he was going quite slowly as the light was fading and he was approaching a bend on a narrow road.'

'That's right.'

'Dr Rickman hadn't spotted that there was a ditch beside the road, so presumably neither had the other driver.'

'Okay.'

'The other car swerved in front of Dr Rickman's Jaguar. Could it be that the aim was to give him a fright?'

Ralph said, 'You mean he only tried to run Greville off the road onto a grass verge ... a tactic designed to scare him ... like the sort of manoeuvre he possibly tried on me?'

Donovan said, 'It's just a theory, but the incident hardly amounted to a high speed crash, did it?'

Donovan had given them something to think about. They could all see the logic behind his reasoning. Even so, it brought them little comfort.

Chapter 29

SUNDAY

On Sunday morning Anne apologised to Donovan as they drove through the village to collect Angela and Dorli.

'Sorry to lumber you with fetching Lucas,' she said. 'When I agreed to take him with us I'd forgotten what a roundabout journey it was, going via the marina.'

'It's okay,' said Donovan. 'I don't suppose we'll need to take him every time we go.'

Angela was on the doorstep with Dorli in her carrying basket when they drew up outside the house. Although Anne was sure Donovan knew the way, she liked to sit with the road atlas open in front of her on journeys. It made her feel she had a useful part to play.

Donovan glanced every few seconds in the rear-view mirror throughout the whole journey, but there was no dark-coloured pursuer that morning. So confident was he that they were unobserved, that he didn't bother with the subterfuge of turning right into First Turn on the outskirts of Oxford. Nevertheless he maintained a careful watch in the mirror for any sign of a car keeping station behind them.

Like Angela, Lucas was waiting for them as soon as they turned into the gates of the marina. He climbed in behind Donovan, plonked Anne's bag on his lap and made himself comfortable. The rest of the journey across country to Brackley was uneventful. At Randall's rectory Anne climbed out and pulled the seat forward to let Angela out from the back of the Beetle. She was amused to see that once again Angela used her own key to enter the house.

From Brackley it was only a short hop to Autumn Lodge, and Donovan straight away found a parking space. He switched off the engine. 'Okay. Here we are. Stand by for a gushing reunion. Can you bring Dorli, Lucas?'

'No problem. Damn!'

Anne looked back at him. 'What's up?'

'Sorry, Anne. I forgot about your bag. I've dropped it on the floor and a load of stuff's fallen out.'

'That's all right. I don't need it anyway.'

Lucas was shamefaced. 'I'll shove back in as much as I can.'

By now Donovan was out of the car, holding the door open. Lucas hurriedly scooped up most of Anne's belongings and slipped them into the bag. He struggled from the back seat with Dorli's basket under one arm and a piece of paper in his free hand. Anne led the way to the house with Donovan behind her, and Lucas with Dorli hurrying to bring up the rear.

No one was surprised when Frau Kreisler emerged from the building with a cry of '*Ach, meine kleine Dorli!*' and the gushing reunion began. Donovan translated Frau Kreisler's greeting as *my little Dorli* while Mrs Albright came out to greet Lucas with a hug. She ushered everyone along to the conservatory and promised that tea was on its way.

Mrs Albright settled beside Lucas on a sofa and leaned forward to take hold of both his hands. At that moment she became aware of the piece of paper that he was holding.

'What's that?' she asked.

'I dropped Anne's bag in the car. Things fell out. It's just a slip of ... oh, it's in fact a photo. D'you want it, Anne?'

He handed it to Mrs Albright to pass to Anne. Mrs Albright glanced at it briefly. 'Relatives of yours, Anne?'

'Second from the left is Ralph, the husband of my friend, Marnie. I work for her. It's an old photo. They're a college tennis team from the time when Ralph was studying for his doctorate.'

'Nice looking young man.' Mrs Albright was extending the photo to Anne when she paused. 'Oh, there's writing on the back.'

'It's their names,' Anne said. 'Marnie's husband is Ralph Lombard. His team won that trophy in the picture.'

Mrs Albright turned the photograph over. 'It's impressive.' She looked back at the names and frowned before studying the photo again. 'That's odd. This isn't quite right.'

'I didn't write the names,' said Anne. 'They were already there.'

Mrs Albright was examining both sides of the photograph, still frowning.

Donovan said, 'What's wrong with it, Mrs Albright?'

'This one on the end.' Mrs Albright held up the picture and pointed. 'According to the writing on the back, he's called Jay Harper, but I'm sure that's not his name. I know him. I've seen him lots of times, and though he's much younger there, I'd recognise him anywhere.'

'Who do you think he is, Mrs Albright?' Anne asked.

'He's called ... let me think, now ... yes, he's Gareth Ellis.'

'How can you be sure?' said Donovan.

'I'm certain of it. He used to visit his sister regularly. She was a patient at the Alberic hospital near Brackley where I worked. You know it, Lucas. 'She lowered her voice. 'It's where you spent some time in rehab, where I first met you.'

'I never saw him,' said Lucas.

'No. Gareth's sister was in the long-term psychiatric unit. It's a separate building.'

In the silence that followed, the only sound was the soft cooing of Frau Kreisler as she stroked Dorli behind the ears, while the cat purred. Eventually Anne spoke.

'What was his sister's name, Mrs Albright?'

'I remember her well ... a lovely lady. So sad to see her there. I recall she had an unusual name.'

'Could it be Rhiannon, Mrs Albright?'

'That's it! A Welsh name, I believe.'

'You're sure?'

'Definite.'

ooo0ooo

'No.' Ralph was adamant. 'The captions are correct. That man in the photograph is definitely Jay Harper.'

They were sitting in the kitchen of the farmhouse late that afternoon. After dropping Angela and Dorli home at the vicarage, Anne and Donovan took Lucas with them back to Glebe Farm. Having heard from Anne on her mobile, Marnie had been keen to get the whole story without delay. She had therefore invited Lucas to join them for supper.

Anne said, 'Mrs Albright seemed convinced she knew the man in the photo as Gareth Ellis. He was apparently the brother of your ... friend, Rhiannon.'

Ralph shook his head. 'The man in the photo is Jay Harper. We were in the same tennis team for three years. For two of those years he was my doubles partner, for example the year we won the varsity trophy, also the year before when we reached the semi-finals. The question is – '

'Why Mrs Albright was so convinced she knew him as Gareth Ellis.' Donovan completed the sentence.

'And that's another thing,' Ralph added. 'I never heard Rhiannon mention a brother. I don't think she even had one.'

'Called Gareth?' said Marnie.

'Called anything. I don't believe there was any such person.'

'Then why did Mrs Albright think otherwise?' Donovan asked the question they were all pondering. 'She seemed to be in no doubt.'

'There's something odd about this.' Ralph looked puzzled.

'I think we all get that picture,' said Marnie.

'No, I mean there's something else,' said Ralph. 'I can't put my finger on it, but there's something about this whole business that bothers me.'

'There's an awful lot that bothers me,' Marnie said. 'In fact that applies to just about everything that's going on at the moment.'

Ralph muttered, 'It was some time back. It seemed just a small thing at the time, but it struck me as odd then, and now I've lost it.'

'It will probably come back to you,' said Marnie.

Ralph looked far from convinced as he sat, racking his brains.

Chapter 30

MONDAY

Ralph was surprised on Monday morning to receive a very early phone call from Greville Rickman. It was soon after seven o'clock and he was still at the breakfast table with Marnie when his mobile began warbling. Marnie smiled to herself, impressed that he knew which button to press to take the call. Not for the first time, Greville began with no greeting or preamble. His agitation was clear.

'Ralph, I think I've remembered that car and where I'd seen it before. You're not going to believe this.'

'Good morning, Greville. Try me.'

'Oh, yes. Good morning, Ralph. I've seen it in the car park at All Saints.'

Ralph was intrigued. 'So it does belong to a member of staff, just as we thought. Any idea whose car it is?'

'Not exactly, though one thing is clear. It doesn't belong to someone in residence.'

'And you know that because ...?'

'It isn't there all the time, just intermittently.'

Ralph considered this and gave it some thought before replying. 'Can you detect a pattern in its attendance, Greville? Do you know if it's been there on the same days each time you've seen it?'

'I can't, Ralph. In fact I've only just persuaded myself that I'd seen it at all.'

'Pity. If we could ascertain precisely when it shows up, we could check the timetable and work out whose it might be.'

'Yes, of course. That would reveal who our man is ... definitely.'

'Assuming it is a man,' Ralph added.

'I thought that had been our assumption all along.'

'It has been just an assumption, Greville. I think we need to keep an open mind. And there is another thing.'

'Another thing?' Greville repeated.

'Yes. That the car you've identified really is the one that's been pursuing us.'

Greville was deflated. 'Yes. I suppose you're right, Ralph. Perhaps I'm getting ahead of myself.'

'No. You're making progress. In fact, Greville, you're the only one of us who is taking things forward.'

'You think so?'

'Definitely. I think we should follow your lead. You need to check the car park each day, starting today, and then keep it under surveillance every day from now on.'

'And if I've been mistaken?'

'Then at least we've been able to eliminate someone as a possible suspect.'

Greville sounded more upbeat. 'You make it sound like a criminal investigation, Ralph.'

'What else do you think it is?' said Ralph.

ooo0ooo

It was while clearing away after breakfast that Marnie had a brainwave. She heard Ralph coming down the stairs. He had gone up to use the bathroom before setting off to his study on *Thyrsis*. Marnie rushed out to the hall to intercept him.

'Ralph, I've had an idea. Who at college would keep a list of cars allowed in to use the car park?'

'Well, the porters would keep one in the lodge.'

'Wouldn't there be other copies somewhere else in college?'

'I suppose there would. What do you have in mind?'

'It seems to me we could make a start by eliminating anyone who had a car that wasn't black or dark blue. No need to wait while Greville Rickman keeps an eye on things.'

'That's a point. There's probably a list in the Master's secretariat. I could check that with Clare Goodall, though ...'

'What is it, Ralph? Have I missed something?'

'Not necessarily, but I'm not sure if that would give any clues about colours. Worth a try, though.'

At that moment the phone rang. Marnie hurried into the kitchen and grabbed the wall phone. It was Anne; Marnie was surprised.

'Aren't you going to be late for college?' she asked.

'That's why I'm ringing. We have no classes this week, Marnie. It's mid-term reading week. We're supposed to use the time to get on with our course wrok.'

'*We?*'

191

'Yes. Donovan's here as well. That's why I'm ringing. I'm wondering if we could come home and work at Glebe Farm. There's only the one table on *Sally Ann* and –'

'Of course you can. That's fine. In fact we could use some of the time to talk about Ralph's ... problem. Greville Rickman has had an idea, and we're working on it. I'll tell you more when you get here.'

ooo0ooo

Despite the early intervention from Greville Rickman, it proved to be a productive morning. Marnie was able to devote herself to design projects; Ralph worked on the next chapter of his book; Anne and Donovan pressed on with their college work. By the time they gathered in the kitchen for a sandwich lunch, Anne could contain her curiosity no longer.

'So what's this new development from Dr Rickman? I'm all agog.'

Ralph gave a summary of their thoughts from earlier that morning.

'Do the secretaries keep a list of the cars allowed in the car park?' Anne asked.

'Yes,' said Ralph. 'But neither Clare nor Rosemary has the slightest idea of the colours of the various cars.'

'What about the porters?' said Donovan. 'Perhaps they have more than a chance of knowing which car is which.'

Ralph nodded. 'I phoned the lodge this morning and asked if the porters had any ideas about colours. They're going to put their heads together and see if they can come up with anything.'

Anne said, 'Why don't you just go round to Jay Harper's house and confront him outright?'

'That's the problem, Anne. I only know he lives somewhere near Bicester. It's a large area to cover.'

'How do you know that?'

'His address is just a Bicester PO Box number.'

Donovan sat up in his chair. 'You have a PO Box number for him?'

'It's the only one I do have.'

Donovan said, 'Can you write it down for me, Ralph.' He took the note and made for the door. 'Leave it with me,' he said.

Marnie and Anne shared the same thought: *man of mystery*

...

ooo0ooo

192

Donovan did not join them again until the time came for their mid-afternoon tea break, though Ralph thought he spotted him from *Thyrsis* walking along the towpath with the mobile phone clamped to his ear. Anne was handing out cups of tea when Donovan walked into the office and handed a slip of paper to Ralph.

Ralph read it and looked up. '16 Langdale Road Bicester? What's this?'

Donovan said, 'Jay Harper's address, known technically as his physical address, and before you can say anything, don't ask.'

Ralph looked baffled. 'I thought a PO Box meant it had to be collected from a sorting office, or something like that.'

Donovan simply shook his head and accepted a mug of coffee from Anne.

ooo0ooo

That night, in Anne's attic room in the office barn, Anne slipped into bed beside Donovan. He reached across to the bedside table and turned out the lights.

In the darkness Anne said, 'I was impressed at how you got that address in Bicester for Ralph.'

'It wasn't difficult. It just took a little time.'

'I did wonder how you managed to do it,' said Anne.

Donovan said, 'I thought Ralph exercised real self-control in not pressing me to explain that.'

'I thought so too,' Anne agreed. 'I also thought I might try and wheedle it out of you.'

Donovan chuckled. 'I was hoping you'd say that.'

Chapter 31

M arnie and Anne were first in the kitchen the next morning, laying the table for breakfast together. Anne was quietly humming something indeterminate to herself as she set out crockery.

'That sounds cheerful,' Marnie said. 'You're obviously in a good mood this morning.'

'Just an old *Blondie* track.' Anne was trying to sound casual. 'I like the classics.'

'That's usually Donovan's line,' Marnie observed. 'He always says that.'

'Yes, he does.'

'Talking of whom,' Marnie began, 'I thought he did very well to get that address for Jay Harper.'

'Mm …' A non-committal murmur.

Marnie persisted. 'Do you know how he got it?'

'Uh-huh.'

'Are you going to tell me … or would you have to kill me if you did?'

Anne smiled and said, 'Donovan had a holiday job with the Royal Mail one Christmas. He still has a few contacts there. He got in touch with one of them and … hey presto!'

'You did well to get him to spill the beans,' said Marnie.

'I just wheedled it out of him,' Anne said modestly, adding archly, 'I can't tell you how.'

Marnie rolled her eyes. 'You just did.'

ooo0ooo

When Ralph appeared for breakfast he was wearing a dark blue suit with a pale blue shirt and burgundy silk tie. He parked a wheeled suitcase in the corner of the room and took his seat. Donovan arrived a few moments later wearing his customary dark grey and black attire. He looked quizzically at Ralph and the luggage.

'What's this, Ralph? Going somewhere?'

'University of York seminar … economic developments in the third world. I'll be away for the next three days.'

'Just when we were making progress with Jay Harper.' Donovan sounded disappointed.

Marnie said, 'Well, I for one feel relieved that Ralph will at least have a few days' respite from all this hassle.'

'Unless Jay follows me up to Yorkshire,' said Ralph, grinning.

Donovan crossed his fingers. Anne sighed. Marnie closed her eyes and slowly shook her head.

ooo0ooo

The rest of the week was quiet. Marnie pressed on with her designs and site meetings. Ralph phoned each evening and had nothing sinister to report apart from excessive exuberance on the part of one or two radical participants in the seminar. Anne and Donovan applied themselves diligently to their college tasks. All in all it was a fruitful week. There was no contact from Greville Rickman, which Marnie interpreted as a good sign.

Ralph returned on Thursday evening and announced that he had had no sighting of the sinister dark car. He rang Greville Rickman who reported that all was quiet on the All Saints front. For a fleeting moment Ralph wondered if this was the calm before a storm, though he said nothing of his misgivings to Marnie.

Over supper that evening they reached a critical decision. On Friday they would travel to Bicester and confront Jay Harper once and for all.

Chapter 32

At the breakfast table in the farmhouse on Friday morning they once again discussed tactics. In bed the previous night, Anne and Donovan had guessed that Ralph would want Marnie to go with him to seek out Jay Harper in Bicester. They were right. The decision was taken to set off after breakfast with the aim of arriving on his doorstep by about nine o'clock. They chose to make the journey in Marnie's Freelander rather than in the Jaguar which Harper would no doubt recognise.

The journey took around forty minutes and they parked at the end of the street. Ralph took a deep breath before climbing out. Mentally he prepared himself to meet a man who for some time seemed determined to destroy him psychologically, professionally and even physically. With a firm step he strode out. His demeanour was resolute, but even so he took Marnie's hand as they walked along the street.

Ralph pressed the doorbell button and took another deep breath. Moments later the door opened and a man stood before them. His expression was blank.

'Yes?'

Ralph was momentarily confused. He glanced quickly at the number beside the door.

'Ah, I was expecting to see Jay Harper,' he said hesitantly.

'Jeremy isn't here,' said the stranger.

'Jeremy,' Ralph muttered. 'Yes, of course.'

'And you are …?'

Ralph extended a hand. 'Sorry, I'm forgetting myself. Ralph Lombard, and this is my wife Marnie.'

'Duncan Harper. I'm Jeremy's brother. How can I help you?' Seeing their evident uncertainty, he added, 'Would you like to come in?'

When the door closed behind them Ralph asked, 'Are you expecting your brother back any time soon?'

'To be honest, I have no idea. I've phoned every day since Sunday and left three messages on the answerphone, but I've had no reply. Let's go into the sitting room.' He ushered them into a small room and gestured to the sofa. 'Perhaps you can tell me what brings you here?'

'It's ... er, a long story, but I really hoped to see your brother.' He added, 'I'm a Fellow at All Saints' College.'

To Marnie, Harper said, 'You're also at the college?'

Marnie reached into her shoulder bag. 'No. I'm an interior designer.' She handed him her business card. 'As Ralph said, I'm his wife.'

Duncan Harper read the card and looked up, desolate. 'I'm worried about Jeremy. He's not himself these days. In fact he had a kind of breakdown about a year or so ago, soon after Rhiannon died.'

'A year ago?' Ralph was astonished. He and Marnie stared at each other in disbelief.

'Yes. In fact longer. It was early summer last year when she died, and Jeremy more or less went to pieces. Did you know her?'

Ralph found himself at a loss for words. Marnie interjected, 'Ralph met her briefly a long time ago.'

'You presumably have a reason for coming to see Jeremy?'

Ralph shook his head. 'Where should I begin? We have reason to believe that Jay – Jeremy – has been acting, shall we say, rather erratically of late.'

'By *we*, you mean you and your wife?'

'No. I mean colleagues at All Saints' College, though I must say I'm not clear where Jay fits in, as far as the college is concerned. He isn't a member of staff.'

'Oh, I can help you there. Jeremy edits *Collegiate* magazine, the university journal. In that role he's in and out of quite a few of the colleges, depending on what articles he's planning to include.'

'So he has access virtually everywhere,' Ralph said, 'at any time.'

'That's right.'

'A familiar sight,' Ralph murmured, 'blending in anywhere in the university.'

'Yes, certainly.'

Marnie said, 'He no doubt has a car. Do you know what he drives?'

Harper looked perplexed. 'His car? I think he bought a new one not long ago. I'm not good on cars, but I think it was some sort of Vauxhall, quite a sporty one. What did he call it? Oh, yes, a *hot hatch*. Does that make sense?'

'Colour?' said Marnie.

'Navy blue, I think, though I couldn't swear to it.' He frowned. 'Why do you ask? In fact, it isn't clear to me why you've come in the first place. Sorry to put it so bluntly.' He turned to Ralph. 'You said Jeremy has been acting erratically. What did you mean?'

Ralph cleared his throat. 'Mr Harper –'

'Duncan.'

Ralph began again. 'Duncan, this is difficult. Can I be absolutely frank with you?'

'I wish you would be. You're obviously concerned about my brother, but I don't really understand what you're getting at ... both of you.'

'You see,' Ralph began, 'your brother appears to have been pursuing me as a kind of ... vendetta.'

'I don't really understand what you mean. How well do you know Jeremy?'

'I used to know him quite well, but it was a long time ago. We were both postgrad students studying for doctorates at All Saints' College, and Jay was for a time my tennis partner.'

'He never completed his DPhil,' said Duncan. 'I expect you knew that.'

In truth, Ralph had forgotten, but excused himself mentally as so much time had elapsed since then. He judged that now was not the time for an admission that could seem uncaring. He simply said, 'What happened?'

'I think this is where I have to ask, if I can be frank with you, Dr Lombard. I'm assuming you did complete your doctorate?'

'I did, but please call me Ralph.'

'Well, the fact is, Ralph, that Jeremy met someone and – to use what now seems a rather outdated term – er, fell in love with him.'

'*Him?*' Marnie and Ralph sat bolt upright and spoke in unison.

Duncan nodded. 'Have I shocked you?'

Ralph stammered, 'Er ... well, er ... not shocked in the sense that you mean, but I think we're probably both ... *surprised*. That is not what I expected you to say.'

'Can you tell us anything more?' Marnie asked. 'I appreciate this is a sensitive subject for you. We are, after all, complete strangers.'

'That's true, but I get the impression that you have Jeremy's wellbeing at heart, despite what you said, Ralph.'

Ralph said, 'Duncan, it's not quite like that. You see, Jeremy _'

Marnie laid a hand on Ralph's arm. To Duncan she said, 'Your brother's ... relationship with this other man. How did it turn out?'

Duncan looked wretched. 'It was a disaster. You see, the other man didn't – couldn't – return Jeremy's affection. He made it clear that he was not that way inclined, though I believe that for a short while he may have given Jeremy a different impression.'

'Why?' said Marnie.

'I think he saw Jeremy as someone who could help him with his studies. He was a first year undergrad, you see. Jeremy had already by then earned a first in History and was doing research. When Jeremy was rejected he took it badly, even tried to ...'

'I didn't realise ...' Ralph murmured. 'You have no idea where your brother might be now?'

'No. That's why I came here today. I've had to take a day off from work, which is why I came so early. I didn't want to waste a minute, you see.'

'I'm sorry we've taken so much of your time,' said Ralph.

Duncan sighed. 'That's all right. I came hoping to see Jeremy, but otherwise I don't know what I expected to find.'

'You've searched everywhere?' said Marnie.

Duncan shrugged. 'I've looked around, but all I've learnt is that his bed hasn't been slept in. I don't know if you have any ideas?'

'Does he have a study in the house?' Ralph asked.

Duncan inclined his head. 'He uses one of the bedrooms. I've already looked in there. What are you thinking?'

'I just wondered if there might be notes for the next edition of the magazine that might give a clue as to what he's doing ... where he might be. I don't know if that would help very much.'

Duncan stood up. 'Might be worth a look. Shall we go upstairs?'

Neither Ralph nor Marnie had any preconceived ideas about what they might learn from Jay Harper's study. It was a small room with one window that looked out onto the side wall of the house next door. Looking down gave a view of the neighbour's dustbins. A bookcase – Ralph identified it absently as probably early Habitat – held a collection of history books, a thesaurus and the odd dictionary. It struck Ralph as a sad place, a den of unfulfilled promise. But perhaps that was because of what he had learnt that morning of Jay Harper's experience of life. He was on the point of suggesting that they should leave, when he spotted a notepad on the corner of the desk. It was well-thumbed with numerous doodles on the cover. Ralph opened it and was surprised at what he found.

ooo0ooo

The writing in the notepad was clear, neat and easy to read. It contained what appeared to be a collection of random thoughts and jottings, and Ralph was intrigued to see that the first note was dated back to the time of their student days. Idly he glanced down the page and, as he read, he became shocked at its content.

> Her hair is black, her eyes are blue. She walks in darkness through my daydreams. She has become fixated on an object of desire, an obsession. There is no knowing where it will end.
>
> To describe her hair merely as black is an understatement. It is the colour of a raven's wings, dense and glossy. It shines with a light of its own. To say that her eyes are blue does them no justice. They are an intense azure, piercing and at the same time languid, provocative.
>
> She carries about her a cloak of despair in the colours of a death-wish. Ghosts hover around her, biding their time. She neither knows nor cares what will become of her.
>
> Her name is Rhiannon.

Ralph handed the open notepad to Marnie. 'Read this.'

As Marnie read the first page, Duncan hovered in the doorway. 'Have you found something?'

Marnie looked up and turned to him. 'Mr Harper, are you sure you're right about your brother's … relationship, that he fell in love with a man?'

'Why? What have you found?'

Marnie passed him the notepad. 'You don't think you might have been mistaken?'

Duncan studied the first page. 'It looks like Jeremy's handwriting. I don't understand. He told me quite distinctly that he'd met –'

They froze as they heard the front door open. Duncan dashed to the landing and called out. 'Jeremy is that you? Your friend Ralph is here to see you.'

Almost immediately the front door slammed shut. Duncan raced down the stairs, quickly followed by Ralph and Marnie. Duncan was reaching for the door when they heard a car engine roar, then a squeal of tyres. With the three of them crowded together in the narrow hallway, it took some seconds for Duncan to pull the door open. As they charged out onto the pavement they were just in time to see a car vanish round the corner at the end of the street with a squeal of tyres. None of them could identify it, but on one point they were all agreed: it was dark blue.

ooo0ooo

'Was it the same car that you've seen before?' Donovan asked. 'Can you be sure of that?'

The Glebe Farm four were sitting over lunch that day in the farmhouse kitchen. Marnie and Ralph had given an account of their visit to Jay Harper's house in Bicester that morning.

Ralph said, 'I couldn't swear to it, but it did seem familiar.'

'What else could it be?' Marnie asked. 'Of course, I've never set eyes on that particular car, but if we'd seen anything but a dark-coloured one racing away, I'd have been very surprised.'

'Me too, I suppose,' Ralph agreed.

Anne said, 'And that strange text in the notepad that you mentioned, Marnie, I wish I could've seen that.'

'You can see it,' said Ralph. He reached down to his jacket that was hanging on the back of the chair and pulled out the notepad. 'I slipped it into my pocket when we all hurried out of the room.' He pushed it across the table to Anne. 'You can read it for yourself.'

'I didn't know you'd done that,' Marnie said. 'Did Duncan Harper know?'

Ralph shook his head. 'No. I'm sure he didn't.'

Marnie looked thoughtful. 'You chose not to ask him. Why was that? Didn't you trust him?'

'What do you think, Marnie?'

'I must say I did wonder, just briefly ...'

'Wonder what?' Ralph said.

'I'm not sure. It was something he did that struck me at the time when –'

Ralph said, 'When he rushed from the room and called out that I was there?'

'Yes. That was it. It was almost as if he was warning Jay about you.'

Anne finished reading the note. She passed it to Donovan as she spoke.

'That's really weird, the way it's written. It's almost like a poem or a fantasy or something.'

Donovan looked up. 'It's like the product of a troubled mind.' He pointed at the page. 'If that's the right date, this is twenty or more years old.'

'I checked the dates of the following entries,' Ralph said. 'That one does seem to be correct.'

Anne leaned back in her chair. 'So he's felt like that about Rhiannon for a very long time.'

Marnie said, 'And he's only taken to direct action now that Rhiannon is no more.'

'He's obviously been brooding about it ever since she died,' said Ralph.

'And yet he was supposed to have been in love with a *man*,' Marnie added. 'Perhaps he felt the same way about her.'

'Who knows?' said Ralph. 'There's obviously more to this than meets the eye.'

'There's another thing,' Donovan said. 'Gareth Ellis … the name given to him by Mrs Albright when she saw Anne's photograph. Are he and Jay Harper one and the same? If not – and Mrs Albright's mistaken – where does this Gareth Ellis fit in?'

'And did Rhiannon really have a brother at all?' Marnie added wearily. 'Things couldn't be more complicated if they tried.'

Within less than an hour Marnie was to be proved wrong.

ooo0ooo

Ralph's wish that afternoon was to be able to press on with writing his latest book about the economics of the Far East. He was poring over data produced by the Tokyo Stock Exchange when his mobile began ringing. He hastily scribbled himself a note before pressing – he hoped – the correct button.

'Lombard.'

'Ralph, sorry to disturb you, but I'm still having problems with the Master.'

'Is that Greville?'

'What? Oh, yes, yes, it's me. It's so frustrating. I don't know what's going on.' He sounded highly agitated.

'And you think it has something to do with me and this plagiarism business?'

'Frankly, Ralph, I don't know what to think. I'm fed up with being fobbed off every time I try to see the Master. Mrs Goodall told me the Master – quote – "couldn't be disturbed". For goodness' sake, I'm supposed to be the Vice Dean of the college! What the hell's going on?'

'Yes,' Ralph agreed. 'It's all very odd. I managed to see him a few weeks ago and –'

'Lucky you!'

'Quite, and he seemed his usual self. Then, of course, there was that awful business when his car was blown up.'

'It's all very peculiar, Ralph. I don't suppose there have been any further developments on the plagiarism front?'

'Actually, we've tracked down the elusive Jay Harper.'

'And?'

'He's still elusive, but we almost made contact with him at his house this morning. Just when we might've collared him he drove off at a hell of a lick. Look, Greville, I'm up against a deadline with this book I'm working on. Can I phone you shortly and bring you up to date? Sorry to put you off, but –'

'No, it's all right, Ralph. I'm used to it these days.' This was said without rancour, and they disconnected.

Ralph had barely returned to his text when there came a knock on the boat's centre doors. He slid back the hatch and pushed open the doors to find Marnie looking flustered.

'I tried phoning but your mobile went straight to voicemail.'

'What's up?'

'It's Jay Harper. He's had an accident … crashed the car. He's in Intensive Care at the hospital in Northampton.'

ooo0ooo

Marnie had a dread of visiting the Intensive Therapy Unit, even though she had received excellent care there when she came close to death a few years earlier. Ralph pressed the bell at the entrance and the two of them waited for a nurse to appear round the corner a short distance away. For a few moments they stood together hand in hand looking out over the car park below them.

The nurse who opened the door looked to be Chinese, and the badge on her uniform gave her rank and name as SRN Wong. Before Ralph could speak, the nurse looked at Marnie and said, 'Are you Rhiannon? He's been asking for you. Come this way, please.'

They followed her at a brisk pace and found only three beds in the unit occupied. Marnie turned to the nurse as she hurried away to another patient, but held back from raising her voice. Jay Harper was hooked up to an array of machinery by a variety of tubes while lights flickered in different colours on a monitor to one side above him. His head was covered in bandages, and his face was dotted with small lacerations. They moved towards the bed.

'Jay,' Ralph said softly and waited.

It was obviously a struggle, but the patient slowly opened his eyes a crack for a glimpse of his visitors. He blinked a few times and closed them again.

In a hoarse whisper he muttered, 'Who ...'

After Jay's voice faded, Ralph said, 'It's me, Jay. Ralph Lombard. I'm here with my wife, Marnie.'

Jay croaked, 'Rhiannon ...?' He stirred.

'No, Jay. She's not here.'

'I know,' he murmured and slumped back.

Nurse Wong returned to check Jay's readings, and Marnie addressed her quietly. 'I'm not Rhiannon. Jay was confused. Rhiannon was an old friend, but she died.'

Nurse Wong looked startled. 'Did you tell him that?'

'No. Is he going to pull through?'

The nurse shrugged and replied softly. 'There are no guarantees for anyone in here. His injuries are serious. We're doing everything we can.'

'I know that. I was a patient here myself some time ago.'

'You're friends of his?'

Marnie hesitated. 'He was a college friend of my husband. They go back a long way. I was wondering about visiting hours.'

The nurse nodded. 'It's open visiting here. You can come at any time as long as the consultants aren't with him and, obviously, depending on his condition.'

'When do you suggest would be appropriate?' Ralph asked.

'It's hard to tell. We don't have regular ward rounds in ITU. Doctors come at different times during the day. Afternoons are probably best.'

Chapter 33

SUNDAY

Marnie and Ralph decided to give Jay a little time to recover before visiting him again. It was early on Sunday afternoon when they made their way to the ITU, where they were admitted by one of the nurses.

'Don't stay too long,' she said. 'He's making reasonably good progress, considering, but you'll find he tires very easily.'

Jay was still wired up to the equipment that was regulating his life, but his eyes were open and he was more alert than before.

'Hello, Jay,' Ralph said quietly. 'It's probably not appropriate to ask how you're feeling.'

Jay's voice was hoarse and weak. 'Why have you come?'

'Good question. I wanted to see how you were and to try to put things right between us ... to try to understand.'

'I doubt if that's possible, Ralph. Let's be clear about that.' He glanced fleetingly at Marnie and closed his eyes.

Ralph said, 'This is my wife ... Marnie.'

Jay stared at her, his expression troubled. 'I thought you were married to ...'

'Her name was Laura,' Marnie said.

'She died several years ago,' Ralph added. 'Look, Jay, I have to ask you this. Why have you been pursuing me?'

Jay closed his eyes again. 'Not today. Perhaps some other time. Now is not ...' His voice, now weaker, faded away.

They hadn't noticed the nurse appear beside them. 'I think that's all you're getting today,' she said quietly.

When they had moved out of earshot, Ralph asked the nurse, 'Is he improving at all?'

She looked non-committal. 'No one is in here without good reason, but I think it's fair to say that your friend is showing some fairly encouraging signs at the moment.'

Your friend. How ironic, Ralph thought. Marnie squeezed his arm as the nurse nodded towards the exit.

ooo0ooo

As Ralph was turning into his slot in the garage barn, Anne and Donovan were loading their bags into the VW Beetle. Marnie climbed out of the Jaguar while Ralph finished parking.

'Leaving already?' she said.

'Not quite,' said Anne. 'Just preparing for off. I've got some messages for Ralph.'

They gathered in the farmhouse kitchen, Donovan armed with the electric kettle, Anne armed with her notepad. She flipped open the pad and tore out a page as the kettle began rattling in the background.

'Here's a number for you to ring in Dublin. It's someone called Liam Kavanagh. He wants you to call him some time on Monday.'

'He phoned today?' Ralph sounded surprised.

'Late Friday afternoon,' said Anne. 'You'd gone to the hospital. He said it wasn't urgent as long as you could ring him at the start of the week. He wants to talk about ...' Anne looked down at her notes with a puzzled expression. '... *tigers*. Can that be right?'

Ralph smiled. 'That's Liam, all right. I've written an article about the booming Irish economy – known as the *Celtic Tiger* – and he's no doubt seen it.'

'He's at a university in Dublin?'

Ralph shook his head. 'He's a senior civil servant in the Finance Ministry. Anything else?'

'Greville Rickman phoned this afternoon. Wants you to phone him back as soon as you can.'

'Did he say why?'

'He said he has some news ... sounded a bit hyper. I've got his mobile number.'

ooo0ooo

Ralph rang Greville from his study on *Thyrsis* in the expectation of more bad news. The call was answered immediately. As usual, Greville dived straight in. Anne had been right about hyper.

'I actually managed to see the Master on Friday.'

206

'You were granted audience?' Ralph chuckled, out of a sense of relief.

'No. I ran into him in the corridor. He *said* – I think I believe him – that he was on his way to see you, and he asked me to pass on a message. Would you look in next time you're in college.'

'Was that it? Nothing else?'

'That's all he said.'

'Okay. Thanks, Greville. Now I have some news for you.'

Ralph gave a detailed account of the visit to Jay Harper's house, the subsequent car crash and the visit to Jay in hospital. He explained that for some reason it appeared that Jay was posing as the brother of Rhiannon Ellis and visiting her in the psychiatric hospital up to the time of her death the previous year. For the next twenty minutes or so they discussed Ralph's story and the possible implications relating to Jay's connection with Rhiannon.

'I don't follow,' said Greville. 'I don't get it at all. You're sure you heard it right, Ralph?'

'Beyond any doubt, and I've since discussed it with Marnie who was with me when I spoke to Jay's brother.'

'He was in love with a *man*,' Greville murmured softly. 'Then why was he so ... whatever it was ... about Rhiannon? Bisexual, do you think?'

'That's what I intend to find out.'

'Ralph, was he hostile towards you?'

'Not exactly, but then he wasn't over-cordial either.'

'Well, at least you know he can't do you any harm from a hospital bed in intensive care.'

I wouldn't be too certain about that, Ralph thought.

They disconnected with the promise to keep in touch.

Chapter 34

MONDAY

On Monday morning Ralph presented himself in the Master's secretariat, but it was the same old story and he felt exasperated.

'Clare, I'm here because the Master gave Dr Rickman a message for me to look in on him.'

Clare Goodall was visibly disconcerted. 'I'm really sorry, professor, but he isn't here. He came in briefly first thing and then went straight out.'

'To ...?' Ralph prompted.

'He didn't say.'

Ralph reflected, taking a few deep breaths. 'Clare, Rosemary, what is going on? Surely you two must be aware of what's happening. I'm not the only one to be confused by the Master's comings and goings. I know for a fact that Dr Rickman is equally baffled.'

Clare Goodall and Rosemary Martin exchanged glances across the room. It was Rosemary who replied.

'Please don't say anything to anyone, professor, but we're frankly worried about the Master's health. He has to dash off to various appointments and he never says where he's going or why.'

'The Master's health?' Ralph repeated. 'I hadn't thought of ... no, surely not. When I saw him recently he seemed like his old self. There's something else going on.'

'I'm sure it's nothing to do with you, professor.'

'Well, I'm naturally concerned about him.'

'Oh, I didn't mean that it was not your business. I meant I didn't think it was because of the ... you know ...'

'You mean the accusations against me?'

Rosemary nodded. 'We really are in the dark about the Master. And that's the honest truth.'

ooo0ooo

Twenty minutes later Ralph was ending his call to Liam Kavanagh in Dublin when there came a knock on the door. Ralph rose from his chair as the Master entered the office.

'Ralph, I owe you an explanation and an apology.'

Ralph indicated a visitor's chair and they sat. 'No, Master. You don't owe me anything, though I must say I've been concerned about you these past few weeks. I was particularly horrified about the bombing of your car.'

The Master twinkled a smile behind his gold-rimmed glasses. 'Well, yes, it wasn't exactly the high point of that week, but I'm over it now. In fact, it was about that that I had to dash out this morning. A loss adjuster turned up unexpectedly at the Master's Lodge, and Gwynedd rang me on the mobile. She was rather flustered about it, I can tell you.'

'It was about your car?'

'I can now go ahead and buy a replacement, so with luck that episode is behind me … or very soon will be.'

'Master, I can't tell you –'

'I think there's no more to be said about it, Ralph. We've both had near-misses as a result of the misdeeds of another party. There have clearly been misunderstandings, and I've come this morning to put the record straight, in as much as it involves me.'

Ralph sat back, folded his arms and waited for the Master to continue.

'Where shall I begin? Forgive me, Ralph, if I seem a little embarrassed by what I'm about to tell you. A few weeks ago I received a letter from the Cabinet Office asking me if I would accept an honour. You know that for political reasons I have reservations about the honours system. I discussed the letter with Gwynedd, who urged me to accept. The next day I was summoned – I think that's the only way to put it – to London on what was described as an *urgent matter*.'

'You were being pressed about the honour, Master?'

'No, this was quite different, and it is even now highly confidential.'

'Please don't feel obliged –'

The Master shook his head. 'I must tell you this, Ralph.' He cleared his throat, evidently embarrassed. 'I'm to be appointed as Regius Professor of Applied Mathematics.'

Ralph shot to his feet and extended his hand. 'Congratulations, Vivian – such an honour and so well-deserved!'

The Master took Ralph's hand and laughed. 'My old friend, I can tell you're as shocked as I am.'

'How do you mean?'

'You've just called me by my Christian name. You never do that.'

Both men laughed, and Ralph resumed his seat. 'I suppose it's what you'd call a *Vivian moment*, Master. But seriously, that is wonderful news. I'm so pleased for you.'

'Thank you, Ralph. There is one further embarrassment, I'm afraid. In all the hullabaloo about the Regius matter, I overlooked the other thing from the Cabinet Office. It appears that I'm being given a knighthood, too.'

'Wow,' Ralph said. 'Hence all the comings and goings.'

'Exactly, and not being allowed to speak about either, of course. But look, that's enough about me. Are you any closer to resolving all this ridiculous accusation business?'

'Actually, Master, we may be making some progress there.'

'Tell me all about it,' said the Master.

ooo0ooo

Ralph was back at Glebe Farm in time for their tea break that afternoon, as Marnie was hurriedly preparing refreshments for the men creating the walled garden behind the farmhouse. Keen to hear Ralph's account of his meeting with the Master, she quickly consulted the list left by Anne itemising the correct beverages for the three men on duty that day. Meanwhile, Ralph made mugs of tea for Marnie and himself and settled in the chair at Anne's desk.

'What's a Regius professor?' Marnie asked. 'And why all the fuss about it? He's already a professor, isn't he?'

'It's a real honour,' said Ralph, 'a sign of distinction. To be a Regius professor, you have to be recognised as outstanding in your field. Traditionally the title is conferred by the monarch, hence the name.'

'And he's getting a knighthood, too,' Marnie said. 'So what will his title be?'

'I think something long-winded like ...' Ralph adopted a stentorian tone. '... Regius Professor Sir Vivian Parry-Jones, plus, no doubt, Master of All Saints' College of the University of Oxford.' He reverted to his normal voice. 'Not bad for a person of such humble beginnings, a boy from the valleys of south Wales, son of an engine driver.'

Marnie looked impressed. 'That's quite a handle.'

Ralph added. 'And my guess is he'll probably hate it.'

'Why?'

'The Master is basically modest and retiring, happiest when he's researching something abstruse in a library or working out a complicated equation.'

'Will you still just address him as "Master"?'

Ralph shrugged. 'Technically, he should be addressed as "Regius".'

'What about the knighthood? Won't he be "Sir Vivian"?

'I think he'll always be the Master to me.'

'And that's what's been taking him out of the college ... secret meetings in high places?'

'That's right, and he's been forbidden to speak of the titles to anyone until they are formally announced. Those are the rules.'

'And that's the tradition you live by,' Marnie added with a smile, 'in your ivory tower.'

A thoughtful smile from Ralph. 'In our ivory tower, yes.'

Chapter 35

WEDNESDAY

Tuesday came and went, filled with their habitual workload. For Marnie there were designs to complete, orders to send, invoices to generate. For Ralph business as usual involved drafting texts, analysing statistics, checking proofs. And, of course, in Anne's absence Marnie fulfilled the role of tea-girl to the gardening contractors. At Glebe Farm Tuesday was a normal day.

Mid-morning on Wednesday Marnie and Ralph set off in the Jaguar to visit Jay in hospital. Even though they knew he was ensconced in the ITU, Ralph could not prevent himself glancing repeatedly in the rear-view mirror, still haunted by the spectre of a dark blue car lurking in the background with sinister intent.

The hospital car park brought the customary hassle and stress. Twice Ralph spotted a possible space, only to find it was being vacated by a much smaller car that had barely managed to squeeze in. He was muttering curses to himself about the narrowness of British parking slots when Marnie pointed to a delivery van vacating a place at the end of a row. It was third time lucky. They paid for a parking ticket and trod the familiar path to the Intensive Therapy Unit.

The nurse who admitted them to the unit explained that Jay was making slow progress. She permitted them to stay for no longer than ten minutes or so; on no account were they to fatigue or upset him. When they approached Jay's bed they found him dozing, still wired up to the machinery that was maintaining his systems. The equipment was soundless, but coloured lights were blinking every few seconds with each measurement taken.

Ralph drew up a visitor's chair for Marnie, plus one for himself. He spoke quietly. 'Jay, it's me. Can you hear me?'

Jay's head moved a fraction towards Ralph and his eyes flickered open. 'I hear you.' The voice was hoarse, little more than a croak.

'I've come with Marnie to see how you are.'

'Marnie ...'

'Yes, my wife.'

'Not ... Laura.'

'No, Jay. Laura has been dead for a long time. I told you that before.'

Marnie glanced at Ralph and whispered, 'Confused.'

Ralph nodded and said, 'The nurse says you're making progress. That's good.'

'She said that?'

'She did. Can I ask you something, Jay?'

'Mm ...'

'It's about Rhiannon. You knew her. I want to ask why you said at the care home that you were her brother, Gareth.'

'Yes ... Gareth.'

'Did she have a brother, Jay?'

'No.'

'But you said you were Gareth, her brother. Why was that?'

'Only relatives could visit. I made out I was ...' His voice faded.

'I understand.'

In the silence that followed, Marnie said softly, 'Did you love Rhiannon, Jay?'

'Love ...?'

'Did you?'

Jay closed his eyes, and Marnie thought that was the end of their talk for the day. She was reaching over to touch Ralph's arm when Jay squinted at her and spoke so quietly that she could barely hear what he said.

'I suffered with her. I knew what it was like to be rejected.' He stared up at the ceiling, his eyes narrow slits. 'I couldn't forgive Ralph for dumping her like that. It was cruel. He was cruel to her.'

Ralph hung his head. 'Yes, Jay, you're right. I agree with you, and although it means very little, I truly am sorry for that.'

Over Ralph's shoulder Marnie noticed that the nurse was hovering. Marnie nodded to her and they left.

ooo0ooo

Ralph was quiet in the car on the drive home. Marnie sensed his inner turmoil and opted not to disturb his thoughts, however troubled they might be. And so she was surprised at his matter-of-fact tone when eventually he spoke.

'I've got it. I know what it was that eluded me a few weeks ago when Jay lured me to that non-existent meeting at the OUP.'

'Something eluded you?'

'Yes. I think I mentioned it a while ago. Don't you remember?'

'Vaguely, I suppose ...'

'It was the name,' Ralph said. 'The anonymous caller – obviously now we know it was Jay – said it was *Gareth* Kempson who wanted a meeting. I knew there was something odd about that, but I just couldn't work out what it was.'

Marnie was none the wiser. 'I think you'll have to spell it out for me, Ralph.'

'Don't you see? He said that *Gareth* Kempson wanted me to meet him.'

'I'm with you so far,' Marnie said.

'That's not his name. He's *Garth* Kempson.'

'And that's significant because ...?'

'Jay was calling himself Gareth ... Gareth Ellis ... Rhiannon's fictitious brother. It must've been a slip of the tongue. He quoted the wrong name to me by mistake. He said *Gareth* when he should have said *Garth*. I was a fool not to have spotted his mistake.'

Marnie nodded. 'I understand. It was an easy slip to make.'

'At the time I just thought I'd misheard him, but now I'm sure I didn't.'

Marnie said, 'That whole business was pretty strange.'

'How d'you mean?'

'Jay calling himself Gareth Ellis, her brother.'

'Well, he did explain that. It was the only way to get to visit her in the psychiatric home. Only relatives were allowed.'

Marnie sighed. 'I keep thinking of what he wrote in that notebook. It was almost like a love poem. I do wonder what his feelings were exactly ... for Rhiannon.'

'Mm ... I wonder if she wasn't some kind of refuge for him.'

'Refuge? In what way, Ralph?'

'Just what Jay said. He'd obviously been rejected by the man that his brother mentioned in the house that day. Jay somehow knew that Rhiannon had been rejected by me and felt that they were kindred spirits.'

'Have you ever been dumped, Ralph?'

'No. You?'

'No, and I've never dumped anyone either.'

'It can obviously stir up strong emotions both ways,' Ralph said with feeling.

'Both ways?'

'The dumper and the ... dumped ... dumpee?'

Marnie frowned. 'Is there such a term as *dumpee*?'

'Does it matter?'

They agreed it did not and drove the rest of the way home in thoughtful silence.

Chapter 36

THURSDAY

How times change. That was Marnie's immediate thought when Greville Rickman rang on Thursday morning. She recalled the first time he'd phoned those few weeks ago. Back then his tone had been disdainful, brusque and dismissive, his attitude towards Ralph decidedly antagonistic. Now they were big buddies, having faced a hostile world together' They were practically brothers in arms.

'Good morning, Marnie. It's Greville. So sorry to bother you. I've been trying to get through to Ralph, but his line's been engaged for a while. Could you possibly give him a message?'

'Of course, Greville. Fire away.'

'Well, actually it's an invitation. Digby Parker-Voss is organising a dinner party for the Master to celebrate his Regius professorship and knighthood.'

'I take it Ralph will know who that is.'

'Oh yes. Digby's the Dean of the college.'

'Fine. I'll pass on the invitation.'

'It includes you too, Marnie, and also … let me see … ah yes, Anne with an "e". Does that make sense?'

'Anne is invited?'

'Apparently the Master is keen for her to attend. Is she perhaps your daughter?'

Marnie chuckled. 'She's my assistant.'

'I see. Well, the Master apparently said he wanted the whole family to attend.'

'We'll be delighted, Greville. Do you have a date?'

'Yes, it's Saturday of next week. Seven-thirty for eight o'clock. Aperitif in the college library, then on to the founder's dining room. Er … Digby said to mention that the dress code is black tie.'

And long frock, Marnie thought.

Chapter 37

FRIDAY

As soon as Anne and Donovan arrived from Oxford on Friday morning, Marnie and Ralph set off to visit Jay in hospital. It was to be a day of surprises.

The first came when they presented themselves at the entrance door to the ITU and pressed the bell. The Chinese nurse – SRN Wong – who had first admitted them on the previous Friday, greeted them with an uncharacteristic smile. She spoke in unaccented English.

'You've come to see Mr Harper? I'm pleased to tell you that he's not here. He was transferred earlier this morning to a private room on the ground floor.'

She gave directions, and Marnie and Ralph retraced their steps. They located the nurses' station leading to the private wing, and moments later were shown into Jay's room. They found him sitting up in bed. No longer connected to machinery by an array of tubes and cables, he had lost his pale complexion and looked more like a normal human being.

Without smiling, Jay pointed to the side of the bed. 'There are chairs, if you like.'

'How are you feeling, Jay?' Ralph asked.

'How d'you think I'm feeling? Did you notice a security guard down the corridor? I haven't seen him, but they told me he's there.' He sneered. 'As if I could run anywhere ...'

'Security guard?' Ralph looked puzzled.

Marnie said, 'Why the guard?'

'I'm to be arrested as soon as I try to leave the hospital.'

'For murder?' Marnie said.

The words had a dramatic effect on Jay, who sat up with a start and at once regretted it. He winced, grimaced and flopped back onto the pillow. When he spoke his voice was little more than a hoarse, rasping whisper.

'What are you talking about?'

'Roland Haddow.'

Jay looked aghast. 'I didn't kill him. In fact, I didn't lay a finger on him.'

'Then what happened?' said Ralph.

Jay fell silent, his expression vacant as he searched his memory. Marnie and Ralph gazed at each other, bewildered.

'Jay?' Ralph prompted.

'I remember ...'

'What do you remember?'

'You and Haddow in that restaurant. I wanted to harangue you, but he came out first and saw me ... asked why I was there. I don't know what I said, only that I wanted to talk to you ... wanted to confront you about Rhiannon, about what you'd done to her.'

'There must have been more than that,' Ralph insisted. 'Roland ended up dead in the river. How did that happen?'

'He tried to brush past me, said he was in a hurry ... a train to catch, or something. I wanted to tell him all about you. He demanded to know if I'd planted the story about you plagiarising his ideas. He denied emphatically that it had anything to do with him, said he'd made no such accusation. He said that I had laid a false accusation against you and that I was a liar.'

Marnie pressed him and said slowly, 'How did he come to fall in the river?'

'I said I didn't even believe you'd done your own research. Don't know why I said that. I was just lashing out by then. He produced a business card of yours showing your title as doctor, the letters after your name: MA, DPhil (Oxon). He thrust it at me, but I grabbed it and pushed it into his top pocket. Then he said he had to dash, but I wanted him to hear me out. He tried to evade me by slipping between the railings at the edge of the walkway. That's when he tripped and fell into the river.'

'You didn't push him?'

'No. I wasn't even near him when he fell. I rushed forward and looked down into the water but he didn't come up. I ran off in the dark. No one was there to see me.'

'You phoned the police?'

'That night ... or the early hours of the morning, I don't know. I told them it was Ralph ... told them he carried a card in his top pocket.'

'Why?'

'I thought it would cause trouble for Ralph, or at least upset him.'

'But you did try to kill me, more than once,' Ralph said.

'No, never. Just wanted to give you a scare. I felt so angry about how badly you'd treated Rhiannon.'

'You were in love with her?' Marnie said.

Jay looked desolate. 'No, not her, not like that ... someone else.'

'A man?'

Jay looked Marnie straight in the eyes, his expression bleak, forlorn. There was no need for words.

'Why the bomb under the Master's car?' Ralph asked.

'I was getting desperate ... never wanted to hurt him.'

'You could've killed him,' Ralph protested.

'No. I was watching ... followed him to the station. I chose my moment. Nobody was hurt.'

'What was the point of that?'

'I wanted everything about you, the college, your associates to be tainted. I wanted you to suffer, the way you had made Rhiannon suffer. You ruined her life. I wanted to ruin yours.'

Marnie said, 'No, Jay. It doesn't work like that. I never knew Rhiannon, of course, but I know enough about people to know that her reaction to losing Ralph was out of all proportion. Ralph couldn't have known how she would behave. You have to understand that. You can't hold him responsible for how she acted.'

'But I do,' Jay almost spat the words out between gritted teeth. 'I hate Ralph for what he did to Rhiannon. There are no excuses.'

Marnie could see that Ralph was deeply shocked. She stood and took Ralph's arm.

'Come on. We're going.'

ooo0ooo

Supper that evening at Glebe Farm was a sombre affair. From the time when he and Marnie left the hospital, Ralph was mired in despondency. The depth of feeling shown by Jay had struck home and only served to increase Ralph's feeling of guilt at his treatment of Rhiannon. Marnie refrained from offering words of comfort, certain that nothing could make Ralph feel less troubled.

They were clearing the table when Anne said, 'What will you do, Ralph?'

'What can I do?' His tone was weary, downcast.

'Well, he admitted that he'd caused Dr Haddow to fall into the river and die. Don't you think you should tell the police?'

219

Marnie said, 'Jay was convinced he'd be arrested once the hospital released him. He told us there was a security guard on duty to prevent him leaving without being apprehended.'

'On what charge?' Donovan asked.

Marnie reflected. 'I don't think that was ever explained.'

'It must have been Greville,' Ralph said. 'I expect he told them he suspected Jay when we gave our statements to the police after the incident when we were almost run down in the street.'

'But you've no actual proof,' Donovan observed, 'only what Jay said to you.'

Marnie said, 'He freely admitted he'd done things to try to scare Ralph, not to mention planting the bomb under the Master's car.'

'So I suppose it's up to you, Ralph,' said Donovan.

Ralph slowly shook his head. 'No. There's no way I'm going to give evidence against Jay. He's suffered enough, and so did Rhiannon.'

'Not your fault,' Marnie said softly.

'Maybe not, but what started it all was down to me.'

'And Haddow? What about him?'

'I know I'll never forget the sight of his body in the mortuary, but he was just in the wrong place at the wrong time. Jay didn't intend to hurt him. I truly believe that.'

'Even so,' said Marnie.

'Whatever happened, the whole sad business was begun by me and what I did to Rhiannon, or what I failed to do.'

'So you want him to go free,' said Anne.

Ralph turned his head to look at her. 'Whatever I do, Anne, I think he'll always be in his own private hell.'

Chapter 38

During the week that followed, Marnie gradually helped Ralph to come to terms with the situation around Rhiannon. He remained adamant that he would neither press charges nor give evidence against Jay. When DS Marriner came to Glebe Farm to interview him, Ralph stubbornly maintained that no proof existed of Jay Harper's involvement in any of the incidents that had occurred in the weeks since Roland Haddow's body had been pulled from the Thames. He refused to speculate on anything. Similarly they learned that Greville Rickman had been unable to make a positive identification of the driver of the 'dark-coloured' car that had run him off the road near Banbury or mounted the pavement and almost run him down with Ralph in Oxford.

When Marriner turned towards Marnie in exasperation, she had simply shrugged and pointed out that she had not been present at any of the 'incidents'. She couldn't be considered any kind of witness, she said.

Muttering under his breath – 'No change there, then' – the detective had walked out of the office barn without another word.

ooo0ooo

Nothing more was heard from the police that week, and life at Glebe Farm resumed its normal pattern. Marnie knew from Ralph's demeanour that he was still brooding over Jay and Rhiannon, and she suspected that he was probably paying less attention to his research than usual. She hoped privately that the celebration dinner for the Master on Saturday evening would help lift his spirits.

For her part, Anne too found concentration difficult that week, but for an entirely different reason. She had arranged with Marnie that they would spend one day together in Oxford on a special quest. It would be the first time in her life when she would set out to choose a long dress for a formal dinner. An expedition was therefore entered in their diaries for Tuesday, and both happily cancelled other commitments for a girls' day out. The mission was a success, and by mid-afternoon Anne was ecstatically disporting herself in front of a full-length mirror in an exclusive boutique, admiring a designer creation in an attractive shade known as Old Rose.

With a shy smile, she turned to Marnie. 'Is it all right?'

'More than all right,' Marnie assured her. 'You look like a character from a Jane Austen novel.'

'Great, though I'll try to avoid all the swearing and blaspheming.'

Marnie rolled her eyes … *that girl!* She knew that for Anne Saturday could not come soon enough.

ooo0ooo

On Saturday evening the party from Glebe Farm comprised Marnie in a dress of midnight blue silk, Anne in her newest – and only – long gown and Ralph in evening dress, complete with black bow tie. Marnie thought he looked more distinguished than ever. She was pleased that he seemed more cheerful than for some weeks, and she suspected that a little of Anne's youthful enthusiasm had got through to him.

They were greeted at the entrance to All Saints' College library by the Master himself. He hugged them all, with a kiss on both cheeks for Marnie. She noticed that Anne's default setting had become a fixed smile and was not surprised when Anne sidled up to her and muttered, 'Marnie, I'm desperate for the loo.'

It was as much as Marnie could do to hold back a guffaw, but after a discreet enquiry of Ralph, she was able to send Anne tottering off in the right direction.

While the Dean received other guests, the Master took Ralph to one side and asked if the 'sorry business' was now concluded. Ralph explained that he thought nothing more would come of it and certainly no repercussions would arise for the college. He added that that had been a prime consideration throughout. The Master nodded thoughtfully then guided Ralph and Marnie towards a table from which college staff – the Master could not bring himself to call them 'servants' – were offering glasses of champagne.

Gazing at the centuries-old rows of bookshelves, the Master said quietly, 'You know, Ralph, the Rhondda Valley boy in me feels guilty at such a privileged life.'

'We are very fortunate,' Ralph replied.

Marnie added, 'When we're growing up, we none of us know which way life will take us.'

'You're quite right, of course, Marnie,' said the Master. 'I was brought up just to do my best and show respect for others. I never expected anything like this.'

On that note the Master excused himself and moved away to attend to other guests. Anne, now armed with a glass of champagne, reappeared beside them.

'The Master's not exactly what I imagined,' she said. 'He seems such a quiet, modest man, for all his honours.'

'His brain is as sharp as a razor,' said Ralph. 'But it's interesting. The academic world can be bitchy and harsh, with rivalries of unbelievable ferocity. Despite that, I've never heard the Master utter an unkind word about anyone.'

'Nor do you,' said Marnie.

She said no more, but a thought crossed her mind. If Ralph had been firmer, less gentle, with Rhiannon from the outset, perhaps things might have turned out differently. Marnie wondered if our qualities can sometimes be separated from our faults by the narrowest of margins.

Marnie had visited the founder's dining room on one or two previous occasions and always found its atmosphere magical. She noticed that Anne, on this her first visit, was similarly enchanted. This was one of the earliest parts of the college, dating back to the beginning of the sixteenth century, with walls clad in linen-fold panelling of dark oak, a low beamed ceiling and small leaded windows overlooking the old quadrangle. The room was lit with candles, supplementing table lamps around the perimeter and brass picture lights illuminating portraits from the Tudor era of the founder, King Henry VII, together with the first Master and the first Dean.

For Marnie, the place reeked of privilege, and she well understood the Master's misgivings. Even so, she wanted to let nothing spoil the occasion for the man in whose honour the dinner was held, and also for Anne who had never before been entertained in such splendour.

Before the guests took their seats the Dean pronounced the grace in Latin. When everyone was seated the staff served wine from crystal decanters. As soon as they withdrew, the Dean made to rise from his chair beside the Master but, to everyone's surprise, the Master placed a hand on his arm, whispered in his ear and got to his feet.

'My dear friends and colleagues, I am deeply touched by your kindness on this occasion, but I have a special wish. There is among us one who has always had the interests of this great college at heart. Despite many hardships and tribulations, I am sure you would all wish to join me in expressing our gratitude, appreciation and friendship to that person.' The Master raised his glass. 'To Mister … Ralph Lombard.'

All the guests stood and raised their glasses in Ralph's direction. To Marnie's great surprise – and Anne's complete bewilderment – everyone muttered, 'Mister Ralph Lombard.'

Only Ralph remained seated, looking profoundly moved at this display of affection and respect from the college's hierarchy. Marnie noticed that the Master raised an eyebrow in Ralph's direction, but Ralph gave the slightest shake of his head and did not move from his place. She thought she detected a certain pinkness in his eyes.

When everyone sat, the Dean stood again and began a short eulogy of congratulation to the Master on his knighthood and especially on his promotion to the rank of Regius Professor. Marnie scarcely heard a word of this oration; her head was buzzing with the words spoken by the Master. Only then did she realise how important it was to the college that Ralph had suffered all the assaults perpetrated on him by Jay Harper without invoking the intervention of the police or the media.

Marnie was musing along these lines when she felt a faint tug at her sleeve. She turned to meet Anne's gaze, an inquisitive frown.

Marnie understood. She inclined her head towards Anne and murmured one word, 'Later.'

ooo0ooo

After the meal, the assembly was invited to withdraw to the senior common room for coffee and liqueurs. Marnie was touched that one by one the other guests, the most senior members of an illustrious institution, came by to offer words of support and friendship to Ralph. Prominent among them was Greville Rickman who had long since ceased to be an adversary and become a close comrade in arms. His lingering presence was no doubt intended as a display of solidarity, though it prevented Anne from asking questions that had been disturbing her throughout the evening.

Soon after ten Ralph announced that he thought they should be heading for home. Marnie and Anne joined him to bid goodnight to the Master and the Dean and, after handshakes, embraces and kissing of cheeks, they walked out to the quadrangle, found the car and set off through half deserted streets towards the northern by-pass and home.

'Are you okay for driving?' Marnie asked.

'Sure. I hardly drank anything and I'm not tired.'

'Can I ask you something, Ralph?' It was a voice from the back seat.

'What is it, Anne?'

'There were things I didn't understand this evening ... all that business about Regius, for a start. What's that all about?'

'It doesn't really mean much outside the academic world. You know that I'm normally addressed as "professor". Well, the Master is also a professor, but now he's a *Regius* professor.'

'Does that change things?' said Marnie.

'Outside the college, other colleagues will now address him simply as "Regius". That's the custom ... the tradition.'

'In your ivory tower?' Anne added.

Ralph chuckled. 'I suppose so. It's how things work in academia, at least in our part of it.'

'And inside the college?' Marnie asked.

'I'll probably go on calling him "Master". I expect some others will too.'

'Ralph ...' Anne spoke hesitantly. 'I don't want to speak out of turn, but why did the Master refer to you as just "*Mister* Ralph Lombard"? Your title's *professor* and before that, you were *doctor*. It's probably a long time since you were just plain *mister*, isn't it?'

'Well ...' Ralph paused, hesitating to continue.

Marnie intervened. 'Actually, Anne, I think I can help you there. You see, I asked Greville Rickman about that. It seems to be another tradition. I don't know if it's just in Oxford, but if someone is referred to as "mister" at that sort of formal dinner, that is a real distinction, especially when it was the Master – who was, after all, the guest of honour – who singled Ralph out like that.'

'So the Master was making Ralph a kind of guest of honour?' Anne said.

'Yes, something like that,' said Marnie. 'At least, that's my understanding.'

She didn't ask Ralph to confirm it, but just left him to drive home in silence.

Arriving back at Glebe Farm, they had been surprised to see Donovan's classic Porsche tucked into its slot in the garage barn. When questioned, he announced that he had driven up from London on a whim just to give the machine a 'run-out'. Nobody had been taken in by that excuse, and they all guessed correctly that he wanted to discover how the 'Jay Harper affair' had turned out. He had forgotten that Marnie, Ralph and Anne would be at the college dinner – or so he said – and he had just waited patiently for their return.

The four of them retired to the sitting room in the farmhouse for a nightcap. Armed with a glass of brandy, Donovan got straight to the point.

'So how have things been resolved?'

Marnie said, 'It was a very pleasant dinner and everyone was delighted for the Master. This Regius professor thing seems to have impressed people rather more than the knighthood.'

Donovan gave her his equivalent of the Death Stare. 'I think you know what I meant, Marnie.'

'Oh … you mean the Jay Harper thing.'

Donovan said nothing. It was Ralph who replied.

'That business is still … undecided.'

'I've been thinking …' Donovan began. 'That bomb attached to the Master's Saab.'

'What about it?'

'Well, it's rather specialised, isn't it? I mean, I'm quite technically-minded, but I wouldn't know how to make one.'

'You'd soon find out, though,' said Anne.

Ralph said, 'I expect Jay probably learnt how to handle explosives during his time in the army.'

Donovan looked puzzled. 'I don't think I knew about that part of his life.'

'No reason why you should. He went on a three year short service commission, I believe, after abandoning his doctoral studies. He'd always intended doing further research but decided he'd had enough of university life and opted for a change.'

'What about you, Ralph? Are you really undecided? After all, he did try to kill you and to destroy your reputation … your whole career.'

Ralph swirled the brandy in his glass and stared into the golden liquid for a long moment.

'One of the reasons why I didn't go to the police about Jay or mount a defence in the media was my concern for the good name of the college. It may be arrogance, but I felt I could certainly take care of myself. Also, I have to admit that the whole problem had been caused by me and my thoughtless treatment of a young woman all those years ago.'

Marnie said quietly, 'You can't hold yourself responsible for Rhiannon, Ralph. I've told you that before.'

'So you've reminded me already, Marnie. But if I'd behaved differently, perhaps she'd not have had that breakdown, and Jay wouldn't have felt compelled to act as he did.'

Donovan said, 'It seems to me that you *have* made up your mind, Ralph.'

'You think Jay's suffered enough already?' said Anne. 'Is that what you're thinking?'

Ralph swallowed the last of his brandy. 'On balance ...'

ooo0ooo

Marnie awoke on Sunday morning to find Ralph gone from the bed beside her. Downstairs there was no indication that he had spent any time in the kitchen. The kettle felt cold to her touch. Dressing quickly, pulling on jeans and a sweatshirt, she grabbed a jacket and dashed through the spinney. Her shoes cracked twigs on the path, and branches snagged her sleeves as she hurried by. Under an overcast autumnal sky, *Thyrsis* lay silent at her mooring.

Marnie crossed rapidly to the side of the boat and peered in through the window of Ralph's study. He was sitting at his desk with a thoughtful expression, one hand supporting his chin, lost in reverie. Marnie hesitated for a few moments, then strolled back to knock on the doors midway along the superstructure. When Ralph opened up, he kissed her lightly and gave her his hand as usual to steady her descent. He led the way to the study. Marnie settled on the small sofa opposite the desk where Ralph took his seat and swivelled round to face her. On the desk lay a small bundle of letters tied with a blue ribbon. The bundle was undisturbed.

'You're up early, Ralph. Are you okay?'

'I'm fine. I just had a lot going through my mind and woke early. I couldn't get back to sleep, so I got up.'

'Shall I make you some coffee? You haven't had breakfast.'

Ralph nodded in the direction of the bundle of letters. 'I found those the other week when the first letter came from Jay.'

'They look as if you haven't untied them.'

'They're the letters that Rhiannon sent me ... back then. I expect you've guessed that.'

'You didn't want to throw them away, yet you haven't re-read them.'

'I have no wish to re-read them, Marnie. I only kept them because it seemed to me it would be churlish to throw them in the bin ... a double rejection.'

'I can understand that, Ralph. I'm sure you'd have regretted it, if you'd just discarded them.'

Ralph nodded. 'You know I regret the way I treated Rhiannon, but I have no regrets about marrying Laura, and I certainly have no regrets about our marriage, Marnie.'

'I know.'

'Like Jay I remember her with sadness, a degree of fondness and no small measure of regret. I can understand why Jay thought of her as he did. Like her, he knew the pain of rejection.'

It was only then that Marnie noticed Jay's notepad lying on the desk beside the letters. Ralph picked it up, and Marnie saw that it was open at the first page. He read the first lines out loud.

'Her hair is black, her eyes are blue. She walks in darkness through my daydreams. She has become fixated on an object of desire, an obsession. There is no knowing where it will end.' Ralph looked across at Marnie. 'Now, all these years later, we know exactly how it ended, and it's not been a happy outcome.'

'Those first two sentences ...' Marnie began. 'They almost read like a love poem.'

Ralph looked down at the text and read the words in silence. 'Yes,' he said. 'Almost.'

'Have you decided what you're going to do about Jay, Ralph?'

For several seconds he stared at Marnie, then slowly, almost imperceptibly, nodded. He closed the notepad, extended his arm and dropped the pad into the waste paper bin.

Marnie said, 'You've decided to take no action? You're not going to the police?'

'No action,' Ralph repeated. 'It's finished now. It's over. No going back.'

228

Also by Leo McNeir

The Marnie Walker series:

Getaway with Murder
Death in Little Venice
Kiss and Tell
Sally Ann's Summer
Devil in the Detail
No Secrets
Smoke and Mirrors
Gifthorse
Stick in the Mud
Smoke without Fire
Witching Hour
To Have and to Hold
Beyond the Grave

The Apostle series:

Gospel Truth
Pilgrims

Novellas:

Angels

and published by Enigma Publishing

Full details are available on the author's website:
www.leomcneir.com

Printed in Great Britain
by Amazon

39803782R00136